Secrets at Seaside

Sweet with Heat: Seaside Summers Series

Addison Cole

ISBN-13: 978-1-941480-75-5
ISBN-10: 1-941480-75-6

SECRETS AT SEASIDE

V1.0

Cover Design: Elizabeth Mackey Designs

WORLD LITERARY PRESS
PRINTED IN THE UNITED STATES OF AMERICA

A Note to Readers

When I began writing Amy and Tony's story, I had no idea how much pain they had both experienced. Their pasts came alive for me during the writing process, and the depth of their love blew me away. I hope you experience the same emotional impact.

Secrets at Seaside by Addison Cole is the sweet edition of the steamy novel, *Seaside Secrets,* and is part of the Sweet with Heat: Seaside Summers series. Sweet with Heat books are the sweet editions of the award-winning, steamy romance collection Love in Bloom written by *New York Times* bestselling author Melissa Foster. Addison Cole is Melissa's sweet alter ego (pen name). The storylines and characters remain the same as the original titles, with minor differences in the positioning of supporting characters. Within the Sweet with Heat series you'll find fiercely loyal heroes and smart, empowered women on their search for true love. They're flawed, funny, and easy to relate to. These emotional romances portray all the passion two people in love convey without any graphic love scenes and little or no harsh language (with the exception of an occasional "damn" or "hell"). Characters from each series appear in future Sweet with Heat series. Sweet with Heat books may be read as stand-alone novels, or as part of the larger series.

Sign up for Addison's Sweet with Heat newsletter to be notified of the next release.
www.Addisoncole.com/Newsletter

For more information on Sweet with Heat titles visit
www.AddisonCole.com

For Amy Manemann,
who is too cute for her own good

Chapter One

"I JUST CAN'T believe that Jamie's the first one to get married. I mean, Jamie? He never even wanted to get married." Amy Maples was three sheets to the wind, sitting in a bar at the Ryder Resort in Boston. That was okay, she rationalized, because it was the night before the wedding of her good friends Jessica Ayers and Jamie Reed, and she and her friends were celebrating. Besides, now that Jessica and Jamie were getting married and her other three besties had gotten engaged, Amy was the only single woman of the group. Drunk was the only way she was going to make it through the weekend.

"But that was before he met Jessica and she rocked his world." Jenna leaned across the table in the dimly lit bar and grabbed Amy's hand.

Amy saw Jenna's lips curve into a smile as she shifted her eyes to Tony Black, another friend they'd known forever, sitting with his arm around Amy, as per usual. Jenna raised her brows with a smile, implying something Amy knew wasn't true. She rolled her eyes in response. Tony always sat with his arm around her, and it didn't mean a thing, no matter how much she wished it did.

Amy and her besties, Jenna Ward, Bella Abbascia, and

Leanna Bray, had grown up spending summers together at the Seaside community in Wellfleet, Massachusetts, and to this day they continued to spend their summers there, along with Jamie and Tony. The six of them had spent eight weeks together every summer for as long as Amy could remember. Their parents had owned the Seaside cottages, which they'd passed down to them. Summers were Amy's favorite time of year. Now that Amy's company, Maples Logistical & Conference Consulting, was so successful, she was able to take eight weeks off while her small staff handled the workload. Amy had spent seven years building and nurturing the business, and over the last three years she had turned it into a six-figure venture with clients varying from accounting to full-on logistical consulting. She could hardly believe how her life, and her summers, had changed. Just four years ago she was working part-time during the summers at one of the local restaurants to keep a modicum of income coming in. She loved summers even more now that she didn't have to work. Of course, her love of summers might also have something to do with being in love with the six-foot-two professional surfer and motivational speaker currently sitting beside her.

If only it were reciprocated. She tipped back her glass and took another swig of her get-over-Tony drink.

"Petey, can you please get me another drink?" Jenna batted her lashes at her fiancé, Pete Lacroux. She and Pete had gotten engaged last year. Pete was a boat craftsman and he also handled the pool maintenance at Seaside. Pete nuzzled against her neck, and Amy slid her eyes away. Maybe if Sky, Pete's sister, were there, she'd feel a little better. Sky wasn't currently dating anyone either, but Sky had to work, so Amy was on her own.

Bella and her fiancé, Caden Grant, were whispering nose to nose, Leanna was sitting on Kurt's lap with her forehead touching his, and Jamie and Jessica were looking at each other like they couldn't wait to tear each other's clothes off. Amy stole a glance at Tony, and her heart did a little dance. Delicious and painful memories from the summer before college tried to edge into her mind. As she'd done for the past fourteen years, she pushed them down deep as Tony leaned in close.

He smelled delicious, like citrus and spice with an undertone of masculinity and sophistication. She knew he wore Dolce & Gabbana's The One. She kept a bottle of The One beside her bed at home in Boston, and every once in a while, in the dead of winter or on the cusp of spring, when months stretched like eons before she'd see Tony again, she'd spray the cologne on her pillow so she could smell him as she drifted off to sleep. It never smelled quite as good as Tony himself. Then again, Tony could be covered in sweat after a five-mile run, or laden with sea salt after a day of surfing, and he'd still smell like heaven on legs. Since they were just friends, and it looked like there was no chance of them becoming more, she relied on her fantasies to keep her warm. When she was alone in bed at night, she held on to the image of Tony wearing only his board shorts, his broad shoulders and muscular chest glistening wet, muscles primed from the surf, and those delicious abs blazing a path to his—

Tony pressed his hand to her shoulder and pulled her against him, bringing her mind back to the present.

"Time for ice water?" he asked just above a whisper.

So much for her fantasy. She was always the *good girl* who did the right thing, the only exception being the occasional extra drink or two when she was with her Seaside friends. At least that's what she led everyone to believe. Only she and Tony knew that wasn't the only exception—and she made sure that was a taboo subject between them. He wouldn't dare bring it up. She might not survive if he did. She sobered a little with the memory and shifted it back into the it-never-happened place she buried deep inside her. Her secret was lonely in that hollow place, being the only one kept under lock and key.

She met Tony's denim-blue eyes and felt a familiar rush of anticipation in her belly. Maybe tonight she wouldn't be the good girl.

"Um, actually, I think I want another drink."

Tony arched a brow in that sexy way that made his eyes look even more intense. He pressed his cheek to hers and whispered, "Ames, you can't show up for the wedding tomorrow with a hangover."

No, she certainly couldn't. But she'd like him to stay right where he was for a while longer, thank you very much. Since she had a life-changing job offer in hand—a dream job worthy of closing down the business she'd spent seven years building and keeping only a handful of clients—she and her girlfriends had decided it was time for Amy to take a chance and lay her feelings on the line with Tony. She picked up her glass and ran her finger around the rim, hoping she looked sexy doing it. Then she sucked that finger into her mouth, feeling a little silly.

I suck at this whole seduction thing.

"I'm a big girl, Tony. I think I know what I can handle." *And I don't want to handle my liquor tonight. I have plans. Big plans.*

Tony rose to his feet with a perturbed look on his face and rubbed his stubbly jaw. "You sure?"

"Mm-hmm." Even as she said it, she considered saying, *Water's good. Just get me water.* She watched him walk up to the bar. At heart, Amy was a good girl. Her courage faltered and she tried to hang on to a shred of it. She needed to know if there was even the slightest chance that she and Tony might end up together. The problem was, she wasn't a seductress. She didn't even know where to begin. That was Jenna's forte, with her hourglass figure and sassy personality. Even Bella, who was as brash as she was loving, had pulled off being seductive with Caden. The sexy-kitten pictures on Amy's pajamas were more seductive than she was.

"Oh my gosh. I thought he'd never leave." Jenna glanced at Caden, Kurt, and Jamie, still enthralled with their fiancées at the other end of the table. She pulled Amy across the table and whispered, "This is your night. I can feel it!" She sat back and swayed to the music in her tight green spaghetti-strap dress with a neckline cut so low Pete could probably get lost in there.

Amy looked down at the slinky black dress the girls had put her in earlier that evening. They were always trying to tart her up. *One look at you in this dress with these sky-high heels and Tony's gonna be all over you*, Jenna had said while Jessica and Bella shimmied the dress down Amy's pin-thin body. *Fits like a glove. A sexy, slither-me-out-of-this glove*, Leanna had added. They'd pushed her into a chair, plied her with wine, and sometime later—Amy had no idea how long, because the alcohol had not only made her body go all loose and soft, but it had turned her brain to mush—they were in the bar with the men, and with her friends' confidence, she'd actually begun to believe that she might be able to pull off being übersexy for a night. Her mind might be foggy, but she'd caught a few words while the girls primped her into a hot, racy woman she didn't recognize. Her friends had thrown out words like *sexy, hot, take him* as if they were handing out doses of confidence.

Now she tugged at the hemline of the dress that barely covered the thong they'd also bought for her and insisted she wear.

She wiggled in her seat, uncomfortable in the lacy butt floss. She should probably give up even trying and just let the new job change her life. Move to Australia, where she'd be too far for any relationship with Tony, and be done with it, but every time she looked at Tony, her stomach got all fluttery. It had done that since she was six years old, so she was pretty sure it wasn't going to change.

Caden, Pete, Jamie, and Kurt must have taken Jenna's whispers and hot stares as a cue, because they headed up to the bar, and Jessica, Bella, and Leanna scooted closer to Amy and Jenna.

"How about you put those puppies away before the guys over at that table drool into their drinks," Leanna said to Jenna while glaring at the three handsome, leering men sitting at the next table. They finally looked away when Bella shot them a threatening stare.

Jenna wrestled her boobs into submission with an annoyed look on her face. She always acted annoyed about her boobs, but Amy knew it was a love-hate annoyance. Jenna wouldn't be Jenna without her boobs always trying to break free.

"Look at our men up there at the bar." Bella wiggled her fingers at Caden. "Pete has his eyes on the drooling men. Kurt and Jamie are eyeing Leanna and Jessica like they're on the menu, and Tony..."

"*Your* men," Amy corrected her. "Tony's not mine, and he looks mad, doesn't he?"

"Sexually frustrated, maybe. Not mad." Bella took a sip of her drink. "But you'll fix that tonight. I mean, be real, Amy. Who tells a girl to *behave and be careful* whenever she goes out if he's not interested? Why would he care? And not just that—he always adds that you can text him if you need him and he'll come running. Just. Like. Always."

Amy couldn't stop the exasperated sound that left her lips. "You read my texts?" That was the only way she could have known that Tony always offered to be there if she needed him.

"Duh. Of course I did. Consider it a recon mission. I had to know what we were dealing with here from his side." Bella had been pulling for Amy and Tony to get together as long as Amy had been in love with him, which was just about forever. She stood and dragged Amy toward the dance floor. "Come on, sweetie. Time to have some fun."

The other girls jumped up and followed them. Amy sensed Tony's eyes on her before she caught sight of him watching them. It made her nervous and excited at once. The music blared with a fast beat. Amy's head was spinning from the alcohol, and as Bella and Jenna dirty danced up and down her body, gyrating with their hands in the air, Amy tried to ignore the rush of anticipation mixing with nervous energy inside her. Leanna and Jessica danced beside them in a far less evocative fashion that was more Amy's speed, but she could no sooner disengage from being the target of Jenna's and Bella's sexy dancing than she could ignore Tony as he moved to the edge of the dance floor. His eyes raked slowly down her body, making her insides twist in delight. His jaw muscles bunched as he slid his eyes around the bar and leveled the leering men at the table a few feet away with a dark stare.

The sexy dancing, the alcohol, and the way Tony was guarding her like she was a precious treasure—his precious treasure?—boosted her confidence. Amy rocked her hips to the beat. She closed her eyes, lifted her hands above her head, and let the music carry her into what she hoped was a plethora of tempting moves.

"You go, girlfriend," Jenna encouraged her. "He's not going to be able to resist you. You're drunk, sexy, and ready for action. What man could resist that?" She wiggled her butt against Amy's hips.

"Oh, please. He'll probably *never* reciprocate my feelings, which is why I'm seriously considering the job offer from Duke Ryder." *Never again, anyway.* Her chest tightened with the thought.

"No, you are *not*." Bella's eyes widened as she froze and pointed her finger at Amy, right there in the middle of the dance floor. "You are not going to move to Australia for two years. You'll never come back to Seaside in the summers if you're in *Australia*. Can't you tell Duke you'll consider nine months out of the year instead of twelve?"

Duke Ryder was a real-estate investor who owned more than a hundred properties throughout the world. He was also Blue and Jake's older brother. Blue Ryder was a specialty carpenter who had renovated Kurt and Leanna's cottage and built an art studio for Jenna and Pete. He'd since become one of the gang and hung out with them often. Jake was an Army Ranger and mountain-rescue specialist. Amy had dated Jake briefly last summer, but he was younger and too wild for her. And…he wasn't Tony.

"No, I can't," Amy answered. "It's a full-time position heading up the creation of the new Ryder Conference Center. The conference center is going to be the focus of international meetings with major corporations. I think I need to be on-site full-time." Amy had worked with Duke on a consulting basis for several years. When Jessica and Jamie had said they were getting married at the Ryder Resort in Boston, Amy had jumped at the chance to help plan the event and work with

Duke and his staff again. Amy had known that Duke was negotiating on a property in Australia, but she hadn't realized he'd sealed the deal until she'd arrived at the resort two days ago and he'd offered her a full-time job as director of operations for the Conference Division Center. She'd never been to Australia, and between all of her friends getting engaged and summer after summer of wasted energy spent on a man who treated her more like an adoring brother than a potential love interest, she decided it was high time she made some changes in her life.

Amy tucked her straight blond hair behind her ears and moved her shoulders to the slow beat of the music. "I'm not sure being here for the summer is smart anyway. It's like torturing myself." She stopped dancing at the thought of not coming back to Seaside for the summers. Could she really do that? Would she even want to? Could she survive not seeing Tony even if she knew for sure he didn't want her?

This was why she had to figure out her life and make a change. She was becoming pathetic.

She sensed Tony's eyes on her again and forced her hips to find the beat as Bella and Leanna danced closer. "It might be time I move on," she said more confidently than she felt.

"Move on from Tony?" Bella took her hand and dragged her back toward the table with the others on their heels.

Amy saw Tony's eyes narrowing as they hurried past. Why was he so angry all of a sudden?

"He's so into you, he won't let you go." Bella elbowed her as they took their seats. "He texts you almost every day."

"Yeah, with stuff like, *Won another competition* and *Check me out in Surfer Mag next month!* He texts me when he's going to miss an event at Seaside. He doesn't text me because he misses me or wants to see me." Tony had started texting her during the summers when they were teenagers, because Amy was the only one who checked her cell phone when they were at the Cape, and at some point, those summer texts had turned into a year-round connection. He'd stopped texting her for a few years when she was in college and he was building his surfing and speaking careers, although she knew the real reason he'd stopped, and it had nothing to do with either. After she'd graduated from college, he'd begun texting again. She hadn't known why he started up again, and after having been without that connection for so long, she didn't ask. She was just glad to have him back. Since then, she'd become his habit, but not exactly the type of habit she wanted to be.

"It's not like what each of you have. I want that, what you have. I want a guy who says I'm the only woman for him and that he can't live without me, like your guys say to you." *I want Tony to say that.*

Seeing her girlfriends so much in love was what really drove home how lonely Amy had become over the past few summers.

"I think he takes care of you like you're *his*. I mean, how many guys text to say they saw a kitty pajama top you'd look adorable in if they aren't gay or interested?" Bella shifted her shoulders in a *Yeah, that's right* way.

"I'm probably the only woman he knows who wears kitty pajamas. He was teasing me, not being flirty or boyfriendish." *Was he?* No, he definitely wasn't. There had been times when Amy had thought Tony was looking at her like he was interested in a more intimate way, but they were fleeting seconds, and they passed as quickly as he'd taken his next breath. She was probably seeing what she wanted to see, not what he really felt, and she'd begun to wonder if she'd really loved him for so long, or if he'd become *her* habit, too.

"You know, he's never brought another woman to Seaside." Leanna's loose dark mane was wavy and tousled. With her golden tan and simple summer dress, she looked like she'd just come from the beach. Her gaze softened in a way that made Amy feel like she wanted to fall into Leanna's arms and disappear. "And look how he treats you. He's always got an arm around you, and when you drink too much at our barbecues, he always carries you home."

Amy wanted to believe them and to see what they apparently saw when he looked at her, but she never had. It was the secret memories of being in Tony's strong arms that long-ago summer, feeling his heart beat against hers, feeling safe and loved, that made her hopeful there would come a day when they'd find themselves there again. But then her mind would travel to the *end* of those recent nights when she'd had too much to drink and he'd carried her home. When he'd tucked her into bed and gone along his merry way back to his own cottage across the road, quickly dousing her hope for more with cold reality. Whatever they'd had that summer, she'd ruined.

"Exactly, Leanna. That's why she's not making a decision about Australia until *after* this weekend," Jenna said. "Right, Ames?"

"Yes. That's my plan. I'm going to talk to Tony, and if he looks me in the eye and says he has no interest in anything more than friendship, then I'm going to take the job. It's pretty stupid, really, because how many times has he had the opportunity to...you know?" She dropped her eyes to her glass and ran her finger along the rim. Amy was as sweet as Bella was brash, and even thinking about trying to seduce Tony and finding out where his heart really stood had her stomach tied in knots. When her friends had come up with the idea of seducing

Tony, she'd fought it, but they'd insisted that once he kissed her, he'd never look back, and she'd grabbed that shred of hope as if it were a brass ring. Now her fingers were slipping a little.

"Talk? That's not the plan," Jenna said.

Jessica shook her head. "So, seduction? You're going to try?"

"If I can muster the courage." Amy drew in a deep breath, hoping she wouldn't back out. As much as she wanted closure, the idea of actually hearing Tony tell her that he didn't see her as anything other than a friend made her almost chicken out. But she didn't want to chicken out. She had a great job opportunity, and at thirty-two, she was ready to settle down and maybe even start a family. But that thought was even more painful than Tony turning her away.

Tony set a disconcerting stare on Amy as he moved confidently across the floor with the other guys, heading for their table. Her pulse ratcheted up a notch as his eyes went dark and narrow. She broke the connection, grazing over his low-slung jeans and short-sleeve button-down shirt, afraid to try to decipher if it was an angry or an interested look in his eyes. She'd probably see only what she really wanted to see anyway.

Big mistake. Now she was even more nervous.

Several women in the bar turned and watched the four gorgeous men crossing the floor, but Amy knew they had to be looking at Tony. She was held prisoner by his sun-drenched skin, sandy hair that brushed his devilishly long lashes, and squared-off features that amped up his ruggedness and made her pulse go a little crazy. She reached for a glass of liquid courage, having no idea whose it was, and drained it as Tony slid in beside her. His thigh met hers, and his irresistible scent made her hot all over again. She grabbed another glass and drained it, and another, until the glasses were all empty and the nervous stirrings in her stomach stilled.

"Since when did you become Beyoncé?" Tony grumbled.

Beyoncé? Was that good or bad? Amy couldn't form an answer. All she could think about was that no matter what the outcome, after tonight her life would never be the same.

TONY HAD SPENT the last three hours watching men ogle Amy in that skimpy dress of hers. What was she thinking, dressing like that? He worried about her when she drank. She was too small to protect herself against unwanted advances, and she exuded sweetness like she was made of sugar, making her an easy target for a savvy guy. And he knew for a fact that Amy Maples was made of sugar—and spice and all things in between that were delicious and worthy of being savored. But that was a long time ago, and he'd spent years making sure Amy was treated as she deserved to be and putting his own desires on the back burner. Or trying to, anyway. He didn't think anyone else noticed that he could barely hold himself together when it came to Amy, and he was grateful for that.

She was looking at him in a way that was reminiscent of that summer years ago, and he assumed it was caused by the far-too-many drinks she'd consumed. She never could hold her alcohol. He ran his hand through his hair and ground his teeth together. Maybe he'd take a walk back up to the bar to get away from the jerks watching her. He'd seen Pete stare them down when they were leering at Jenna, but Pete was Jenna's fiancé. She was his to protect.

Well, he wasn't Amy's fiancé, but she needed protecting too.

She's with Bella and the girls. They'll protect her. He mulled that over for a minute or two. *Bella and the girls.* Yeah, they'd protect Amy. They were about as protective of Amy as he was, but the idea of moving from Amy's side and having some jerk saunter over and hit on her messed with his mind. She was so darn beautiful and way too naive for her own good. One of her gorgeous smiles could stop a man cold, and she was clueless to that fact. It was so easy not to think about those things when they were in different states during the year, but summers? They were torture. And these last few summers, watching his summer friends fall in love, made this time with Amy even more difficult. But they'd crossed that line years ago, and not only had it not ended well, but Amy seemed to have moved on just fine, while Tony never really had.

He thought about all the summer nights since then that he'd spent checking up on her, making sure she got home safely. The summer she'd turned twenty-two and insisted on going out with that bonehead, Kevin Palish. Tony'd stalked his window that night until she'd arrived home safely. Normally he tried to ignore the Seaside gossip about who Amy was dating, and she seemed to keep guys away from the complex, as far as he could see, but a few summers ago she'd dated that other guy who came around more than a handful of times. What was his name? Mr. Tall, Dark, and Annoying? Tony had waited up every night for a week to make sure Amy got home okay—and to make sure the dude left shortly after dropping her off at her cottage. Not that it was any of his business or that he could have done anything about it if they'd spent the night together. That was the problem. It wasn't his business. Luckily, Amy had come to her senses and broken up with the guy before Tony ever woke up to the guy's truck in her driveway.

Amy wiggled in the seat beside him, tugging at that way-too-short dress. Her thigh pressed against his, and it suddenly got way too hot in there. He unbuttoned another button of his shirt and exhaled loudly, trying to talk himself out of going up to the bar. He should stay right there to ward off looks, like the one the dark-haired guy from the table of oglers was giving her. Amy smiled and fidgeted with the hem of her dress again. *For the love of...* Tony's thoughts drifted to last summer when she'd dated bad-boy, mountain-rescuer, handsome-as-Brad-Freaking-Pitt Jake Ryder. Tony had seen all the women at the beach party eyeing Jake, and Amy had acted the same adorably nervous way around him. Jake was younger than Amy, too, which pissed Tony off even more, and he was friends with Jake. He actually liked the guy. But she needed a man, not a boy.

Enough already. If he couldn't be the man she deserved, he could at least make sure no other guy treated her badly. He laced his fingers with hers and set their hands on her thigh.

"What?" Amy asked.

Tony nodded at the guy at the next table. "No need to flirt with a guy like that. He'll only hurt you."

"Then maybe you should take me back to my room." She said it with wide, innocent eyes that tore right through him like lightning.

He rose to his feet and pulled Amy up with him.

"We're calling it a night," he said to their friends. He needed to get her to her room before she got herself into trouble—or before he got himself into trouble. "I'm going to walk Amy back to her hotel room. Jamie, Jessica, enjoy your last night of freedom."

"You're kidding, right?" Jamie rubbed noses with Jessica. "Who needs freedom? All I want is to wake up with Jessica in my arms for the rest of my life."

Yeah, and all I want is to wake up with Amy in my arms.

He shifted his eyes to Amy, standing before him pink-cheeked, glassy-eyed, and sexier than anything in that skimpy little black number that looked painted on and high heels that did something amazing to her long, lean legs. He forced his eyes north, to the sleek line of her collarbone, which he wanted to trace with his tongue. Her hair fell over one of her heavy-lidded green eyes, giving her a sultry look that sent heat through his body. When she trapped her lower lip between her teeth, it took all his effort to force something other than, *Man, you look hot,* from his lips. Well…how was he supposed to resist her now?

She slid her arm around his waist and leaned her head against his chest.

"Okay, big guy. Take me home."

If she only knew what those words coming from her while dressed in that outfit did to him. As he'd done for too many years to count, he bit back his desires and walked her back to her room. He pulled her room card from his pocket, and it dawned on him that he always carried Amy's stuff. Her keys, her wallet, her phone. At some point, his pockets had become her pocketbook.

Tony held the door open for Amy and kept one hand on her hip as she walked unsteadily past him.

He closed the door and took in her hotel room. Standard upscale fare, it looked like his room, with a king-size bed, a long dresser and mirror, and a decent-size sitting area. Amy's perfume and lotions were lined up neatly on the dresser, along with her birth control pills, which made his gut twist a little. He didn't want to think about Amy having sex with anyone. Well, except maybe him, but—

"Hey." Amy reeled around on him, stepping forward in those sky-high heels. He didn't need to inhale to know that she smelled like warm vanilla, a scent that haunted him at night.

She wobbled a little, and instinct brought his hand to her waist. He'd held Amy in his arms a million times, comforting her when she was sad, carrying her when she was a little too drunk to be steady on her feet. He'd cared for her when she was sick and sat up with her after each of her girlfriends had fallen in love, when she simply couldn't handle being alone. He had a feeling those nights were their little secrets, because he'd never heard Bella, Jenna, or Leanna ever make reference to them, and those girls talked about everything. Now, as she stepped closer and touched his stomach with one finger and looked at him like she had years ago, not like the sweet, too-good-to-be-true Amy that she never strayed from around him unless she was drinking, he found himself struggling to remain detached enough to keep his feelings in check.

He forced himself to act casual. "What's up, Ames?"

She trapped that lower lip of hers again, and his body warmed.

Amy stumbled on her heels and caught herself against his chest. She slid her hands up the front of his shirt, and his body responded like Pavlov's dog. Amy had that effect on him, but he'd always been good about keeping it under wraps. What was happening to him? Was it the romance of the impending wedding? Watching his best buddies whisper and nuzzle their fiancées while he had walls so thick around his heart that he didn't know if he'd ever be able to move forward and love anyone else again?

She gazed up at him with naive curiosity in her eyes, and it was that innocence that threatened his steely resolve. It almost did him in every time they were alone together. Only this time she had the whole hips-swaying, chest-pushing-against-him thing going on.

He covered her hands with his and breathed deeply. With those heels, they were much closer in height. A bow of his head and he could finally taste her sweet mouth again.

With that selfish thought, he pressed her hands to his chest to keep them from roaming and to keep himself from becoming any more aroused. She gazed up at him, looking a little confused and so sexy it was all he could do to squelch his desire to take her in his arms and devour her.

"What do you need, Ames?"

"I'm pretty sure you know what I need," she said in a husky voice as she pressed her hips to his.

You don't mean that. You're just drunk. He clenched his jaw against his mounting desire. She was all he'd ever wanted, and she was the one person he knew he should walk away from.

"Amy."

"Tony." Her voice was thin and shaky.

"You're drunk." He peeled her hands from his chest. She got like this when she was drunk: sultry, sexier, eager. As adults, she'd never taken it this far. She'd made innuendos over the years, but more in jest than anything else. He wasn't an idiot. He knew Amy cared about him, but he also knew she sometimes forgot things. Important things. Life-altering events that were less painful if forgotten. He was certain it was why she drank when they were together and why he'd spent years protecting her. Not that she needed protecting often. Drinking was a summer thing for Amy, and really, she rarely drank too much. She didn't drink when she wasn't at the Cape. He knew this because over recent years, after Amy had graduated from college and settled into her business, he'd begun texting her more often. He'd been unable to ignore his need for a connection to her any longer. He could count on one hand how many times she'd made reference to drinking.

"I might be a little drunk." Her sweet lips curved into a nervous smile. "But I think I know what *you* want."

What I want and what I'll let myself have are two very different things.

He exhaled, took her hand, and turned toward the bed. "Sit down and let me help you get out of your heels and then I'll go back to my room. I don't want you to break your ankle."

She swayed on her heels and attached herself to his side again. "I don't want you to go to your room."

Tony stepped back. The back of his legs met the dresser. "Amy—"

"Tony," she said huskily, taking him by surprise.

"Ames," he whispered. She was killing him. Any other man would have silenced her with a kiss, carried her to the bed, pushed that sexy dress up to her neck, and given her what she wanted. But Tony had made a career out of resisting Amy, protecting her. He respected her too much to let her make a mistake she would only regret when she sobered up.

He gripped her forearms and held her at a safe distance.

She narrowed her eyes and reached for him.

For a breath he closed his eyes and let himself enjoy the feel of her touching him. Every muscle in his body corded tight as her hand slid down his chest. He reluctantly gripped her wrist.

"Amy, stop." He'd learned his lesson with her when he was a teenager, and he was never letting either of them go back to that well of hurt. "We're not doing this."

The dark seductiveness that had filled her eyes when she was touching him was gone as quickly as it had appeared. Her shoulders rounded forward, and hurt filled her eyes.

"Why?"

He felt like a heel. An idiot. A guy who *should* have taken her to bed, if only to love her as she deserved to be loved. Even if she might not remember or appreciate it in the morning. He draped an arm over her shoulder and pulled her into a hug.

"Come on, Amy. You're drunk and you won't remember any of this tomorrow. Let me help you get ready for bed."

"Don't you want me?"

Her broken voice nearly did him in, and when her arms went limp, he tightened his grip on her. "Amy," he whispered again.

In the space of a few seconds she pushed away from him, determination written in the tension around her mouth and the fisting of her hands.

"Tell me why you don't want me. What is it? Am I too flat-chested? Too unattractive?"

"No." *You're the sexiest woman I know.* Anger felt so wrong coming from her that it momentarily numbed him.

"I know I suck at seduction, but don't these take-me high heels or this stupid dress turn you on? Even a little?"

"Your take-me heels? Boy, you are drunk. You don't realize what you're saying. Come on." He reached for her hand and she shrugged him off again.

"Come on, Amy. Let me help you." *Before I give in to what I really want and lay your vulnerable, gorgeous, sexy body down and devour you.*

"So that's it. I don't turn you on." She paced the room on wobbly ankles, looking like she was playing dress up in her mother's high heels—and it did crazy things to Tony's body.

He followed beside her in case she stumbled, fighting the urge to give in and show her just how much she turned him on.

"Maybe if I had bigger boobs, or if I were better at acting sexy, or if I were smarter, you'd want me."

It surprised him that she avoided the secret they'd buried so long ago, but then again, after that summer, she'd never said another word about it. And he'd let her get away with that, believing it was the only way she could survive what had happened. Just like him.

"Amy, it's none of those things." He did *not* want to have this conversation with her. He wanted to fold her in his arms and kiss the worry away.

Tears slipped down her cheeks.

Tony could handle a lot of things, but Amy's tears melted his heart, and that he'd caused them was further proof he wasn't the right guy for her.

"Then why, Tony? Just tell me once and for all. Why don't you want me? I need to know so I can decide about taking this job in Australia."

Tony opened his mouth to answer, but his thoughts were jumbled as he processed what she'd said. "Australia? I thought you said you weren't taking it."

She crossed her arms, and he hated knowing it was to protect herself from his rejection. Tony felt like a heel, but he knew that taking Amy up on her seduction would only dredge up bad memories and lead to hurting her. They'd spent a lifetime denying the past between them existed, even to themselves.

"I said I wasn't sure what I was going to do." She dropped her eyes to the floor, and he slid a hand in hers, as he'd done a million times before. It was a natural reaction. Taking care of her. Protecting her. Helping her feel safe. He knew it could send her mixed messages, but he just couldn't help himself. His hand had already claimed its spot with hers.

"You'd give up everything you've built to run Duke's resort? You'd move to Australia?" He had nothing against Duke Ryder. But the idea that Amy would change her life to help him just pissed Tony off.

She sank down onto the bed and buried her face in her hands.

He wrapped an arm around her shoulder, and when she tried to pull away, he tightened his grip and kissed the top of her head.

"Amy, you're sexy, smart, and everything a guy could want."

She cocked her head to the side and narrowed her damp eyes. He felt like the biggest jerk on earth, and at the same time, his own heart was fighting tooth and nail against the space he was trying to maintain between them.

He scrubbed his hand down his face. "You are all those things, Amy, and so much more, but…"

"But you like me as a friend."

He'd never seen so much hurt concentrated in one person's eyes, and even if he had, it wouldn't have compared to seeing it in Amy's. He touched his forehead to hers, and he did the only thing he knew how to do without doing irreparable damage to their friendship.

His lie came in a whisper. "No. I *love* you as a friend."

He loved Bella, Caden, and the others. But what he felt for Amy was so much bigger than friendship, it threatened to stop his heart.

She didn't say a word, just nodded, and Tony knew in that moment that she wasn't drunk enough to forget what he'd said by the morning—and he almost wished she were.

Chapter Two

THERE WERE TIMES in a woman's life when she needed to be anywhere but in her own head. This was one of those times. Amy stood on the side of the dance floor at Jamie and Jessica's wedding reception, reflecting on all that had transpired the night before. Amy had spent the entire night trying to separate herself from her heart and trying to convince herself that she could live a perfectly happy life without Tony in it.

And she'd failed.

Miserably.

She was surprised her bed hadn't fallen through the floor with the weight of her tears last night. Amy had no business trying to seduce Tony. She hadn't a clue what she was doing. Did her friends really think that after all these years he'd suddenly look at her and profess his love to her? *Did I?* She must be a glutton for punishment.

He. Doesn't. Love. Me.

It had taken Jenna an hour to cover every splotch and conceal the dark moons under Amy's eyes. Before the ceremony, Leanna and Jessica had given her such good pep talks that she almost believed Tony was no longer worthy of her thoughts. Bella, however, hadn't been quite as ready to let him go. She'd wanted Tony's head on a platter.

At least they'd made it through the ceremony without any head chopping, and it turned out that Amy *did* have more tears to shed. She'd cried when Jessica and Jamie exchanged their wedding vows. Jessica looked radiant in a chiffon sheath wedding dress with a sweetheart neckline and crisscross bodice. It was the perfect combination of elegance and simplicity. Jamie couldn't have been more handsome in his dark tux with the look of love in his eyes so thick and palpable Amy felt like a voyeur.

The reception was half over, and so far Amy had successfully avoided saying two words to Tony. With Bella on the warpath, she was pretty sure that Tony was keeping his distance in order to save the wedding from a scene. She'd been busy keeping her distance from her father. She adored him, but he was so overprotective that she didn't think she could stand his scrutiny on the heels of her very messed up seduction. Luckily, he'd been too busy talking with Jamie's grandmother, Vera, and Leanna's parents to track her down.

She allowed herself one small peek at Tony. She was annoyed at how her stomach fluttered at the sight of him. Holy mother of hotness, did he have to look so good in that tux? His shoulders seemed impossibly broad. Tuxes weren't supposed to fit tightly, but heck if his biceps didn't stretch that fancy material every time he lifted his drink. His hair needed a trim. His hair always needed a trim. Amy liked the way his sandy blond hair brushed his thick lashes. She found it even more attractive that he wasn't perfectly manicured, as was all the rage.

She remembered all the summers their families had spent together at the Cape, the way she'd watched his body change over the years, hoping he'd notice hers. She thought of the tall and lanky boy he'd been the summer after high school and the way their young bodies had fit together like they were made for each other. She fought hard to push those intimate thoughts away again, thinking instead of the years when she'd been in college and he'd been surfing around the world, making a name for himself. He'd broadened and become muscled to heart-throbbing proportions over those years when they hadn't seen each other much. They'd drifted apart, making it easier to allow their past to drift away, too. But her feelings had never changed. She'd loved him then and she loved him now. Even if he didn't love her back the way she wanted him to.

"Amy."

Bella's voice startled her, and when she lifted her eyes, they were all there for her. Her saviors. Her Seaside sisters. Bella, Leanna, Jenna, Jessica, and even Sky.

"Hey." Amy smoothed her royal-blue bridesmaid dress. Jessica had chosen short dresses that were chic enough to wear to the wedding but casual enough to wear again to a fancy dinner or out on the town. Jenna had kept her dark hair longer this summer, nearly the same length as Bella's, Leanna's, and Amy's, to the middle of their backs, which would look nice in the wedding pictures.

"Come on, gorgeous." Bella reached for her hand. "We're not going to sulk over surfer boy."

"No, I'm definitely not," she lied.

"Besides, your father is about ten feet behind you. I figured you needed backup." Bella shifted her eyes over Amy's shoulder.

"Oh no," Amy whispered. Her mother and father had divorced when she was twelve, and while she'd split her time between the two of them during the year, after their divorce, she'd continued spending the summers with her father at the

Cape. It had been her mother who'd initiated the divorce with a need to find herself, whatever that meant to her, and Amy had always felt bad for her father. She was very much a daddy's girl before the divorce, and after, having felt bad for him, she'd tried even harder to please him.

She felt his hand on her shoulder and smelled his Old Spice cologne before he said a word. She feigned a smile and turned. "Hi, Dad."

"How's my princess?" He hugged her close, and before she could get a word out, he said, "I'm so proud of you, Amy. When you called to say you increased your business revenue by thirty percent, I had to brag to all of my cohorts."

Of course you did. "I'm glad you're proud, Dad." Her father was in his late fifties. His once-thick blond hair was now flecked with white and thinning on top. He wasn't a heavy man, but his face had lost any signs of youth, and his jowls showed his age.

"I told you Brown would pay off. A chip off the old block, that's what you are." He draped an arm over her shoulder and pulled her in close. "That's my girl."

"Thanks, Dad."

"It's your focus that has you rising to the top, princess. You're smarter and more determined than any other woman out there."

As if he only just realized the others were there, he smiled at them. "Girls, you all look lovely."

"Thank you," they said collectively.

Bella reached for Amy's hand and pulled her out from her father's grasp. Amy wanted to thank her, but she knew better than to let on that she was being saved.

"Mr. Maples, if you don't mind, we have some bridesmaidy things to attend to," Bella said.

"Oh." His thick brows drew together. "Princess, I'm proud of you. We'll catch up. Call me sometime soon. I want to go over your business plan for next year."

It was all Amy could do to keep from rolling her eyes. "I will, Dad." She took the opportunity to turn away and speak to Jessica, hoping her father would take the hint. "Jess, that was the most beautiful wedding I've ever been to." Luckily, her father turned his attention to someone else. She breathed a little easier with him out of the picture. "Thanks, Bella."

"The man would rule every minute of your life if you let him, but I think he means well," Bella said.

"He does mean well. He just…means too well. Anyway, now it's time for you, Leanna, and Jenna to get married."

"No way." Jenna draped an arm over her shoulder. "We made a deal. The four of us are getting married together, remember?"

"In case you haven't noticed, I'm not even dating." Amy smiled at the thought that they would even consider waiting for her after last night's debacle.

"Ha! I see eligible bachelors." Jenna pointed across the room to Blue Ryder, standing with Duke, both looking incredibly hot in their suits. What was it about men in suits that made them look sexier?

"I'm sure Sky wouldn't want me to go out with Blue, and Duke might be my new boss. I think I'm okay by myself. Besides, I have you guys. I don't need a man."

Sky rolled her eyes and flipped her long brown hair over her shoulders. She was a total throwback from the seventies, with her bohemian style and laid-back nature. "Blue and I are just friends. I've told you guys that a hundred times."

"Whatever. Then you're crazy." Bella laughed. "What is it

with people being so obviously interested in each other and fighting it?"

"*I'm* not fighting a darn thing. Or at least I wasn't trying to." Amy glanced at Tony as a tall, curvy brunette made a beeline for him.

Jessica followed her gaze and cringed. "Sorry, Amy. That's one of my symphony friends. She's a Worthington. Very rich, a little snotty. Not the type of woman Tony would like, I'm sure." Jessica played the cello for the Boston Symphony Orchestra.

Bella spun Amy around so her back was to Tony. "Anyway… About that job. I think that regardless of what happened with Tony, you shouldn't take it unless you can get summers off."

"I know you do, Bella. I'm talking to Duke tomorrow to find out a few more details. But honestly, Tony made his feelings, or lack thereof, very clear to me last night. I think I just need to accept it and move on. And maybe moving on means not seeing him for eight weeks every summer."

They turned back to their friends as Jamie swept Jessica out to the dance floor. Caden and Pete were right behind them.

"Babe?" Caden held a hand out to Bella and nodded toward the dance floor.

Bella turned compassionate eyes to Amy. "Ames?"

"I'm fine. Go." She watched her friends wrapped in their loved ones' arms. Even Blue and Sky were dancing cheek to cheek, just friends or not. She'd like to be dancing cheek to cheek with Tony. *I love you as a friend.* Could she accept his honesty and still have the same friendship they'd always shared? On some level she knew that just because she now had her answer, their friendship shouldn't change. If anything, it should

get stronger. Now that she clearly understoo
she should be able to remove the hope and antic
having more.

She watched the couples on the dance floor and
friend of Jessica's dancing with his teenage daughte Tony passed behind them, and suddenly the sight of that teenage girl threw Amy off-kilter, sending her mind back to when she and Tony were teenagers.

Tony turned and their eyes locked. Her knees weakened. This was too much. He was too much.

Who was she kidding?

He wasn't just too much.

He was everything.

TONY WATCHED AS Amy lowered herself into a chair and shifted her eyes away, but not before he saw the look in her eyes. Maybe she hadn't buried the past so deeply after all.

She'd been avoiding him all day, and he hated that as much as he hated the idea of her being with anyone else. She looked stunning in her blue strapless dress, but no amount of makeup could hide the pain he'd read in her eyes. Her eyes never lied. Not when she was a teenager and not as an adult. Not even last night, when they'd been full of love and lust and when they'd clouded over with hurt. He needed to apologize for hurting her. He wished he could save himself from the pain, too, but that was his cross to bear.

While he was busy mulling over the line he'd drawn in the sand, Duke joined Amy at the table. Duke had about two inches on Tony. All of the Ryders were six three or six four, with athletic builds and a look of determination in their eyes. Duke reminded Tony of every surfing competitor he'd ever had: savvy, always sizing up his surroundings. But beneath that carefully devised exterior, he had a friendly nature, and he was always talking about his family. He was a good man, and he'd make a good boss for Amy. And Tony knew by Duke's protectiveness over his own sister that he'd watch out for Amy.

Duke sat beside her and leaned in close, talking about who knew what. The job, probably. Amy was smiling, but it wasn't the same smile Tony knew and loved. It was forced, and it never reached her eyes. He wondered if Duke could see that, too, or if he was oblivious the way new employers usually were.

"Hey there, handsome."

Tony clenched his jaw. Cher Worthington was Jessica's friend from work, a clingy brunette with big knockers and an hourglass figure. There was never a shortage of attractive women wanting to accompany Tony in a night of no-strings-attached sex. He could have his pick of jailbait to cougar, groupie to celebrity. Since Tony had long ago built a fortress around his heart, the whole no-strings scenario had always suited him just fine. But at thirty-four, he was no longer interested in overenthusiastic twenty-three-year-olds, lecherous cougars looking to ease the pain of aging, or anyone in between.

"Hi, Cher." He walked toward Amy and Duke. Over the last few summers, as Tony watched his friends at Seaside fall in love and move toward the altar, his interests had narrowed. So much so that they were heading backward.

Cher draped her hand possessively on Tony's shoulder. Her breath brushed against his ear. "Help a lady ease her loneliness? Dance with me?"

Amy lifted hopeful eyes to Tony as he headed her way. Her

gaze slid to Cher, hanging on Tony like a second shirt, and all that hope evaporated as if it had never existed. What the heck was wrong with him? This was just one reason why he couldn't be with Amy. Inside he was pining for Amy, tearing himself up over hurting her and wanting her more than he'd ever wanted another woman—and he hadn't thought to shake Cher off. He'd become so used to attention from women that he'd ignored it and had inadvertently hurt Amy again.

This was so messed up.

He glanced at the dance floor. Caden was gazing into Bella's eyes. Pete and Jenna were smooching, and Jamie and Jessica, well, were they ever not lusting after each other? And Kurt and Leanna? Those two emitted love from a thousand miles away.

Like Amy. Sweet Amy. She looked at him with more emotion than any of their friends looked at each other. If he had a sliver of a chance of being the man she deserved, he'd give up everything else in his life just to be with her.

"Excuse me, Cher." He stepped away and closed the gap between him and Amy. He would give up surfing, motivational speaking. He'd give up breathing if he could be good enough for her, but he wasn't even sure he knew how to own his feelings anymore after repressing them for so long.

"Hi, Tony." Duke nodded, smiled. "I caught your competition in the spring. Nice win." He had deep-set eyes, a jaw that could chisel granite, and a strong voice that commanded attention.

As Tony shook his hand, he noticed Cher giving Duke a lascivious leer. *Better him than me.*

"Thanks, man. It was a good year."

"Well, now that I've got the Australia resort, why don't you stay there when you compete out that way? I'll make it a point to be there, and we can celebrate together." Duke smiled at Amy. "And if I'm lucky, Amy'll be running the conference center operations, so she can join us."

"Sounds great," Tony said more gruffly than he'd intended.

"Excuse me, Amy. I'll give you two some privacy."

Tony nodded in response, unable to find his voice. He wondered what was going on in Amy's mind. Was she thinking about how much she hated him after last night? Did she have any hope left that he'd come around? Because if she did, that was a dangerous thing for both of them. How long was a man expected to ward off the only woman he really wanted? His mind was tangled up in all that couldn't be—and all that he'd become. He maintained a bit of a player lifestyle. It kept him from getting hurt, and Amy had the power to slay him. This he knew firsthand…She'd done it once—no, he wouldn't go there.

"Hi." Her voice slid over his skin, with a hint of regret that he knew was all his fault.

He reached for her hand, and she lowered her eyes in contemplation. He'd always held her hand, hadn't he? They'd sat arm in arm around the bonfires at Seaside forever. They'd held hands when they were all out as a group. He had a key to her cottage, and she to his. She didn't take his hand this time, and when she lifted her eyes to his, the pain was back, blazing a path of sorrow and dark history between them, slaying him again, only this time it was his own doing.

His mind reeled back fourteen years. He could still feel the damp sea air. She was eighteen; he was just two years older. Her hair was long and straight and hung well past the middle of her back, just the way he loved it. He could still smell her perfume, Angel by Victoria's Secret. He'd thought it was strange that sweet Amy had worn a perfume from such a risqué store, but that had been the least of his surprises that summer. He'd learned a few hours later that Amy had a few secrets of her own. *I've loved you since you saved the crayfish at Sheep Pond for me, and I'll love you until the day I die. Please love me back.* She'd pledged her love for him with wide eyes and an open heart. He'd saved those crayfish when she was six, and in the years after, he'd thought she looked at him with trust and love that went deeper than infatuation. *Impossible*, he'd told himself for all those years, but then she'd confessed the truth.

Once he'd known how she felt, he could no longer deny his feelings for her. Still he'd held back from doing anything, or he'd tried, for a week, maybe two. Even then he'd known that his feelings for Amy were bigger than he was capable of keeping boxed inside. He'd tried so hard to resist because she was Amy Maples, a girl so pure and good, and he was Tony Black, the older, more experienced guy, on his way to a very public life as a pro surfer.

His feelings for Amy had scared him. He'd been terrified to touch her despite the love they'd shared. How did he get so lucky to have Amy fall in love with him? He'd been scared that the moment their bodies connected, he'd never be able to rein in his feelings again. And there was so much at stake. Their families had known each other forever. Her father had high expectations for her, none of which included traveling with a surfer boyfriend—a guy her father liked well enough, but probably wouldn't approve of as a partner for his perfect daughter. The guy whose own father had taught him everything there was to know about being successful but thought a career in surfing was for losers. There wasn't room in her life for him in the way that she wanted and begged him for. He knew better. Her father was a high-powered, well-respected lawyer, and Amy was set to leave for Brown University at the end of the summer. Then she'd said the words that broke down the walls he'd been hiding behind since he was old enough to define the feelings that swelled within him every time he was near her. *Don't just be my first; be my only.* She hadn't just wanted to sleep with him. She'd asked him for forever, and he'd been ready to promise her the world.

Only then had he allowed himself to give in to the emotions that blanketed him every night and pulled him through the long winter months in anticipation of seeing her. In the darkness by the dunes, he'd folded her into his arms that first time, felt her slender body against his, and cupped her beautiful cheeks in his hands. And as the world around them fell away, their lips brushed. A sliding of skin, the scent of a kiss. He could barely breathe as the moment he'd imagined for so long was upon them. In the next moment, their mouths were sealed as one, their tongues colliding with love and lust and more emotion than either of them knew what to do with. It was a powerful kiss that bound them together and left them wanting more.

After that they'd stolen away for a few precious moments alone every time they were able. Sneaking out of their cottages at night, sharing a sleeping bag beneath the trees in the woods behind the pool. Sharing kisses, and then, a few days later, groping, touching, learning and loving the curves of each other's bodies.

In the blink of an eye, he'd gone from holding back everything in his heart to laying it out for her to soak up, and soak up she did. She was so open to him, so wanting, so caring. She treated him like he was all she ever wanted, and he knew she was all he ever wanted—even though their relationship was secret. Amy had insisted that not even Bella, Jenna, and Leanna find out, because, she'd explained, this part of her life, this intimacy that was so new to her, so all-consuming, would kill her father if he found out. Her father was so protective of her, and he had made it clear to Amy that she couldn't afford any distractions from her schoolwork if she was going to get *anywhere* in life. She'd spent her whole life trying not to disappoint him, and she wasn't taking any chances. He'd fought her on it at first, knowing he'd be unable to hide his feelings. But she'd been adamant. His love for her left him powerless to argue, and he'd reluctantly relented.

Only they *had* taken a chance. One chance. One time, a week after they'd first shared their feelings. Too overcome with passion to slow down and take precautions. *It'll be okay*, she'd said. *You can pull out.* He was older than her, more experienced. He knew the risks. *I don't know*, he'd said halfheartedly. *Love me, Tony. Please love me.* He shouldn't have given in, but he'd been powerless when it came to Amy. He'd loved her so much, he would have turned himself inside out for her. And oh, the way she'd looked at him that night as they made love. Even now, it made his chest feel full.

They'd made love a dozen or so times over the ensuing eight weeks, and when the summer was over, they made secret plans to return to Seaside for a weekend alone. A weekend that Tony would have given his life for—a weekend when they didn't have to hide their relationship.

Three weeks after their families left Seaside and Amy had gone off to Brown University, they'd returned for that secret weekend together. They'd been a couple just shy of twelve weeks. It had been the best twelve weeks of Tony's life. He had Amy. Sweet, precious Amy, and she loved him the way he loved her, with his whole being. She loved him with a heart so big it swallowed him. Amy had said she wanted to talk, but he'd wanted to surf before the sun went down.

The waves were big that weekend, following a storm during the week. Amy may have been lean, but she was strong, with the balance of a gymnast. But that afternoon, she'd turned to look for him just as a wave caught her board, and her foot twisted. Tony's heart had stopped cold as he watched her wipe out. He dove for her as the waves pummeled her against the ocean's rocky floor. At first Tony had no idea what was happening. Blood pooled in her suit. Had she gotten her period? There was too much blood for that. Amy's eyes had bored right through him. She'd clutched his wet skin, digging her nails into him and crying. *Oh no. Oh no. Oh no*, she'd cried. Tony carried her to the car and drove her straight to the hospital.

A miscarriage. He hadn't even known she was pregnant. Amy was too distraught to talk. She lay silent and still in the hospital bed, staring with emotionless eyes at the curtain, and that nurse, that stupid nurse, had looked at him with her beady eyes and hissed, *How could you let your pregnant girlfriend go surfing?*

It was his fault. All of it.

He'd taken Amy back to his cottage that evening, cared for her, loved her, wept with her, and in the morning she'd said she needed time and space. *Time.* The word loomed between them as she packed her bag. *Space.* Tony had felt his heart shatter inside his chest with that one. He felt the change when he hugged her goodbye. She'd held him at a distance, in a cold, halfhearted embrace. He'd wanted to tell her that he'd love her forever, regardless of what happened. He'd wanted to promise her that they'd have a big family one day with as many children as she wanted when she was ready.

But Amy had had other plans.

Plans that didn't include upsetting his budding career or upsetting her father's expectations. Plans that no longer included Tony.

She'd pushed at his chest, eyes wide and...fearful? He could never be sure what he'd seen. *I can't, I'm sorry,* she'd said, before getting into her car and driving away. He'd gone after her, but she'd driven too fast, ignored his texts and phone calls.

Weeks went by without a word from her, and when he'd shown up at her dorm two weeks later, she'd offered nothing. There was no reconciliation, no discussion of the two treacherous weeks that had passed, and no explanation to her reticence beyond a lame excuse of not remembering a thing about the moment that he'd never forget.

He'd tried to bring it up. *We should talk about what happened.* She looked at him like he was crazy. *Happened? I have no idea what you're talking about.* She'd acted like they'd never loved each other. She'd ignored his calls and texts after that, and for several years Tony had avoided going back to the Cape during the summers for more than a few days. Until after she'd graduated from college, when he'd seen her at Seaside and she still acted like nothing had ever happened between them, but at least she was talking to him. Their friendship resumed as if nothing had ever happened—except it had. Tony hadn't forgotten and never would, and from that day on, he'd protected Amy as if she were his only love, all the while reminding himself why she never could be again.

It had been his fault she'd gotten pregnant at a time when she should have had no cares other than having a good time in college. It was his fault she'd gone surfing, his fault she had the miscarriage.

"Tony, did you want something?"

Her voice brought him spinning back into the moment. He recognized the sadness in her eyes as his own, reflecting back at him. He had to save them both from this endless torture, but he couldn't let her go. Not yet. He needed one dance, one last chance to hold her before he set her free forever.

"Dance with me?" He watched her eyes fall to the dance floor and skate over the friends they loved. When her eyes found his again, the air between them chilled. The years they'd shared hovered between them.

"I don't think that's such a good idea."

The sharp edges of her voice sliced right through him. She did what he'd been too chicken to do. He craved one last dance, but she knew he was going to set her free. She probably read his eyes as easily as he'd read hers, and she was doing it first. He'd asked for this outcome, and he shouldn't be surprised by it.

He shouldn't feel like he was losing his best friend.

But as his heart cracked right down the center, he knew what he had to do.

"I think you should take the job in Australia."

Chapter Three

"ARE YOU SURE you don't want me to stick around and drive back with you?" Bella hugged Amy so tightly she thought she'd break a rib.

"Nah. I'll be back at Seaside later tonight. I told Duke I would stay to go over some of the details about the job." Amy didn't want to get Bella any more pissed off at Tony than she already was, so she didn't tell her that he'd told her to take the job. She'd sucked it up last night and pretended that everything was cool, when she felt as though she were dying inside.

"Remember"—Bella narrowed her eyes and pointed at Amy—"negotiate summers at the Cape, or I'll negotiate it for you."

"Oh, please. Don't put that pressure on her." Jenna hugged Amy.

Jamie and Jessica had left early that morning for their honeymoon, and Leanna and Kurt had left at the crack of dawn so Leanna would be back in Wellfleet in time to sell her jams at the flea market. Leanna owned Luscious Leanna's Sweet Treats, and it had taken off over the past few years. Restaurants and stores across the Cape sold her jams, and her flea-market traffic had nearly doubled.

"Are you sure you're okay with the whole Tony thing?" Jenna asked. "I still think he'll come around. He's always been careful with you, Ames. He's just being extra careful now."

I don't think telling me to go to Australia is being careful.

"Speak of the devil." Bella nodded toward the door to the resort.

Tony came through the doors in a dark suit with a crisp white shirt. His cuff links sparkled, and Amy wondered if he was wearing the ones she'd given him two Christmases ago, but she didn't dare get close enough to look. His sexy baby blues were serious as he glanced at his watch.

"Why is he dressed up?" Amy asked.

"He has a speaking engagement at the Marriott this morning," Jenna explained. "Didn't you know he was staying in Boston today?"

"No. I…I haven't talked to him since, well, you know." *Since he told me to take the job in Australia.*

"Hey," Tony said with a wave. "You guys heading out?"

Pete and Caden pulled up in front of the hotel in Bella's SUV.

"Yeah." Bella handed her suitcase to Caden. "Good luck at your talk."

"Oh, so you're speaking to me today?" He smiled at Bella.

Amy sensed that he was purposely not looking at her, and she hated it.

"Yes. Of course I'm talking to you." Bella sidled up to Amy. "But I hate you for hurting Amy."

"Bella!" Amy hissed. She felt her cheeks flush.

"What? I do. I mean I love him, of course. We all do, but still." Bella punched Tony's arm.

Tony arched a brow at Caden in a *what's up with your wom-*

an way. Caden held his hands up in surrender. "Dude, what can I say? I think you and Amy were meant for each other, and I've only known you a few years."

"Oh my gosh." Amy groaned. "Okay, this has to stop. Tony is not obligated to be with me. And, Bella…" She glared at her. "I can't believe you told Caden! Can't we just pretend that things are like they used to be? Please?" She needed to mend the fence between her and Tony. It was giving her splinters at every turn. They'd been friends for too long to let her broken heart come between them.

Tony draped an arm over Amy's shoulder. Obviously telling her to go to Australia hadn't affected him as badly as it had affected her. Despite her hurt feelings, her body betrayed her by getting that tingly feeling of anticipation all over. Her stomach fluttered and her mind instantly skipped down the *maybe one day* path.

"Listen, I love Amy like I love each of you, and that's never going to change. Right, Ames?"

Tony's words kicked her off that path and right into the ugly ditch of reality.

TONY'S MOTIVATIONAL-SPEAKING engagements and pro-surfing career earned him a comfortable seven figures a year. Normally, he loved every second of his dual career, from the awed look of the seminar attendees to the repetitive questions about his success. A few years into his surfing career, he'd found that he was continually giving impromptu talks about his path to success. His agent took note and talked him into putting on a seminar about creating one's own success. Over the years the seminar that had once hosted twenty participants blossomed into hundreds of attendees across the country, with multiple engagements. Tony now spoke not only about creating one's own path to success, but overcoming fears and other obstacles and paying it forward along the way.

For the first time ever, Tony had to feign the positivity and confidence he usually exuded naturally. He hated knowing that Amy was spending the day with Duke. She'd probably already accepted the position, and now there'd be no turning back. Everything he'd done over the past two days pissed him off. He needed to hit the waves and clear his head, work off some steam.

He looked out over the sea of attendees, wishing every blond head was Amy. He'd felt her body go rigid beneath his arm earlier that morning when he'd said he loved her like he loved the others. It was only afterward that he realized how much those words had probably stung. She couldn't know that he adored everything about her. She couldn't know that it was her face he conjured up in the middle of the night, or that half the time he texted her, he did it just to feel the connection to her. There was so much that she didn't know about the way he felt because he kept it buried deep inside, beneath the anger and confusion of his youth, beneath the womanizing and the refusal to get close to any woman for more than a few nights. Buried so deep that sometimes he wondered if he'd ever be able to move past it. Until this weekend, he'd never wanted to.

He forced himself to focus on the seminar he was giving on creating one's life. The irony was not lost on him that while he'd created his own life, he was doing a real good job of messing up the only part that really mattered.

Chapter Four

AMY DECIDED THAT she would remember this summer as the *summer of perspective*. She realized that in previous years, she and the girls had been there for one another in a different way than they were now. They'd practically been each other's significant others, filling the gaps that boyfriends usually occupied. Now all of that had changed. Each of her friends had taken determined steps to change their lives the way *they* wanted them. They weren't driven by what someone else felt or didn't feel about them, and in the process they'd found their forever loves. Amy realized that she was the only one who hadn't changed. She was the same girl pining after the same guy she'd loved since she was six years old.

It was time for a change, and if she'd had any doubts about moving on without longing for Tony Black, he'd made things perfectly clear for her. Three times.

Three painfully honest times.

She spent the day with Duke going over his ideas for the opening of the Australia resort. He was a savvy businessman with solid plans for the property and an endless budget. The more she learned about the job he had offered her, the more excited Amy became. She wasn't thrilled about giving up the business she'd put her heart and soul into, but as with most things in life, where there was a meaningful gain, there was usually an equally meaningful loss.

Duke had lunch and dinner brought in, and they worked straight through until after seven. Duke was easy to work with, and Amy had a good feeling about him. Not only were he and Blue close, but during their all-day meeting he'd taken calls from both his sister, Trish, and his brother Gage. He hadn't rushed them, which might have turned off another new employee, but Amy found his loyalty to his family refreshing, and it made her happy she'd be working for such a family-oriented man. Selling Amy on Australia hadn't taken much. She'd never been anywhere beyond the East Coast, and once she'd made up her mind to pull up her big-girl panties and try to move on from Tony—and after he'd told her to take the job—she knew that being far away could only help ease the pain.

By the time she left the resort, she'd convinced herself she'd done the right thing by accepting the job, but she couldn't shake the feeling that she needed to see Tony one last time. She didn't want to talk to him, and she definitely didn't want to try to convince him that he was wrong. She was done putting herself in *that* particular position. She just needed to see his face with a clear definition of where he belonged in her heart—in the friend category forevermore—before seeing him again at Seaside.

On the way back to the Cape, she stopped at the Boston Marriott. *A quick stop.* She'd peek into his seminar, get one last look, then be on her way with a new job in hand and a new perspective on her love life.

This was good.

It was the right thing to do. Then she could put this part of their relationship—or lack thereof—away forever.

She parked the car and headed into the hotel. She wasn't even sure Tony would still be there. She knew his seminars were all-day affairs, but he hadn't texted her for days. She didn't know his schedule.

Listen to her. *Know his schedule. Sheesh.* What had she been thinking?

She'd known his summer schedules forever. Now that she was thinking about it, hadn't she known his schedule for the past few winters, springs, and falls, too? She'd downplayed to the girls exactly how often Tony had texted her. She'd had to. It would have been too painful to admit that while she'd become his *habit*, he'd become her everything.

Inside the resort her nerves got all prickly. She followed the signs to the Presidential Conference Room, where Tony's seminar was taking place. She was in luck. It was scheduled to end at eight, and it was seven fifty. She had time to peek and run.

Outside the conference room doors, her brain stopped firing. *Open the door.* Her hands wouldn't budge. *Just open the door and look. One last look and you can put him into the* friend file *forever.*

Tony had always been in her *heartthrob* file. Her *I love you* file. Her *someday* file. He'd been the only person to ever inhabit those places in her mind.

She drew in a deep breath and smoothed her skirt and blouse. Maybe she should have changed after her meeting. Why was she still dressed up? Why was she thinking about clothing when she was about to say goodbye to the *someday* Tony and welcome the *friend-only* Tony?

Taking the job was the right thing to do.

She opened the door with a shaky hand and peered inside the large conference room. The seminar must have just wrapped up. Tony stood at the front of the room surrounded by a slew of people. Amy's eyes locked on the tall man at the head of the group. The man who never teased her about being flat-chested or chicken-legged. The man who knew she could handle only two drinks but often indulged in three with her Seaside friends. The man who carried her home on those nights and never gave her a hard time for it the next day. His handsome, tanned features stood out against all the rest of the people in the room. He was smiling, his eyes friendly and sharp. She knew that look. It was his game face. His *on* face. His game face was miles apart from his natural smile. The one that sucked her into the warm, loving, capable man that was Tony Black and clutched her so tightly sometimes she thought she'd forget how to walk.

Turn around. Walk away. You'll be done with him forever.

Forever is a very long time.

Chapter Five

THE SALTY OCEAN air swept up the dunes of Cahoon Hollow Beach, bringing with it too many sweet and painful memories. Amy sat with Bella, Leanna, and Jenna later that evening as they tried to comfort her. Bless them for not giving up on her, because she was acting as sullen as a brooding teenage girl. She tipped back the bottle of Middle Sister wine she'd bought on her way there and wiped the tears from her eyes. How many times had she come to watch Tony surf without him knowing? How many years had she watched his muscles bunch and flex as he waxed his board, knowing those muscles would look even more enticing if she were the object of his efforts, lying with him as he learned about her more mature, womanly body and made it sing? How many summer nights had she lain in her bed wondering if he might appear at her window with confessions of love instead of the girls wanting to go skinny-dipping?

She felt Jenna scoot closer, smushing their legs together.

"That's good, Ames. Cry it out. Cry out that Tony love." Jenna took the bottle from her and drank from it; then she handed it to Bella.

"Don't cry it all out," Leanna said. "I refuse to believe that this is it. I know that stubborn surfer loves you, Amy. I feel it in my bones."

"Not helping," Amy said quietly. "I need to let him go."

"She's right. That big oaf may love her, but now…He doesn't deserve her. Look how sad she is." Bella rose to her feet and pulled out her phone. A minute later the sound of Hedley's "Anything" filled the air.

"We need to spin this positive." Bella pulled Amy to her feet. "You can do anything, Amy." She bumped Amy's hip with her own.

"He *does* deserve me." Amy swayed from the alcohol, not to the music, and put her hand on Jenna's shoulder to steady herself. "He's a good man. He's honest, Bella. He's more honest than any man I know."

Jenna rose to her feet and straightened Amy's hoodie, which had clung to her waist. "I think she's right, Bella. You want to hate him, but we can't. He cut her loose. That's the only way she'd be able to move forward. You know that."

Bella rolled her eyes. "Whatever. I can't look at Amy being so sad and think a good thought about Tony. He caused this." She held her phone up to make the music louder.

Leanna reached for Amy's hand and tugged her toward the steep path on the dune that led down to the beach. "Come on, girls."

They stumbled down the path clinging to one another. Jenna crossed her arms over her boobs as she ran. "Slow down! These puppies are going to give me a black eye."

They laughed and held one another up as they reached the beach. The sand was cold on Amy's bare feet, but the laughter of her friends warmed her. They were always there for her—when she wasn't hiding secrets from them.

He was always there for her.

He wasn't always going to be there for her, and she needed to get used to that.

Jenna headed straight to the edge of the water. "Help me find rocks." Jenna had collected rocks for years. Every room of her cottage and her and Pete's beach house had rocks of all shapes and sizes in them. On the floors, on the tables, in glass bowls, and along windowsills. She was very particular about the rocks she brought home, and she would study each rock like some people studied diamonds, making sure the ones she selected met her expectations, which changed from summer to summer.

"I have a better idea. Let's wash Tony off of me. Literally." If she was really going to turn over a new Tonyless leaf, she had to stop being afraid to hold back. She needed to be brave and to take control of her life. Amy pulled her hoodie over her head. Goose bumps chased the cold air up her torso.

"Amy, what are you doing?" Leanna's eyes widened.

"Starting over." Amy stood in her pink bra and shimmied out of her jeans. She had always done the right thing, and that included being careful and modest. With the exception of skinny-dipping—or chunky-dunking, as she and the girls called it—at the pool at Seaside in the middle of the night, she'd never done anything like *this* before. It was so out of character for her that she even surprised herself, but she felt braver than she ever had, so she was going with it.

"You are not going in there." Leanna picked up Amy's jeans and held them out to her. "Shark bait, remember? How many times has Tony told us not to swim at night?"

Amy set her hand on her hip. "All the more reason for me to do it. He's not the boss of me. And he doesn't own my heart anymore, remember? Now, are you joining me or standing on the beach like a mother hen?"

Jenna whipped off her sweatshirt. "I'm in!"

"You guys are nuts." Bella pulled her sweatshirt off. "I'm only going in to make sure you go no deeper than your knees. Idiots."

"You guys..." Leanna pulled off her sweatshirt. "What if you get bitten by a shark?"

"Oh please. I have no meat on my bones. They don't want me." Amy shimmied out of her underwear and tossed her bra behind her as she strutted naked toward the water, feeling liberated. Thank goodness for Middle Sister wine, which she just might start calling Courage in a Bottle.

"Even Tony doesn't want me. I'm done being Goody Two-shoes, by the way. I'm done being the one who does the right thing."

She sensed them all behind her and felt empowered. More confident than she had in her life. She reached her hands out behind her and wiggled her fingers.

Seaside sisters, help me start a new life. She felt Jenna grab her right hand, Bella took her left, and Leanna took Jenna's other hand. The four of them stood buck naked before the sea, and Amy's mind drifted back to the summer before she left for college. Painful memories tried to claw their way into her mind—the blood, the fear on Tony's face, the ache in her heart. She squeezed the hands of her girlfriends a little tighter and told herself that that summer had never happened. With a hard swallow to push down the lie, she raised her hands in the air and said, "Let's cleanse Tony right off of me!"

They walked toward the water. *I'm doing this. I'm really doing this. There's no looking back. Once I get in there, he's out of my system.*

No matter what.

A wave broke over their feet, and they squealed and ran back up on the beach.

"*Brr!* That's cold!" Bella crossed her arms over her chest.

"Chilly nipples! *Chipples*!" Jenna laughed.

"Oh my gosh. Oh my gosh." Leanna bounced from one foot to the other.

"Holy fudgenuggets, it's cold. But I *need* to do this." Amy steeled herself against the cold and held out her hands again. It took only a second for the others to join her.

"All for one and all that." Bella's teeth chattered.

"Goodbye, Tony. Hello, Australia!" Amy ran into the ice-cold water, clinging tightly to her friends' hands. She sucked in a breath as the water consumed her thighs and sent piercing shocks of cold water up to her waist.

Jenna shrieked. "Under!"

They all dunked under the water at once, then burst through the surface, laughing as they sprinted back up the beach, kicking sand everywhere. Cold and wet, and covered with sticky salt water, they shivered and snatched up their clothes.

"You…." Bella's voice shook. "You took…" She pulled her hoodie over her head. "The job?"

"Uh…huh." Amy pulled on her jeans. Her fingers were numb and her entire body was sticky, but she felt better than she had in the last two days.

"Summers off?" Bella asked.

"No." Amy finished dressing and beckoned the others to come closer. They huddled together, teeth chattering, bodies shaking with cold. She swallowed hard against the tears threatening to silence her.

"He…He told me to go…" She closed her eyes to ward off the cold. "I don't think I'm strong enough…" A shiver stole her breath. "To see him next summer. I'll come…" She clenched her jaw against her trembling teeth. "For two or three weeks the following summer."

They huddled together.

"He *told* you to? Tony did?" Bella narrowed her eyes as Amy nodded. "That idiot. I'm going to kill him."

"Amy…" Leanna put her arm around Amy.

Jenna did the same on her other side. Bella plastered her body against Amy from the front, and they came together in a group hug. Amy lifted her eyes to the dunes. This was where it all started so many years ago. She remembered when they were little girls searching for rocks for Jenna and playing in the waves while their parents sat on the blankets reading and talking and doing whatever else grown-ups did back then.

She was a grown-up now.

It was her turn to watch *her* children play in the surf. The thought stung.

She'd always hoped she'd do those things with her best friends, and she'd always believed that sitting right beside her, passing knowing glances and silent looks of love, would be Tony.

Her eyes caught on headlights in the parking lot at the top of the dunes. Caden was on duty tonight, and he always checked up on them if they were out late. The glare of the headlights made it impossible for her to tell if it was him or not. A tall, wide-shouldered silhouette came into focus. There was no mistaking the thick-legged man standing at the top of the dune in a pair of board shorts, powerful arms arcing out from his body. Arms that had carried Amy to the safety of her cottage so many nights that she could feel them now, wrapped around her, warming her.

But they weren't wrapped around her now. Those were the arms of her girlfriends holding her close. The ones whom she'd told she'd washed away the remnants of the man looking down upon them in the moonlight.

The ones she'd lied to in order to protect her heart.

She closed her eyes for a beat. When she opened them, Tony was gone, and her heart was just as broken as it had been before she'd tried to wash him away. Only now it ached even more, because she knew that if willing him away while she was nestled in the arms of her best girlfriends couldn't do the job, nothing ever would.

Chapter Six

TONY PADDLED HARD to catch his second wave of the morning. He'd been up half the night, frustrated and angry over what was happening with Amy, and had finally decided to go out on dawn patrol—a surfer term for catching early-morning waves. He felt like they'd broken up, which was crazy, considering they weren't dating. After his seminar last night, he'd gone back to Seaside and taken the back entrance so he didn't have to pass Amy's cottage, but that didn't help. Every single thing felt different. Her cottage was across the street and only two cottages up from his. He could practically smell when she was home, and last night he'd known that even though her car was in the driveway, she wasn't there. The complex felt empty despite Pete and Kurt having drinks on Kurt's deck. Even Pepper, Kurt and Leanna's energetic Labradoodle, didn't make him feel better. And Pepper was so darn cute he could make anyone smile.

He knew Amy had to be out with the girls, and he knew Amy well enough to know exactly where she'd gone. He'd finally given up trying to ignore the urge to make sure she was okay and he'd driven out to Cahoon Hollow. How was he going to get through this? Just seeing her had brought his feelings for her rushing back in. He couldn't help but think he'd made the biggest mistake of his life by telling her to take that stupid job.

He'd stayed up until she'd returned to her cottage, as he always did. He had to know she was safe. Would that need ever subside? Would he ever be able to stay at his cottage again when she and the girls were skinny-dipping in the pool and *not* listen for her giggle as she walked by on her way to her cottage? He pictured her sweet smile and her green eyes, alit with happiness, which seemed to follow him everywhere. He thought of their group barbecues in the quad, the grassy area between the cottages. *Ames, can you grab some ketchup from my place?* They'd always been comfortable in each other's homes, and now that would all change. It was changing already.

Was she going to take the job and move to Australia? He'd been there, of course. Bells Beach was one of the great point breaks, located south of the Victorian coastline of Australia. The last time he'd been there, he'd called Amy before his competition. He did that often. As often as he said his silent mantra before the ride. *This one's for you, Ames.* There was a time he used to say that to her out loud. When they were teenagers and he'd run into the surf to catch a wave. Even before that summer they'd come together, she'd watched him with wide eyes that made him feel special. Like he was her whole world. Every single time he ran into the surf, it was for her. Now that world he adored was crumbling down around him. When he'd seen her last night, he'd wanted to scoop her into his arms and tell her he'd lied, that he'd never loved her as just a friend, and the last thing he wanted was for her to go to Australia.

But that wouldn't have been fair, and he hoped like crazy that the waves would do what they always did—help him forget.

Everything. Her smile, her touch. Her sweet laugh. The way her eyes crinkled around the corners when that smile was genuine and the way her deep green eyes held his gaze for a beat longer than they needed to.

The wave hit the underside of his board, and the familiar sense of exhilaration and greed swept through him. The power of the water traveled up his legs to his core, testing his strength, fighting his balance, but he was Tony Black. He was one with the ocean. He harnessed the magnificent energy of the swell, and there was only him and the sea. He craved the challenge of the waves, the newness and complexity of each one. He longed for its intensity. Anticipation tortured his body as momentum grew, tensing and easing. He was lost in the moment, and when that wave hit, it was over way too fast, leaving him temporarily sated but always craving more.

He rode the whitewater, the ridge of turbulence and foam after the break.

He lowered himself to his board and paddled back out, barely taking time to catch his breath. He'd achieved what he needed, a clearer head, but one glance at the empty dunes sent his thoughts spiraling right back to where they were the happiest: drenched in images of Amy.

An hour later he dragged himself from the water feeling invigorated, slightly numb, and still frustrated. He had to talk to her. He had to mend the friendship they both depended on. He set his board in the sand, and as he stripped his wet suit from his limbs, he decided he'd do just that.

"Hey, jerkface."

Tony turned at the sound of Bella's angry voice. She, Jenna, and Leanna were dressed in their typical attire, short sundresses over bathing suits. Bella stomped across the sand, hands fisted, an angry scowl on her face. If looks could kill, he'd be dead two times over by now. Jenna and Leanna had serious looks on their faces, but they were more tentative, as if they were there to ensure that Bella didn't take things too far. *Great.*

He tossed his wet suit onto his board and faced the firing squad. "Ladies."

"Don't you *ladies* us. What did you say to Amy?" Bella was tall; she came almost to Tony's chin and stood as near as the close talkers Seinfeld hated.

Tony held his ground *and* her steady gaze. "That I loved her like a friend."

She pushed his chest. "You're a jerkface. What else did you tell her?"

"Bella, chill out." Jenna touched her arm and Bella shrugged her off.

"I will not chill out." Bella poked Tony in the chest. "You are a total, complete idiot. She's moving to Australia because you told her to. Do you even know who you're talking about? Do you care at all?"

Her eyes dampened, and Tony opened his mouth to respond, but she beat him to it.

"This is Amy. Not Leanna, who can pick up and go anywhere, anytime, without blinking an eye. Sweet, trusting Amy. Stable, consistent Amy. She worked to build her business for seven years, meticulously building a rapport with each and every client, nurturing relationships as if they were her very best friends. And now she's giving all that up because you are too scared to tell her that you love her. What's the deal, Tony?" She was breathing so hard her face was red.

"Bella—"

"No. Don't *Bella* me. I've been here, remember? All these

summers I've watched you care for her, hold her hair back when she pukes. What's going on, Tony? What's. The. Deal?"

Tony scrubbed his hand down his face. As if self-torture wasn't enough. He didn't need this guilt trip, even if she was right. "Come on, Bella. What do you want me to do? Amy is good and sweet and, you know she deserves a guy way better than me."

"Bull."

Leanna stepped between them. Her dark hair was pulled back in a ponytail, and her dress had streaks of red jam on it, as most of her clothing did. "Tony, what are you talking about? She adores you."

"Yeah, no kidding. I'm not blind, Leanna." *Just stupid.*

"So why did you tell her to go to Australia?" Leanna's tone softened.

Tony shook his head. He wanted to have this conversation with Amy, not them. Who was he kidding? They were a package deal. Everyone in the whole complex was, and he loved them for it. He just hated being in the center of this nightmare, knowing he was the cause of it.

He blew out a breath and clenched his jaw a few times to gain control of his emotions. "Because it's a great opportunity for her, and she deserves it." There was no way he was going to tell them anything before he told Amy. He'd already decided he needed to clear the air with her. That's what he intended to do, but first he had to get them off his back.

"Look, Amy's a big girl. She can make decisions for herself. I know you care about her, but you can't bully me into doing anything, Bella."

Bella plunked herself down on his beach chair. "Forget you."

"Bella." Jenna touched her shoulder, and Bella shrugged her off again.

"Bella, look." Tony crouched beside her. "I've got a lot of stuff to deal with in my own head, all right? You can hate me, and if I were you, I'd probably tell me to kiss off, too. But you gotta know one thing if you know me at all. Hurting Amy is not something I ever wanted to do."

"Tony," Jenna said. "Are you sure this is what you want? If you are, well, you are. We care about you and we'll respect your decision. But if you're not, you're about to lose a woman who really loves you."

I think I already have.

AMY SPENT THE afternoon at Duck Harbor, reading a romance novel. She didn't care that the sun had long ago set, or that she had goose bumps all over her body. She was lost in the love of two fictional people, which was a heck of a lot better than thinking about her own broken heart. She decided to revel in the fictional world for a while longer. What did she have to rush home to? There was a barbecue tonight in the quad, and she knew exactly how that would go, didn't she? She'd gotten a nice little preview of things to come at the hotel. The girls loved her and they loved Tony, but their loyalty to her was thick as tar. Sticky, mucky tar that she counted on to pull her through. But the thought of them being mad at Tony for not wanting her made her a little queasy. She knew Tony's friendships with the girls were treasured as much as hers was. She didn't want to be the cause of trouble between any of them.

She was also clued in to herself to realize that she sure as heck wasn't experienced enough in love to figure it all out on her own. Her heart knew and loved Tony. Beyond that, not much made sense. Would she ever be able to tuck away those feelings and allow another man to replace him? She wasn't sure, but she had to go back to her cottage and face the music. Tony and the girls were her friends, and she needed to fix things between them.

On her way back to Seaside, she stopped at the Wellfleet Market to pick up wine, chicken for the barbecue, and to check out the new books they had on the shelves. She read through each title, but she'd sort of had her fill of romance for the day, and mysteries were too intense. She was more a romance or literary-fiction girl. But today even literary fiction wasn't piquing her interest. She didn't want to read about anything too heavy. She turned toward the register and spotted a rack of greeting cards. She loved cards. A cute picture and a few words could change someone's whole day. Maybe she'd find something funny for the girls and surprise them with it. She turned the rack away from the birthday section and read a few of the Girlfriend cards. *Ugh.* The cards were all about men and relationships. Couldn't she escape that for just one day? Her friends had guys. Perfect, romantic, loving guys who would do anything for them.

She gave the rack another spin and plucked a card from the thin wire shelf. There was a picture of a little boy and girl sitting on a stoop; the boy was whispering in the girl's ear. *Cute.* She flipped it open and read the inscription. *My life's just better with you in it.* She shoved it back in the rack and tried to block the thoughts of Tony that stupid card conjured up. She should have known better than to pick it up. She snagged a card that had a picture of a bottle of wine and an unattractive man on the front and flipped it open. *Drink up. He'll look good by the time you finish.*

When had greeting cards become so lame? She nixed the card idea, and her eyes caught on a little surfboard key chain hanging from a display next to the card rack. She unhooked it from the display and ran her fingers over the inscription, *#1 Surfer Dude.* She felt herself smile and then chided herself for thinking of Tony.

Yeah, right. Don't think of Tony. Like that has a chance of happening.

She took the key chain and her other groceries and headed for the cashier.

The barbecue was in full swing when she arrived at Seaside. The bonfire was lit, Tony, Kurt, and Bella were manning the barbecue on Leanna's deck, and Pete and Caden were carrying a table from Bella and Caden's deck into the quad. Jenna and Bella followed, each carrying a deck chair. Leanna was on her way up from the pool, walking Pepper along the side of the road. Within seconds of Amy reaching her driveway, Jenna, Leanna, and Bella were there to greet her.

"We've been wondering when you'd get here." Bella took the grocery bag from Amy's arms while Amy grabbed her beach bag and towel from the trunk.

"I told you I was going to Duck Harbor to chill." Amy willed herself not to turn around and look at Tony. She hurried up the steps to her cottage with the girls following behind her.

"Have you talked to Tony?" Jenna asked as they walked inside.

"No, why?" *Did he say something?* As quickly as the thought formed, she pushed it away.

"Just wondering." Jenna emptied Amy's groceries while

Amy went to hang her beach towel over the railing of her deck. Okay, so maybe it was an excuse to get a glimpse of Tony. She *was* only human. He lived in his board shorts, and sweet mother of hot and sexy, did he fill them out nicely. Tonight he was wearing a gray tank top, giving Amy a lovely view of his bulging biceps and his sculpted lats.

Had he thought about her at all today? Or was she alone in her agony?

"Hey, honey." Leanna joined her on the deck. "You okay? Jenna wanted to know if that chicken was for tonight."

Amy shook her head to clear the lust from her brain. "Yeah, I'm good."

"Is this going to be too awkward? We can eat here if you want. Let the guys eat together over there."

"No, Lea, it's okay. I want to talk to Tony and clear the air." She stole one more glance at him just as he looked over his shoulder. Their eyes connected, and for a brief second Amy's mind tried to go down the *maybe tonight* trail again…And then she remembered. There was never going to be a *tonight* in that sense for them.

She held his gaze, unable to look away. She knew Tony well enough to read the clench of his jaw. *Worry*. The widening of his eyes. *You want to tell me something.* And then he lifted his chin, his lips quirked up in a semi-smile, and he raised his hand and waved, confusing and elating her all at once.

"Aren't you going to wave?" Leanna whispered.

Amy felt herself swallowing past the thickening in her throat. She told her arm to move, but it didn't budge. Her body had betrayed her enough times by now that she was getting used to it. She forced a shaky, nervous, *are we okay* smile that earned her a furrowed brow and a nod from Tony.

She breathed a little easier. Maybe she could survive the summer with their friendship intact. It might not be what she'd hoped for, but it was better than nothing.

Amy went back inside with Leanna. "I need to shower. Can you guys take the chicken over for me?" She went into her bedroom to grab clean clothes and called out to them, "Don't forget the teriyaki sauce. The one Tony likes is on the door of the fridge." She clutched her clothes to her chest. "Fudgenuggets."

Bella stuck her head in the bedroom. "Fudgenuggets?"

Amy rolled her eyes. "I need to stop thinking about him."

Bella handed her a glass of wine. "Here. This will help."

Amy sucked the wine down in one gulp. "I think I'm gonna need the whole bottle."

BY TEN O'CLOCK Kurt and Leanna had already called it a night. Tony sat on the bench beside Amy in their usual spot, only he didn't put his arm around her. He wanted to, ached to, had to fight the urge not to, but she'd been acting distant all evening, and he didn't want to cause any more of a fissure between them by overstepping his own very clearly defined boundaries.

"We're going into Chatham tomorrow." Bella snuggled in closer to Caden, and it magnified the emptiness beneath Tony's arm—the spot where Amy should have been. "Anyone want to join us?"

Jenna rested her head on Peter's shoulder. "Pete? We could go to the Chatham Pier Fish Market and pick up lobsters for dinner."

"Whatever you want, babe. I've got to work on the boat at some point, but if we take two cars, I can head home around two and you can hang with Bella if you want." Pete was refitting a thirty-foot Bristol sailboat. He kissed Jenna's cheek and whispered something in her ear, causing her to giggle.

The fire crackled in the breeze. Amy folded her arms across her belly and curled her legs beneath her. "I was thinking about hitting the beach tomorrow. It's supposed to be eighty and sunny." She shifted again beside Tony and pulled her sweatshirt down over her knees.

"I'm hitting the surf early tomorrow, but thanks, Bella." Tony saw Amy's arms press in to her body with a shiver. He gave in to his feelings and did what he would have done if they'd never had the love-you-like-a-friend conversation. He pulled her against him and wrapped his arms around hers. She stiffened against him and it felt like a kick to the gut, but he didn't relent. He held her until she gave in and at least some of the tension in her shoulders eased.

A few minutes later Bella and Jenna pulled Caden and Pete to their feet.

"We're calling it a night," Jenna said with a mischievous grin aimed at Pete.

"Us too," Bella said.

"We'll catch you tomorrow, man," Caden said to Tony.

"Sure thing." Tony felt Amy lean forward. "Stay," he whispered to her, and heck if her body didn't tense up again. He had to clear the air and save their friendship. He might not be able to be the man she needed, but he sure could be a friend. Even if it killed him.

After the others left, Tony sat with Amy, trying to figure out how to break the uncomfortable silence that had settled in around them like an unwanted guest.

"I have to go." Amy moved from under his arm.

"Don't you want to talk about this?" He held her steady gaze as emotions washed over her face. Worry filled her eyes, then morphed to sadness, drawing her lips downward. Her eyes followed.

"I'm sorry, Amy. I never wanted to hurt you."

Amy lifted cold eyes to him. Her mouth closed tight. But her determined mask faded fast, unlike the night in her hotel room, when it had threatened to slaughter him. She was putting on a brave face, and he respected her for it, but of all times, did she have to pick this moment to be strong? He'd selfishly hoped that she'd look at him like she used to and maybe his resolve would melt.

"You did me a favor." She rose to her feet. "I could have spent the next ten years pining over you." She laughed, a sad little laugh that drove his pain even deeper.

A favor. That's exactly what he had thought he was doing when he'd told her to take the job, but now he wasn't so sure. Was he doing himself a favor by making her move so far away that a relationship would be impossible? She might be out of sight, but Amy Maples was never far from his mind. Why did it take the threat of her leaving the country for him to realize how much he didn't want to lose her?

"Would it have been so bad to keep liking me?" he said lightly. He rose and draped an arm over her shoulder, intending to walk her home.

She shrugged him off and took a step away. "Honestly? Yeah, probably."

"I'm sorry." He reached for her hand. "I'll walk you home."

"It's okay. I need to get used to this." She shoved her hands in her pockets and headed across the grassy quad toward her cottage.

He almost wished she'd had too much to drink so he could carry her back to her cottage and put her to bed. How was it possible to miss someone who was right there in front of him? And how could it hurt so much? It hadn't exactly been easy all these years to keep his feelings for Amy at bay, but it had been doable. He'd dated enough women to satisfy his carnal needs, and Amy had always been right there during the summers, across the gravel road. The possibility of her not being there was beginning to settle in, and it felt wrong and painful.

On the way to his cottage he passed Leanna's bedroom window and heard Leanna giggling. *Stupid windows.* Listening to Leanna and Kurt make love was a running joke around Seaside. They always forgot to close their windows. Usually he could laugh it off or ignore it. Tonight, as Leanna's giggle turned to a low moan, it only made him miss Amy more.

Chapter Seven

MIDNIGHT CAME AND went, and Amy was tired of staring at her stupid clock. She'd wanted to climb into Tony's arms and fall back into the closeness they'd had before her seduction-gone-bad, when he'd revealed his true feelings for her. But there was no going back. She was in love with an incredibly smart, handsome man who was a numbskull for not seeing her for who she was. She tossed off her blankets, stripped off her favorite pajama top—the one with a kitty lying on its side like Marilyn Monroe, propped up on one elbow, legs crossed, with the words *Let me show you what purrfect feels like*—and peeled off her underwear. She stomped into the bathroom, grabbed a towel, and secured it around her naked body, then headed outside to her deck. The cold air sent shivers up her body. She didn't care. It was a dark, moonless night, and she needed dark. She felt dark. The water would be cold, but that was okay, too. She needed to shock her system to rid it of Tony again.

She stepped off her deck and onto the driveway. Darn it. She'd forgotten her flip-flops. Oh well. Bare feet beware, because Amy Maples was on a mission. She walked on her tiptoes across the gravel road to Leanna's bedroom window and prayed she and Kurt were done with their frisk-fest. All was quiet on the bedroom front, but Amy wasn't tall enough to see in, and she worried about waking Pepper, so she tiptoed over to Jenna's back deck and went to her bedroom window instead. The inside of Jenna's cottage was always immaculately organized, as was the house on the bay where she and Pete spent half their time. The interior was painted white with orange, black, and *rock* accents. Jenna had a wicked rock obsession, and she kept rocks she'd hand selected from the beaches over the years in every room. A quick glance inside confirmed that she and Pete were sleeping. Pete was lying on his back with the sheets bunched around his waist—*thank goodness*—and Jenna was draped over his chest. Joey, their female golden retriever, was sprawled across her doggy bed in the corner of the room.

"Jenna," Amy whispered.

Jenna didn't budge. Joey lifted her fuzzy head.

"Jenna," she whispered louder. Joey yawned, put her head back down, and closed her eyes.

"Amy."

Startled, Amy squealed. Bella covered Amy's mouth and they dropped to the deck like lead.

"Shut up." Bella was also wearing a towel and she'd remembered her flip-flops. Her tangled and messy hair had that mattress-romp look.

Had everyone but Amy had sex tonight? She sighed and pushed Bella's hand from her mouth.

"You scared the life out of me."

"I was coming to get you," Bella whispered. "I thought you could use some cheering up."

"Yeah, well, great minds think alike."

They got up on their knees and peered into the bedroom. Jenna and Pete were still zonked.

"They both sleep like logs." Bella put her mouth up to the screen and whispered loudly, "Jenna."

Jenna lifted her head and blinked several times. A smile formed quickly as she slid from the bed and ran naked to the window. "Chunky-dunking?"

"Heck yeah, and don't wake Pete. We'll go get Leanna." Bella took Amy's hand and dragged her off the deck and across the grass.

"Ouch. Slow down. I don't have my flip-flops." Amy clung to Bella's arm as Jenna darted off her deck and across the quad with a towel clutched to her chest.

"It's gonna be a chipples night," Jenna whispered.

"It's always a chipples night with you around," Amy teased. "Put your towel on. Jeez, Jenna. And how can you sleep naked like that with your windows wide open?"

Jenna rolled her eyes and wrapped her towel around her body, tucking the top securely. "Happy?"

"Not really, but happy about your towel, yes."

"Shh." Bella glared at them as they approached Leanna's window. Bella was the tallest of the group, towering over Jenna's four-foot-eleven stature and a couple of inches taller than Amy at five four. She peeked into the window, then crouched with her back against the house. "She's not in there."

"What?" Jenna stood and started jumping up to try to see in the window. Bella yanked her back down, and she fell across Bella's lap, laughing. Bella slapped her hand over Jenna's mouth.

"Shh. Do you think I'm blind?" Bella hissed.

"No, but sometimes I wish you were mute," Leanna said as she came around the corner of the house. "Get away from the window before Pepper hears you." She motioned them over to the road. "I heard you guys before you even reached the windows, *chipples* crew."

Jenna covered her mouth and laughed.

Arm in arm, they walked down to the pool at a snail's pace, thanks to Amy's bare feet. Leanna was the only one who'd remembered to bring her pool key.

"What would you do without me?" Leanna teased as she unlocked the gate.

"We'd probably get more sleep." Jenna crossed her arms over her chest and puckered her lips. "*Oh, Kurt. Yes, more, baby, please…*"

Leanna swatted her arm. "Shut up before you wake up Theresa, and get in the pool." Theresa Ottoline was another resident at Seaside. She was also the property manager, and she was a stickler for the rules. Swimming was prohibited after eight o'clock at night, but that never stopped the girls from indulging in their favorite rule-breaking activity.

Chunky-dunking was a ritual that hadn't changed much over the years. It usually involved wine or cookie dough, but Amy had been too distraught over Tony to think of anything other than being with the girls and washing away the hurt of rejection.

"Theresa's not here. She had to go back home, but she said she'd be back in a few days," Leanna explained as Jenna went running by buck naked. Jenna always dropped her towel by the gate, then ran to the far end of the pool to use the stairs. She'd done it for years, and why she dropped her towel so far away when everyone else wore theirs to the far side of the pool was a mystery. Then again, much of what their obsessive-compulsive friend did was a mystery, like collecting rocks and organizing every little thing she could get her hands on.

The girls descended the stairs and dunked under to their shoulders. Amy missed Jessica and the way she always said, *Cold, cold, cold,* when she dunked under the water. She hoped she and Jamie were having a wonderful honeymoon, and knew that it wouldn't matter where they were, as long as they were together. They would be happy in a cardboard box if they had each other.

I'd be happy with Tony in a cardboard box. Naked.

Stop…

"This is freaking cold." Bella reached for the foam noodles and tossed one to each of the girls. They'd all forgotten to pin up their hair, and each had a halo of tendrils floating around them.

Amy's teeth chattered. "I need the cold. I need to freeze thoughts of Tony out of me." Amy kicked her feet to keep warm as they drifted toward the deep end of the pool.

"Don't give up on him, Ames." Leanna swam over to her.

"Yeah. He looked like a caged tiger tonight before he finally put his arm around you," Bella added.

"Um, yeah, right. He as much as told me to give up on him, and he only held me because I was cold." Amy sidestroked away from the group, needing a moment to breathe. She hadn't counted on them urging her to try again.

"Because he cares," Jenna added. "If he didn't care, he'd have let you freeze."

"Kinda like we are right now." Leanna laughed. "This would have been easier if we were drunk. Hey, are we having breakfast tomorrow?"

"Of course. I'll bring the coffee," Jenna offered.

"Muffins from me. Bella's house?" Leanna asked.

"Sure." Bella swam over to Amy. "How can we help, Amy?

Want me to beat the stuffing out of him?"

"No one can beat the stuffing out of Tony. He's..." Amy mulled over her answer. *Hot, strong, sexy, frustrating, and totally not in love with me.* "Total alpha." *Just not my alpha.* She swallowed the sadness before it could swallow her.

Jenna let go of her noodle and hung on to Leanna's with her. They kicked across the pool and joined Amy and Bella.

"He's not a total alpha," Jenna said. "I think only a beta would turn down sex with you."

Amy rolled her eyes.

"What?" Jenna grabbed Amy's orange foam noodle and hung on to it beside her.

"He's totally not a beta. He's just being thoughtful." *Too darn thoughtful.* "He was doing the right thing. I'm so sick of doing the right thing." As the words left her lips, they tasted acidic and wrong. She knew all too well what doing the wrong thing could lead to.

Leanna and Bella positioned themselves in front of Amy and Jenna and held on to their noodles.

"So this is it? You're giving up on him?" Bella asked. "Because I'm on the fence. Well, on the noodle really." She chuckled.

"I don't think I can ever give up on him, but I want more. I'm ready for real, reciprocated love. A real relationship. I am ready for what each of you have. I don't know if I can ever open myself up to any other man, but I have to try." Amy gazed up at Tony's cottage. She'd spent countless hours on his deck, in his kitchen, sitting on his couch. *Mooning over him.* She thought of the way he protected her, how he looked at her when the others were talking and something secret and silent passed between them, like they could read each other's thoughts. Like when any of the girls were so into snuggling with their guys that Amy wanted to turn away, and Tony caught her eye and flashed that smile that said, *She's your friend. Smile and suck it up.*

Only that wasn't what Amy had hoped to see. She wanted to see the devilish grin that was dark and naughty. The one that she'd dreamed of that said, *Come here, baby. Let's show them how it's done.*

TONY HAD NEVER felt like a stalker before. Not in all the years he'd watched over Amy to ensure she got back to her cottage safely after she was out late. Granted, he'd never waited beside her deck, lurking in the darkness before tonight either. He wasn't actually lurking. He was waiting beneath the tree beside her deck so the others didn't see him. He'd heard them go down to the pool. Heck, who hadn't? They laughed like schoolgirls when they were together. It was one of the things he loved about all of his friends at Seaside. The camaraderie of the group and friendship they could all count on. He couldn't even blame Bella for coming after him like she had at the beach.

Amy and the girls walked up the hill practically on top of one another, clutching their towels and whispering, then bursting out in bouts of laughter. Amy looked adorable with the ends of her hair wet, sticking to her lean shoulders, but even from the short distance away he heard a difference in Amy's laugh. It wasn't the carefree laugh he'd come to love. It was laden with emptiness or sadness. Loneliness, maybe? He felt all of those things, but she seemed to be detaching herself quite easily from him, which was why he was there. Waiting. Hoping to explain where he was coming from so they could…What? Go back to the way they were? Yeah, well, that would be a start. He wasn't certain exactly where tonight would take them, but he was determined to find out, and the missing spark in her laughter made him want to take an even closer look.

"See you guys for breakfast." Amy's sweet voice carried in the night air.

Tony waited until the others had gone inside before stepping out of the shadows. He hated that they didn't wait for her to reach her deck before heading in themselves, even though he knew Seaside was safe. He was wearing his favorite jeans, worn thin on the thighs and threadbare on the bottoms, a black shirt, and a pair of Corona flip-flops. He was probably near invisible in the dark.

Amy was humming a little tune as she approached her deck.

"Amy."

Startled, she stumbled backward, her eyes wide and fearful.

"It's okay. It's only me." He slid an arm over her bare, chilly shoulder and out of habit drew her trembling body against his chest.

"You scared me." She clutched his shirt, then flattened her hand and stroked his ribs. He'd forgotten he'd worn her favorite T-shirt. She loved its softness, and seemed to cuddle up against it every time he wore it.

Okay, so maybe he hadn't forgotten.

"I'm sorry. I just wanted to talk." He lowered his hand to her hip and led her up the stairs of the deck. "Come on. Let's get you warm first." He followed her inside and almost immediately felt the tension in his shoulders ease. He was surrounded by her essence. Her simple, feminine touch was everywhere. In the pale blue walls and cream-colored sofa with white and pink accent pillows and the light wooden floors with shaggy throw rugs overtop. Even the photos of the Seaside gang mixed in with beachy, textured artwork felt very *Amy*.

Amy sat on the couch, shivering, and Tony settled in beside her.

"Don't you want to get dressed?"

"Yeah, but…" Her teeth chattered, and she lowered her voice. "Why are you here?"

He rose to his feet. "Let me get you a sweatshirt; then we'll talk."

She took his hand and pulled him back down to the couch. "Tony, please." Her whisper wasn't seductive. It was something between anxious and put out. The way she gently held his hand and the trusting look in her eyes coalesced with the gravity of the years they'd been friends, and it brought him back to the couch beside her.

He cupped his hands around hers and brought them to his lips, then breathed warm air over her cold fingers. He scooted closer to her and drew her body against his, warming her as he stroked her back. He heard her uneven breathing caused by the cold, and he assumed—*hoped?*—by the heat between them that he couldn't ignore. He held her until her trembling calmed. She felt so good, so right in his arms, and even covered in chlorine she smelled like *Amy*. He reluctantly drew away from her, and she shivered again.

He knew he was sending her mixed signals, but he couldn't stop himself from being close to her or taking care of her. He was drawn to her, and it was getting more difficult by the second to maintain his distance. He pushed from the couch. "At least let me get you a blanket."

She shook her head and pulled him down beside her again. She could be so sweetly stubborn. He reached behind him and tugged his shirt over his head, then pulled it gently over hers and lifted her arms through the sleeves. The shirt billowed over her petite frame. The sleeves hung to her elbows. He settled it around her body, then loosened her towel beneath, careful to keep her covered but wanting to get the wet towel away from her skin. She gazed up, and her eyes stilled on his bare chest. Tony knew how other women reacted to his muscular physique, but all he cared about was how Amy reacted to him. Her breathing quickened, and she dropped her eyes, nibbling on her lower lip. At least he still had some effect on her. All hope wasn't lost. He wasn't even sure exactly what he was hoping for, but he knew he didn't want Amy to stop being part of his life.

"Thank you," she whispered.

"Amy…" He touched his forehead to hers and breathed her in. "This is so hard."

"Tell me about it."

He reluctantly sat back and moved his arm to the back of the couch, giving her space, hoping she wouldn't send him away before they had a chance to talk.

"How did you know I'd go swimming tonight?" She fiddled with the edge of his T-shirt, her eyes still not venturing to his.

He sighed. It was time for complete honesty, no matter what the cost. "I always know."

That brought her eyes to his. She shook her head, and confusion wrinkled her brow. A strand of wet hair stuck to her cheek, and he carefully moved it away with his index finger.

"I have always known, Amy. I wait up and watch you walk home, just to be sure you don't fall or run into trouble."

"You watch? Like…" Her cheeks bloomed with embarrassment.

"No, babe. I don't watch you down at the pool. Just up

here, to make sure you get home okay after the others have gone inside." Not that he wouldn't love to see her skinny-dip. He'd like nothing more than to skinny-dip with her, to feel her gentle curves sliding against him.

"How long?"

Tony tried to blink away his lascivious thoughts. "Um…" *Nine inches?* Typical guy thoughts and responses came easily to him. Denial. Protective mode. Those came reflexively. It was the other stuff, the stuff from the heart that didn't come as easily.

"How long have you watched me?"

"I don't know," he lied. He knew exactly how long. Since the first time he caught wind that they'd been skinny-dipping, when they were teenagers. He wanted to be honest with her. "Forever, I guess."

She nodded, and her eyes grew serious as they dropped to his chest again. "You have a new scar."

He glanced down at the thin white scar that snaked along his left pectoral muscle. "Yeah. Rough ride in the spring. I texted you about it. Cane Garden Bay, remember? In the Caribbean."

She held her finger an inch from his chest, her eyes trained on his, as if she were waiting for him to stop her. When he didn't, she ran her finger over the scar. "I remember."

He felt himself getting aroused and laced his fingers with hers to keep from losing his mind. The cottage was quiet, save for the sounds of the leaves rustling in the wind through the back window screen. He wanted to pull her against him and close his eyes, drift away to sleep with her warm and safe against him. He wished that she'd somehow inherently know what he was there to say. But as he looked at her expectant, trusting eyes, he knew it was time to tell her the truth. It was time to tell her all the things she'd never let him say fourteen years ago.

"Amy, I'm sorry I hurt you."

Her eyes dropped to her lap, and he drew her chin up so he could see them again.

"Tony, please. You did me a favor. My feelings for you were holding me back, and now..." She shrugged, but she didn't look thankful.

Thank heaven for that.

"It's okay that I'm not your type, Tony. I get it. I'm—"

"Not my..." His breathing quickened. "Amy, you are one hundred percent my type. Can't you see that? Can't you see how hard this is for me?" He didn't mean to raise his voice, and when he saw her shaking her head and withdrawing from him, he was sure he'd blown it.

"Stop." She crossed her arms over her chest. "Just...stop."

"No, Amy. I won't stop. You need to know how I feel. How I really feel. How I've felt for years."

She looked away, and he got up and paced, too frustrated to sit any longer. "Don't you see? You're *Amy Maples*. You're sweet and good and all things tender wrapped up in this beautiful person. You're generous and giving, and—"

Amy pushed to her feet. The towel fell to the floor, and gravity sent his T-shirt down to her upper thighs. "And not your type." She crossed her arms and the shirt inched up higher.

Tony forced himself to look into her hurt-filled eyes.

"That's not true. I said that because I'm not the man you *need*, Amy, not because I don't *want* you." He closed the distance between them and couldn't help touching her arms. *Everything* felt different, more intense, more important and urgent. He knew he'd been fooling himself by thinking that after knowing she might be gone forever he wouldn't do everything he could to keep her with him. Her lower lip was trembling, and he was pretty sure it wasn't from the cold, because he could feel heat coming off of her, drawing them together until their thighs collided. It was all he could do to remain focused on making her understand where he was coming from. But he had to. It was now or never. He couldn't let her drift further away.

"Amy, you deserve to be put on a pedestal. You deserve flowers and candy and a man who will always put you first. You deserve a man who will spend every minute of every day taking care of you, loving you."

Her hands splayed across his abs, causing his thoughts to teeter between apology and desire.

"And you're not that guy."

It wasn't a question, and he didn't try to respond. Silence stretched between them, doing nothing to dampen the heat that spread like wildfire beneath her palms.

"I want it to be you," she said with hopeful eyes.

"So do I, Amy, but..." Had she buried their past so deep that she truly didn't remember? "Amy, what happened between us wasn't a mistake."

She turned away. "I don't know what you're talking about."

Her shoulders rounded forward. Tony touched her arm with his fingertips, just to ground her. To let her know he wasn't going anywhere, and he wasn't going to let her send him away this time.

"Yes, you do," he said firmly.

Her wet hair stuck to her back as she shook her head.

"Amy, we were in love. We were kids. We didn't—"

She covered her ears with her hands.

Tony took a deep breath and pushed on. "We made love a dozen times, and I know it was my fault. I never should have made love to you without protection. I take full responsibility, but please, Amy. Please don't shut me out this time."

He felt her trembling and stepped closer, pressing his chest to her back and circling her waist with his arms.

"I never meant to hurt you. I wanted to be there for you."

She broke free and crossed the room, waving her hands behind her, motioning for him to stop. To leave. To shut up.

"Amy…"

"Stop it, okay? Stop it. Just stop. I can't go there." Her words were garbled by sobs as she leaned both palms on the kitchen counter and bowed her head.

He wasn't going to lose her again. He'd come this far. He had to say his piece, no matter how much she fought him on it.

"We never dealt with it, Amy, and we have to."

She spun around with venom in her eyes. "I dealt with it, Tony. I moved on. It never happened."

In three determined steps they were toe to toe. He didn't touch her, didn't want to get her any angrier.

"It happened," he insisted just above a whisper.

She shook her head, and her body trembled.

"It happened, Amy, and it wasn't your fault. It was mine."

Tears streaked her cheeks as she inhaled a jagged breath. "I…No."

"Yes, Amy. It happened. Look at me. Please."

She stared at the floor as she whispered, "I never blamed you."

"You didn't have to. I blamed myself. Every minute of every day."

She lifted her red-rimmed eyes. "It wasn't your fault," she

whispered. "It was mine."

Tony couldn't keep himself from touching her, comforting her. He brought his hands to her cheeks and looked directly into her haunted eyes.

"Baby, you're wrong. So very wrong."

For a few seconds they stared into each other's eyes. Years of hurt passing between them like shards of glass, until Amy shrugged from his grip again and crossed the room with too much rancor in each step. It cut Tony to his core. How long could she pretend she was okay?

"I moved on. You did, too, so let it be. No one knows. I made sure of that."

Man, that's what he'd thought. She'd taken the burden alone, without him, without the girls, and who knew how that had eaten her up. How had she survived it? He'd done the same, shouldered the burden of their loss alone, but he was a man, used to dealing with hard knocks and difficult situations. He'd wanted to be there to help Amy, to share the pain and help her heal. To build a life together, a future…the only future he ever wanted.

"I haven't moved on," he admitted.

Amy blew out a half laugh, half breath. "Yeah, right. You have girlfriends galore. You have a successful business. You're an amazing surfer—"

"No kidding, Amy. You know me. If anyone in this blessed world knows me, it's you. Burying my feelings, using that frustration to excel in other ways and try to prove myself worthy is what I do best. Wearing a coat of armor so thick it smothers me but never showing it to the world. That's me. Those women were camouflage." He turned his back to try to gain control of the burn in his gut.

"Don't you know why I take care of you? Why I make sure you don't get hurt by other jerks who are only looking out for themselves? Don't you see how hard it is for me to leave when I carry you home? How I nearly lost my mind when the guys at that bar were checking you out? Don't you know why I've never had a single long-term relationship?" He turned around and closed the distance between them again.

She turned her back to him and wrapped her arms around herself.

"Because of you, Amy. Because of us. Those women were substitutes. Every single one of them. I don't know if I can be the man you want and the man you need, but darn it, I want to try."

She turned back around, her gaze and voice softer. "You're the best man I know, Tony."

"Bull. The best man wouldn't have given up when you sent me away. The best man would never have made love to you without protection and risked a pregnancy in the first place."

She circled her arms around his waist and rested her chin on his chest, and his anger turned to sadness, softening his tone.

"The best man wouldn't have filled the gaps with other women."

"Tony..."

His body was shaking now, darn it. He felt like he could barely breathe.

"You're strong and sensitive. You're thoughtful and more of a man than Rambo. Any guy would have..." Fresh tears filled her eyes. "Would have been with other women. You did what you had to in order to move on, to *survive*, just like I did."

He closed his eyes to try to center his thoughts. When he opened them, he nearly gave in to her trusting, honest gaze and the desire building within him, but she'd sent him away once before, and he knew he couldn't survive it again. And he'd turned her away so many times, he wasn't sure she could survive it if it wasn't real. He had to be sure this time. Sure of her love and sure that he could be all she'd ever need.

Her eyes remained trained on his as she drew her shoulders back and spoke in a confident, warm tone. "And you're the only man I want."

His breath left his lungs in a rush. He'd waited fourteen years to hear those words, and now he wasn't sure he was worthy. He moved her wet hair from her shoulders and stroked her cheek. His words tumbled painfully from his lips.

"I'm not the best man, Amy. You're the only woman I want in my life, and I didn't protect you at a time when it mattered most."

She stepped back and looked up at him through wet lashes. "You did what mattered most. You loved me."

He pulled her against him again, needing her close in case she didn't want anything to do with him after everything they'd said and what was yet to be said. In case this was all he'd ever have. He drew in a deep breath and held it, preparing for her response, clenching his teeth a few times to strengthen his resolve for honesty.

"We were so careful all those nights we made love that summer. That night in the woods, I was too weak. I'm a man, Amy. I should have been thinking of you, not me. You should always come first. All I could think about was being intimate with you, loving you, joining together in a way that would make me feel whole again. Only you could make me feel so loved, and damn it…"

He swallowed against the tears welling in his eyes with the

memories of how she'd freed him. She was the only one who had noticed the changes in his father that summer. How many times had he hammered Tony's worthlessness into his head? *You won't amount to anything. A surfer? Surfing is for losers. Get a job.* Tony had never told a soul. Not once. He hadn't even told Amy. But Amy had known. He had no idea how. His father had been careful to say things when no one was around. He'd been slick like that those few difficult weeks, so different from the man he'd been before that summer. But Amy knew. She'd eased all the hurt from what his father had said when she'd told Tony at the beginning of that summer, just as she told him now, *You're the best man I know.* But that humid June night he hadn't been the best man. He'd been selfish.

And she'd never wavered from loving him over the following weeks. Until after she'd gone to college, when they'd returned for that fateful weekend. The weekend they'd lost the baby he'd had no idea they'd conceived.

"I knew it was risky. I knew that withdrawing wasn't foolproof. I was older than you. I *knew* the risks, and I still did it. You need a guy who won't ever be that weak." He looked away, not wanting to see the disappointment he was sure was filling her eyes.

She laughed, a sweet, unexpected, tear-laced laugh.

Laughed.

He looked down at her, and she was smiling through her tears.

"Did you take a vow of chastity that I'm not aware of?" she asked.

He couldn't even form a response. He couldn't find one funny thing about their discussion.

"Tony..." She pressed her lips to the center of his chest, and he felt the walls around his heart crumble a little more. "I can't deal with the past, not now. But you're human. Any man would have made love to me in that way and filled that empty place with other women when I sent you away."

"Not when they loved someone else."

She dropped her eyes, and in that moment he realized what she *wasn't* saying. She'd been with other men. Of course she had. He'd known that, hadn't he?

"Yeah, they would," she whispered.

He pushed away thoughts of her with anyone else and focused on them. "Bull. Caden and Peter, do you think they would be with other women? Even for a second? Kurt, for Pete's sake?"

She laughed again. "Uh, yeah. If they'd been…if they'd gone through…"

She couldn't even say the words, and he knew, at least on some level, that they'd never be able to move forward until they *both* dealt with their loss.

"It's normal," she whispered.

"I never wanted to keep things secret back then, and I allowed myself to be swayed. If there's one thing I'm certain of, it's that you deserve a man who is better than normal."

"Tony, I don't know where you got the idea that I should be put on a pedestal, but I shouldn't. I'm the one who sent you away. I'm the one who couldn't handle it." Her thighs were still pressed against his. She had to feel how just being close to her again, allowing himself to *feel* again, *with her*, changed his very being, swamping him with memories of their love and the connection he'd never stopped feeling—memories of their bodies as close as conjoined twins.

"Don't sell yourself short," he said.

"Tony." She sighed. "I'm addicted to my label maker. I have the body of a prepubescent girl, and I can't hold my liquor." She ran her fingers up his back, sending heat to all the right—and wrong-for-the-moment—places. "I can't deal with heavy things. I hide from them. I don't deserve a second look, much less to be put up on a pedestal."

"Let me be the judge of what you deserve, okay?"

She leaned in so close her breath brushed over his bare chest. Torture. Pure, unadulterated torture.

"No," she whispered. "You aren't a good judge of what I need, because what I need is right here, right now. We don't have to deal with the past. I have no idea why you think you're not good enough to be with me, but from the feel of things, I think you want to be."

He narrowed his eyes and gripped her shoulders. "I never said I wasn't good enough. I said you *deserved* better. There's a difference." He was powerless to resist sliding his hand down her hip to the curve of her thigh, inciting a sexy mew from Amy.

"You're the best, Tony. Can't you see that? You're one of the top three surfers in the country. People pay money for you to tell them *how* to live their lives. Who could be better than you?" Her breathing became shallow as he dropped his other hand to her thigh.

He had driven himself to succeed in his career, but he'd never pushed himself to be the best boyfriend he could be. He'd pretty much spent his life avoiding being a boyfriend, because every other woman was a substitute for the one he really wanted. The one he really needed. The woman he truly believed deserved more than a guy who hadn't fought for her all those years ago when she'd sent him away, a guy who had never been able to commit to a long-term relationship since—and worried now that he might let her down.

"It's not about how successful I am, Amy. I need to prove to myself that I can be the man you deserve, and I need to prove it to you before I can call you mine again. I need to know I'll never risk your health again. I mean, I know it already, but I need to prove it to us both." He wanted to kiss her, to slide his hands across her beautiful body and finally take what had felt like *his* for way too long, but he held back. They needed to deal with the past, but he couldn't say that now. She'd come a long way. For the first time in fourteen years, she acknowledged that they'd been together. That was huge. A start. A frigging blessing.

"Maybe you don't know what I need after all," she challenged.

He breathed deeply, trying to ignore the way every bit of him wanted to give in to what she wanted. But Tony wasn't a man who believed in doing things he'd regret. Not anymore, and especially not with Amy.

"I know you better than you know yourself. Can't you see that?" He tangled his hands in her hair and tilted her head back. "You're everything to me, Amy. You're the first thing I think of when I wake up and the last thing I think of before I fall asleep." He pulled her impossibly closer and lowered his mouth so their lips were a heartbeat away.

"It's your voice I hear pushing me through those treacherous swells, and it's your voice I hear in my head right now, guiding me to do the right thing by you."

He had to kiss her. Just one kiss. He wasn't strong enough to leave without one kiss, restaking his claim, showing her how much he loved her.

"I'm not worthy of a pedestal," she whispered.

"You're so very worthy." He paused to keep himself from lowering his lips to hers.

"Statues are put on pedestals," she whispered, blinking up at him. Her fingernails, which had grazed his skin so lightly, dug into his back. "Statues are cold and hard. I'm warm and soft in all the right places, not at all like a statue."

She was reaching so far out of the way she normally behaved that he clenched his jaw just to try to remain in control.

"You say all the right things, Amy, but I know you. You're going to wake up conflicted tomorrow, and I don't blame you."

His heart threatened to burst through his chest as he tightened his grip in her silky hair and whispered, "I'm sorry. I shouldn't do this. It will only muddy the waters, but, Amy…I can't wait a second longer."

He sealed his lips over hers, and years of want and lust came crashing like a wave, holding him spellbound as she opened her mouth to him and slid her tongue over his. A storm of emotions rocked through him: greed, lust, disbelief, and a swell of love that seemed as endless as the sea. She tasted sweet and ripe, like she'd been waiting her whole life for this moment. Her body molded to his effortlessly, naturally, as he lifted her in his arms and carried her into the bedroom, feeling the tension and excitement as real as when he entered the barrel of a wave, knowing it had the ability to drown him and needing it too badly to turn away.

He lowered her to the bed and followed her down. She circled his neck with her arms and arched up with a needy moan when he tried to reluctantly draw away from her. He moved beside her on the bed, finally pulling back from her delicious mouth and their mind-numbing kiss. He brushed her hair from her forehead and kissed the corners of her mouth, feeling her hot breath against his cheeks, spurring him to take more than he intended. He kissed her forehead, the soft indentation beside her eye, her jaw, and heaven help him for being weak, he allowed himself a luscious taste of her collarbone. She was his drug, even after all these years.

She arched her neck and fisted her hands in his hair, jolting him back to reality.

"Yes." Her needy whisper cut him to his core.

He needed more of her. All of her. He didn't want to leave. He wasn't ready. Would he ever be? He sealed his lips over hers, probing, memorizing, claiming her mouth as his. She met him stroke for eager stroke. His hand slid down her rib cage to the hem of his T-shirt she was wearing and met her bare hip bone.

What was he doing?

He forced himself to tear his lips from hers and pulled back with a gasp for air.

"We have to stop."

"No." She pulled him toward her again.

He smiled at her determination, so reminiscent of that incredible—and treacherous—summer.

"Tony, please."

He was quickly careening toward giving himself up to her. To be one hundred percent utterly and completely hers once again was everything he wanted. He was weakening again. She needed strong.

He needed to stop.

Now.

"Babe," he panted out. "We have to stop."

"Noooooo." She buried her face in his chest and clutched his arms for dear life.

"I'll never forgive myself if we do this, Amy. Not now."

Not until I know we can deal with the past and move forward without regret. Not until I'm sure you won't send me away again. He couldn't say either of those things; all he could do was frame it in a way that hopefully wouldn't scare her off.

"Not until I can prove to myself, and to you, that I can be the man you deserve and the only man you'll ever need."

Chapter Eight

THE NEXT MORNING Amy sat on Bella's deck wearing Tony's T-shirt from last night and her sleeping shorts, with four sets of eyes on her. *Four*, not three. *Four*. Apparently Sky had had a nagging intuition that something big was going on at Seaside and she didn't want to miss out. Sky had grown up on the Cape. She'd come back to help run their father's hardware store when their father went into rehab two summers ago, and she'd fallen back in love with the area and was here to stay. She'd also quickly become another Seaside bestie. At the moment she had her feet tucked beneath her legs, her long cotton skirt tangled around her knees, and her tie-dyed tank top slipping off one shoulder while Jenna painted her fingernails a deep shade of purple.

"Well?" Bella pushed. She and the other girls were still wearing their pajamas, too, all of them braless. Bella wore a tank top and shorts, while Leanna and Jenna had on camis and silky shorts to match.

I really need to sex up my sleepwear. She glanced down at Tony's shirt and decided she'd rather wear Tony's shirt than sexy lingerie any day of the week.

Amy glanced at Tony's empty driveway. He'd gone surfing,

of course. He lived and breathed surfing. He scheduled his summer days around the surf as much as she tried not to schedule hers around anything. It was one of the things she'd always loved about him. He was dedicated to being the best in everything he did, which was why, after he'd left last night and her hormones had finally calmed down, she understood his need to be the best for her, too. If only he'd understand that to her he was already the best.

"As I said." She lowered her voice to a whisper even though Tony was gone. Kurt was at his keyboard on Leanna's deck, and Caden and his almost eighteen-year-old son, Evan, had run out to pick up a few things that Evan needed for his first semester of college in the fall.

The girls leaned forward expectantly.

"We talked." She was still a little numb. She could still hardly believe they had kissed after all these years, and while she wanted to stand on the table and shout, *I finally kissed Tony Black!* she worried that it might jinx whatever chance they had for something more. What if he hadn't meant all the things he'd said? Maybe she'd pushed too hard and he'd given in just because he didn't want to hurt her any more than he already had.

Bella threw her hands up in the air. "Seriously? All this afterglow is caused by a talk? You freaking have a freshly satisfied grin on your face. I'm not buying it one bit."

Leanna patted Bella's shoulder and spoke softly. "Bella, give her a little space. It's okay if all they did was talk. Depending on what they said, that could be a much bigger deal than having sex."

Bella rolled her eyes. That seemed to be the theme for the morning.

"I agree." Sky waved her wet fingernails in the air. "When I fall in love, like *really* fall in love, I'm going to wait to have sex."

Jenna threw her head back and laughed, loud and hearty.

"You have no idea what you'll do, Sky." Jenna put her foot up on her chair and began painting her toenails. "I know Petey's your brother and you probably don't want to hear this, but there is no way I could have waited any longer to be in his arms. Love is like this amazing, all-consuming force that sneaks up on you and steals all those brain cells that make you think rationally and replaces them with emotions so powerful that you're impotent to change their course."

"I gotta say, I totally agree," Leanna said. "But I also agree with Sky's idea. I mean, I couldn't have resisted my feelings for Kurt, but I think there's some value in waiting to have sex."

Bella patted Sky's foot. "You're trying to tell me that you haven't slept with Blue?" She laughed.

"Seriously?" Sky slapped her hands on the table. "You ask me that all the time. No. No. And no, again. I told you we're just really good friends."

"Hey, you're the one who sleeps at his place," Bella said.

"We're friends. We watch movies and hang out," Sky explained.

"Either you're a very good liar, missy, or you're full of it." Bella pointed at Sky. "Either way, fifty bucks says when you either fess up about Blue or find the man who is your forever love, there is no way you'll be able to hold back from the big bang."

Amy arched a brow. "The *big bang*, Bella? Can't it be a little more romantic, like the *big love*, or *lovingly naughty*?"

"Your sweetness is showing, sugar," Bella said.

Amy was deflecting, as she had done for years. She wanted

to pull her closest friends around her like a shield and share the secret that had nearly killed her in college. The secret she'd been denying existed for fourteen years. The secret that, if she hadn't buried it deeper than the earth's core, she wouldn't have survived.

She'd lost Tony's child.

Our child.

She should have told Tony that summer afternoon instead of agreeing to go surfing first. She shouldn't have wanted one last time to feel that high of the waves with him behind her, watching her, being proud of what she could do. She'd loved sharing in the one thing that brought him freedom from the confines of his father's overbearing nature that summer, and she'd just wanted one more moment of it before telling him she was pregnant. She knew he'd never let her surf if he'd known.

She'd been so afraid that someone would get wind of their relationship and that they'd had sex that summer, and then her father would have… Gosh, to this day she had no idea what he would have done. If she hadn't lost the baby, they'd have told him, wouldn't they? How would he have reacted? She hadn't thought of that since the night she lost the baby. She'd always been the light of his life, his *little girl.* She'd never stepped over his carefully outlined boundaries or breached his confidence and trust…until that summer, when she couldn't hold back. Denying her feelings for Tony would have killed her. And now, as she looked into the eyes of the women who had been there for as long as she could remember, her betrayal of their trust hit her like the wave that had taken her under so long ago.

Jenna clapped her hands. "I've got it! The *deep impact*! Or…or…" Her eyes lit up. "In Tony's case, the *big wave*."

"Well, he does surf on an ocean. How about the *big O*?"

Leanna laughed.

"Oh, oh, oh! Surfer words! I've got this. I surfed when I was a teenager." Sky waved her hands in the air. "*Pumping the pipe! Banging the barrel?* Or how about *riding the bomb*?"

Amy wasn't laughing. Listening to them reference sex and surfing brought her back in time. Would she ever get past it completely? She remembered the panic attacks she'd succumbed to when she'd gone to Brown after that fateful summer. She'd barely saved her grades and learned to overcome them with the help of a counselor. But she *had* overcome them, and she was strong enough to push away those memories now and enjoy her friends, who were doing what they always did, keeping things real. If only they knew how real things had become that summer.

Banging the barrel? "You guys, stop," Amy pleaded. "This is *Tony* we're talking about."

"Exactly." Bella raised her brows. "Ready to fess up?"

"We kissed, okay? One toe-curling, earth-shattering kiss that left me unable to even say goodbye when he left." She exhaled loudly, relieved to get their kiss off her chest.

"Wow." Bella sat back and smiled.

"Toe curling? A toe-curling kiss?" Sky twisted the ends of her hair around her finger. "See? You didn't even need sex."

Leanna touched Amy's knee. "Does that mean that you're not moving?"

"Honestly? I don't know what it means. He said I deserve a better man than him."

"A better man than a walking Adonis? Right." Jenna laughed. "Like they're a dime a dozen. What's got into him? Oh, I know. No lovin', that'll do it."

"While I totally get what Jenna's saying…" Sky smiled at

Jenna. "Talking is where it's at. Your relationship gets much deeper by talking. But," she waggled her brows, "there's lots of *fun* to be had after you're done."

Amy held her hands up in surrender. "I'm so sorry I said anything. We aren't like that." *Not that I don't want to be.* "We're in the talking stage. Part of me thinks he kissed me just because I wanted him to so badly, but it didn't feel like that kind of kiss."

"Oh, honey," Leanna said. "You're just worrying because this has been so many years in the making. When are you seeing him again?"

Amy shrugged, as if maybe Leanna were right, but she knew the truth. Their past was like an ocean between them, rising and falling with their thoughts and heated glances, waiting to rise up and come crashing down again.

"We didn't really talk about seeing each other. He just apologized and said some of the nicest things a guy could ever say. Then…we kissed." Tony's words floated through her mind for the millionth time that morning. *You're everything to me, Amy. You're the first thing I think of when I wake up and the last thing I think of before I fall asleep.*

"Care to elaborate on *nicest things*?" Bella asked.

"No. It's too easy to latch on to them and hope he meant them. There was something in his eyes when he said them. It wasn't doubt, but hesitation, maybe?" Maybe even mistrust. How could he ever trust her again after she'd turned him away so harshly when all he'd wanted to do was heal their pain?

"Well, if he thinks you deserve a better guy than him, that's total baloney," Leanna said. "Maybe he got cold feet. I don't know for sure, but he probably did feel a little hesitant to reveal how he felt."

"Well...he is a bit of a player," Bella added with a soft tone and a compassionate gaze.

Amy kicked her under the table. "Thanks. As if I wasn't doubting the moment enough already." She crossed her arms on the table and rested her forehead on them, trying to rein in her hopes.

"I don't mean it like that. I just mean that he doesn't really have a track record of long-term relationships," Bella explained. "He's probably scared to death of actually committing."

"None of us had a particularly great track record of long-term relationships, Bella." Leanna layered a croissant with jam and slid it over to Amy. "Amy, try my new flavor, Sweet Heat. Food always helps."

Amy lifted her eyes to Leanna. "Sweet Heat?"

"Just taste it. I promise it'll make you feel better. My friend Joanie from the flea market suggested I try to create something sweet and spicy." She pushed the plate closer to Amy. "Come on."

Amy sat up, pulled off a corner of the croissant, and popped it into her mouth. Her mouth exploded with the savory sensation of jalapeños and something sweet and tart. "Oh my! This is crazy good, and the name is perfect. It tastes kind of sexy." She picked up the jar of Luscious Leanna's Sweet Treats jam and looked over the green and red label. "Sweet Heat. I love it." She pushed the plate to the center of the table. "You guys have to taste this."

While they *ooh*ed and *aah*ed over Leanna's new flavor, Amy mulled over the sweet heat she'd experienced last night. While she was over the moon about finally kissing the man she loved with all her heart, she had to wonder—if he didn't trust himself to be the man she deserved, should she?

TONY STOOD AT the edge of the surf with a handful of other surfers who had also come out early to catch the waves. As with any sport, there was an unspoken kinship among surfers. One glance spoke volumes about sucky waves, riptides, the agony of defeat, or the elation of a perfect ride. Tony tried to keep a low profile when he surfed at the Cape, but in the surfing world he was a celebrity, and there wasn't an easy way to hide his identity when he had a board under his arm.

Even in his wet suit he knew he was bulkier than most of the surfers on the Cape. Most were surfing for fun, not competition. Tony got up early for his five-mile runs, spent hour upon hour surfing, and trained in just about every fashion his body could handle. His fitness regimen didn't stop there. He fueled his body with as much planning as he used for his workouts, and his mental abilities were just as honed, studying the physicality of all sports—not just surfing—and staying abreast of medical treatments for injuries and current events. Tony believed in being well rounded. There was a reason he was a leader in everything he did—and he probably had his father to thank for that. Proving himself to the man he'd spent years looking up to, and their last summer together, loathing in equal measure, had been just the impetus he'd needed to push himself to the edge.

That was also the reason he would become the best man he could for Amy. No matter what it took. If he was capable of succeeding in other aspects of his life, he was capable of using that same determination for her. Although, as he stood on the shore beside the other surfers, gauging the water and thinking of Amy, he knew he was overlooking the most important part of the equation. There was one thing he had never been able to overcome, and last night's kiss brought it all home once again. He hadn't ever overcome the devastation that she'd cast him aside so easily. She'd moved on without ever looking back, and he'd nearly drowned in her wake. He wondered if he'd be able, or willing, to push past that and open his heart to her completely, the way he had back then.

"Mom! That's him. I told you he was here!" A little boy ran up to Tony, kicking sand all over his feet, and grinned up at him. He was all knees and elbows, topped off with a spiky mop of dark hair.

"Jonah, slow down. Don't bother him." His mother trailed behind him wearing a black one-piece bathing suit and an embarrassed smile.

"It's all right," Tony said casually as the kid tugged on his wet suit. "What's up, buddy?"

"You're Tony Black."

Tony laughed. "Yeah, I am. What's your name?"

"Jonah. Jonah Mickelow. I'm gonna be a surfer when I get older. Mom says I have to be eight, so I have two more years before I can learn, but I'm gonna do it. And I'm gonna break your records and be better than you." His dark eyes were wide, his voice high and excited.

"Another two years, huh? Then I'd better do my best over the next two years."

"Yeah, 'cause I'm gonna be good." The little boy turned toward his mother. "This is my mom. She and her friends said you're hot. I wanna be hot when I'm old like you."

His mother turned a shade of crimson and mumbled, "Oh geez, Jonah."

Tony laughed. Out of habit, his eyes rose to the dune,

where Amy often sat and watched him surf. His heart nearly stopped. She was there, her knees pulled up to her chest, arms crossed over them, and her chin resting smack-dab in the center.

She'd watched him a million times, almost always by herself, and she never came down to the beach. She'd stay for a while, and he'd get engrossed in surfing and look for her a while later, and she'd be gone. He didn't want her gone this time.

The little boy tugged on his suit again. "Can you autograph something for me?"

"Absolutely." Tony glanced at Amy again, excited that she was there; then he looked at the boy's mother.

"Oh. Um. I don't really have anything to write on, honey."

"I've got you covered, buddy." Tony headed up the beach toward his gear. He had a soft spot for children, and over the years he'd gotten in the habit of having a pen and paper on hand. He remembered the excitement of watching the pros in action and the anticipation of one day meeting them, stalking the beaches they frequented and waiting for the perfect opportunity. Having been the eager kid and knowing it was that eagerness that led to determination, Tony made sure that no kid seeking an autograph went home empty-handed. Now he looked down at the enthusiastic little boy and wondered if his feeling toward kids had more to do with the loss he'd experienced with Amy and less to do with stalking pro surfers when he was younger.

"Are you sure?" his mother asked. "We don't want to interrupt your surfing. I'm Lydia, by the way."

"No worries," he said to Lydia. He glanced back up the dune at Amy and hurriedly scribbled a personal message for Jonah so he could go talk to Amy before she disappeared like the wind. He crouched beside the little boy.

"Here you go, buddy. Surfing takes a lot of energy and dedication, just like school does. So you do as well in school as you want to do on the waves—got it?"

"Got it, Mr. Black. Thank you." He reached for his mother's hand and smiled up at her. "Look, Mom. I have Tony Black's autograph."

Lydia batted her eyes at Tony. "Thank you, and thank you for wrapping a little lesson in there with it." Her eyes took a slow stroll down his body.

Meaningless sex had become something he loathed. He could no longer hide from what he really wanted, to share all of his life with someone he loved.

And as he lifted his eyes to the dune, he knew there was only one person who could fill that gap. And she was heading for the parking lot.

Tony ignored Lydia's leer, tossed the pad and pen into his backpack, and darted down the beach toward the wide, steep path that led up the dune to the parking lot.

He reached the top of the hill as Amy drove toward the exit, and Tony sprinted through the parking lot, barefoot and thankful for all his training. He reached Amy's car just as she stopped in the line of cars waiting to exit. He knocked on her window, startling her.

She rolled it down with a shy smile that made him glad he'd reached her. The memory of their kiss was so fresh he nearly leaned in and kissed her again.

"Hey." He was out of breath. She was wearing his favorite bikini, the pale blue one that reminded him of her cottage, which brought his mind back to her bed and the feel of her body for that brief moment last night.

"Hey."

"Why are you leaving?"

She shifted her eyes away. "I…Um. I just came to hang out for a while."

"Stay with me."

"I don't know. You looked pretty busy down there." She ran her finger over the steering wheel. When the car ahead of her pulled onto the road and her car rolled forward, Tony walked alongside, gripping the door.

Something in her voice made him take a deeper look at her expression, and that's when he noticed it. He'd been so excited to see her that he'd missed the conflicting emotions in her beautiful eyes.

"Please?"

"Tony…I'm…I'm not ready to give up the job in Australia."

"I…" He hadn't thought she'd still go. He hadn't put Australia into the picture at all since last night. Why would she just give up on them like that? "I just want time with you."

She sighed. "You came here to surf." Despite the efforts he could see her making to restrain it, a smile curved her luscious lips.

And now he knew just how delicious they were. "Come on, Ames. It'll be fun."

Her finger tapped the steering wheel.

"We'll take a walk and find the ugliest bathing suit."

She smiled at that. She must have allowed that memory to resurface just as he had. The summer they were together they'd stalked the beach claiming they were seeking out the ugliest bathing suits as a cover for just wanting time alone. Their ruse had worked perfectly—their friends made fun of them for doing something so lame and never wanted to tag along. They couldn't kiss in front of their friends, but after walking a mile down the beach, they kissed like kisses were food and they were starving.

"But after everything..."

"We need this, Ames." He ran his knuckle down her cheek, and she closed her eyes for only a second, but that second was enough for him to know she was more on his side of the fence than not. "Please?"

They walked down the beach with the sun at their backs and silence filling the distance between them. Amy looked sexy and sweet, something only she could pull off so effortlessly. She wasn't walking with tension in her steps, but Tony didn't have to see the tension to know it existed.

The ease of their friendship was strained by the past. Tony didn't have a goal when he'd asked Amy to stay with him. He just wanted to be with her, see where things went, in the same way he'd fallen in love with her all those years ago. He hadn't planned it. He'd fallen more in love with her second after second, day after day, year after year. He hadn't tried, and at first he hadn't even realized it was happening. They'd been drawn together in a way that felt natural and very real.

Tony knew by the way her eyes were dragging over every person they walked past that Amy was searching for the ugliest suit. The thought made him smile. They no longer needed to use the game as a cover, and they were no longer confined by keeping their attraction a secret, but it felt as though they were facing new barriers. Barriers dividing the past from the present and another line of hurdles between the present and the future.

The summer they'd found each other, he'd known his feelings were bigger than anything he'd ever experienced, and now, despite the barriers that seemed insurmountable and the pain he knew lay in wait, those feelings rushed forward at breakneck speed, with the intensity of a board snapping in two, hard and fast.

Unstoppable.

Chapter Nine

"ORANGE BATHING SUIT," Tony whispered in her ear.

Amy scanned the beach, glad for the distraction from her thoughts. Her eyes landed on an old man wearing neon-orange bathing trunks.

"That's a winner." She was so nervous that she had no idea how she was walking, much less talking. She silently prayed that Tony wouldn't try to bring up the past, and battling with those thoughts were equally as determined wishes that things could go back to the way their relationship had been a week ago. When they were able to walk with his arm slung over her shoulder and her only worry was if it was because he liked her or if he was just being Tony. But she'd wanted answers, and now she had them—and she was glad she had them—but that didn't make all this discomfort any easier.

She tried to focus on the positive. At least now she knew the truth.

She knew what *just being Tony* meant. He was protecting her, getting close in the only way he could, but she wasn't ready to turn away her dream job for a tenuous relationship teetering on intangible things she wasn't sure she could handle. And yet even having taken the job in Australia, she wanted more with

Tony. She didn't want to revisit the past, but she darn well wanted a future with him, even if she had no idea how to make it work. It was time to suck up her fear and face the music.

She reached for his hand, and for the first time ever, she felt the slightest hesitation in his grip. Was she pushing him away? Losing him over her unwillingness to face the past? The thought scared her. She drew in a breath of courage and walked closer to him. He glanced at her, the sun striking his bangs as they dusted his eyes, and his mouth quirked up in a half smile. She wrapped her other hand around his biceps. Leaning her cheek against his arm didn't feel as unnatural as she feared it might after last night, and when he leaned down and kissed the top of her head, she knew everything had changed and stayed the same all at once.

Which only made whatever they were doing more confusing. But still she was unwilling to pull away and dissect it like she should.

"I've missed you," Tony said as he kicked the surf.

"I'm always around." She knew that wasn't what he meant, but her nerves weren't making it easy to find the right response.

"No. I mean I've missed you for all these years, Ames." He gazed down at her with a piercing stare that told her exactly what he meant.

He wanted this. Her. *Them.*

She opened her mouth to respond, but no words came. He unlaced their fingers and draped an arm over her shoulder. When he pulled her against him, she felt like she was on the precipice of the past and the present. How could she cross that line without getting lost in the pain?

Tony stopped walking and turned her toward him. He slid his hands beneath her hair and tilted her head up. It was the same intimate caress that they'd shared so many times that summer, and it still made her insides hot and melty.

"Everyone has a past. I have mine, you have yours, and we have ours. No matter what it takes, I will prove to you that our past, no matter how hurtful, didn't ruin the future we could have. Only we can either make that happen or run from it. It's our decision this time, Amy. There are no outside influences that can push us one way or the other. There's only you and me and what could be."

Amy didn't think as she went up on her toes and reached her hand around his neck. He met her halfway, and their lips came together in a warm and wonderful kiss, filled with passion and sprinkled with worry. It was sweet and rough at once, like the path they had to travel to figure out their lives.

When they finally drew apart, Tony pressed another soft kiss to her mouth, then her forehead, before settling his cheek against hers and whispering, "I've made my decision. I'm going to prove I'm your man."

"Tony."

He searched her eyes. She wished she could pretend she didn't feel doubt or pain, but they were there, lingering in the corners of her mind.

"I'm not perfect, Amy, but I'm going to try."

She trapped her lip between her teeth to steel herself against tears over the sincerity in his voice. Her dreams were coming true, and she was scared to pieces.

"All I ask is that if you decide you're going to walk away this time, please, Amy, don't go silently. Talk to me first. Give me a chance. I can't take being thrown away again. Not by you. Not if I take down my walls and let you in."

She lost the battle, and tears streamed down her cheeks.

Tony wiped them away with his thumb. "Please," he whispered.

She managed a nod, feeling sick to her stomach for having hurt him so badly. They began walking down the beach again, and she forced her voice to work. He deserved to hear what she'd been hiding behind for so long.

"I was scared." She didn't recognize the tentative strain in her voice, though it resonated with her feelings as she fought to tell Tony the truth.

"I know. So was I. I thought I'd lost you forever."

"I was scared for *you*." She felt his step falter a moment, then regain its momentum. "I was already worried about my father finding out about us, but then after I got pregnant, I worried that your father would use it against you."

He squeezed her shoulder. "I could have handled him."

She nodded. "I know. Even at twenty you were the most confident man I knew. It was one of the things that drew me in. Still does. I knew you could handle anything, but I didn't want you to have to."

"I understand," he said quietly, and she wondered if he really did.

They walked in silence a little farther. "When I came to your school, I was going to tell you not to worry, that it wouldn't change anything between us." He paused as those words sank in. "But as an adult, I realize how misguided that was."

Amy stopped walking. *Misguided?* Her entire world had changed that last night at the Cape. Her outlook, her goals, her desires. Everything. And now she was learning that he'd been misguided? How? Was their love misguided? After everything he'd said to her just now?

"I think I need to sit down."

"Sure, of course." They were on an empty stretch of beach. Tony led her up the shore to the crest of a hill. They sat in silence and watched the breaking waves.

Tony leaned back on his palms. Amy missed the comfort and closeness of his arm over her shoulder.

"Are you okay?" he asked. "I know it's a lot to process. All of this. Us."

"Yeah." She was not okay. But she wanted to be.

"Amy, I know now what I couldn't see clearly then. You can't go through something like what we did without it changing who we are, at least on some level." He slid his feet closer, leaned his arms over his knees, and folded his hands together. "But I wanted to be there with you, no matter what it meant."

"I changed, Tony. I was barely hanging on when I got back to school. I tried to stuff all the hurt and the self-loathing into a box and shove it as far away as I could, but no matter how far I kicked it, it returned. And when I saw you..." Her eyes welled with fresh tears. This was so darn hard. How could she put into words what she felt? It was too much, too hurtful.

Tony put his arm around her. She drew strength from his touch, feeling guilty for doing so after the way she'd shut him out, and at the same time, feeling relieved that he was giving her another chance.

"I've never loved anyone like I love you, and everything hurt after that. It hurt to sleep, to eat, to think. To *feel.*" She turned away, ashamed by the constant flow of tears.

He drew her chin back toward him, and it was all Amy could do to look into his compassionate eyes and not break down sobbing. She reached for his other hand and held on tight.

"I'm so sorry. I know…" Tears blurred her vision. "I was scared. I didn't know if I'd survive how empty and scared I felt, and I was so worried that I'd ruin your career, and you were just starting out and doing so well…"

He pulled her against his chest and caressed her back. "It's okay," he whispered.

"No. It isn't, and it never was. I faked my way through the next few years, until faking it became so real that I could no longer tell the difference between who I really was and who I was pretending to be."

"Oh, baby. I'm so sorry." He pressed his lips to the top of her head, holding her cheek against his chest. "I never wanted you to experience that. It's no way to live."

She listened to his heartbeat, remembering all those nights they'd snuck out and fallen into each other's arms, and afterward, how she'd lay on his chest and count his heartbeats beating in time with her own.

"It was the only way I could live…" Her voice faded into the sound of the waves.

"Are you still wearing that armor, Amy? Even with me?"

She shifted away from his chest and met his gaze. "I don't know. It's been so long that I'm no longer sure."

He searched her eyes and then his became serious. "I know who you were, and I know the woman you are now. You know who I was, and I mean who I really was. Not the guy covering his feelings. Not the guy everyone else thought they knew."

Amy felt the impact of his words, the intimacy of their relationship winding its way deeper into her. She did know him, and he knew her, better than anyone else ever could. She hated that she'd hurt him and hated hearing the pain in his voice now. She watched his lips move, and she had the overwhelming desire to climb into his lap and kiss the pain away, but she was unable to move.

"Together we can figure out who we are now. We can find the people we were before we lost…"

He lowered his eyes and she felt her chest tighten. He cleared his throat, and when he spoke again, his voice was not quite as solid.

"Before." He met her gaze. "Together we can figure out who we are now, without our armor. Together we can become the people, the couple, we should be."

She stayed where she was, sitting beside him and leaning across his chest, the weight of fourteen years pinning her in place.

"Do you want to see if we can salvage our relationship?" he asked. "Or do you only want a relationship with me if I can pretend the past never happened?"

She'd been asking herself that for the past hour. She'd been so in love with him for so long that she hadn't considered that if they ever got back together, their relationship was dependent upon her confronting their past. And ever since they'd kissed, she'd thought of nothing else. She knew the only answer she could give was one he wouldn't want to hear. How could she tell him that she didn't know if she would ever be able to deal with the past? Or that she was scared they might not survive uncovering all the hurt they'd survived? How could she tell him that she feared that discussing it would cost her any chance she had with him? The longer she remained silent, the more worried his eyes became, and then, as if he were remembering a joke, his lips curved into a smile and he stroked her cheek.

"Take your time, babe. I deserve the torture."

She wasn't out to torture him, although this whole conversation was torturous for them both. She asked herself again how she could tell him the truth, and the answer became clear. Because the truth was the only answer she *could* give.

"I don't know what I can handle. But I know I want you."

Chapter Ten

"A DATE!" JENNA sat on the edge of Amy's bed in a pair of daisy dukes and a purple tank top that made her tiny waist look even smaller. She fell onto her back, kicked her feet up in the air, and wiggled her purple toenails. "A real date with Tony. Oh, Amy, this is amazing!"

Amy stood in her closet, fidgeting with the edge of her shorts. "I don't know about amazing, but…Who am I kidding? Yeah, it's pretty amazing." She was thrilled that Tony wanted to try to be like a normal couple. *Date, talk, and see where things go.* It was the talking part that frightened her. She really didn't know what she was capable of handling without panicking. Or running away. She definitely did not want to run away. All of the excitement over Tony overshadowed her lingering indecision about the job in Australia. And now, as Leanna waltzed in and out of Amy's closet, holding up dresses and outfits, and Bella paced the room, a whole new panic was setting in.

She couldn't betray her friends' trust any longer. When the past was put away completely—safely tucked away in the land of denial—she could pretend she wasn't keeping such a big secret from them, but now that she and Tony had opened Pandora's box, the guilt pressed in on her.

"This will be interesting, Amy. I mean, how do you decide if you stay at his cottage or yours?" Bella crossed her arms and stared up at the ceiling. "Or maybe you go back and forth. One night there, one night here."

"But remember to close the windows," Leanna said as she held up a blue sundress. "This would be pretty."

Close the windows. Maybe she could close the windows on her past. Or rather, keep them closed and continue to pretend it never happened. Did her friends really need to know?

Jenna jumped off the bed and headed into the closet. "No. She needs something sexier."

"Oh my gosh. Amy." Bella grabbed her arm. Her blond hair was pinned up in a messy ponytail, and she was still wearing her bathing suit beneath her sundress. "You took the job in Australia. What will you tell Duke?"

She hadn't thought that far ahead. To be fair to Duke, she probably needed to make a decision sooner rather than later. But she wasn't ready to make a decision. Her heart screamed for her to stay with Tony, but they were like a garden that had just been seeded, and she wasn't sure that one big storm wouldn't wash them away. She needed time to think things through, and tonight she'd barely been able to think about getting dressed.

"It's too early to worry about that, don't you think? I mean, we're just going on a date." Now she was lying to herself *and* to her friends. She knew perfectly well that she and Tony were rekindling a summer of the deepest love she'd ever known, and the only love she'd ever wanted.

"When are you supposed to start the job?" Bella asked.

"December. I was going to give my clients enough notice to try to hire someone to replace me, well, the few who wouldn't be able to continue working with me remotely."

Jenna tugged at Amy's T-shirt. "Take this off."

Amy pulled her shirt over her head.

"Put this on." Jenna handed her a slinky silver dress.

"I am not wearing that. This is *Tony*, remember? Think casual, comfortable, sexy but subtle. I don't want to wear something that makes me feel like I'm someone I'm not." *I'm having enough trouble figuring out who I am at the moment.* "I need a dress that says, *It's me, only better.*" She reached past Jenna and pulled out a green print halter-top dress with a beaded neckline that gathered in the middle.

"This is one I'm comfortable in. I love the black and yellow flowers at the bottom, and I think it makes my little boobs look at least a little bigger. Don't you think?" Amy put it on and twirled in a circle.

"Oh, Ames," Jenna said. "You're going to knock his socks off. You're so lucky. You don't need extra-sexy clothes. You look like a million bucks."

"A million *sexy* bucks." Leanna handed her a pair of silver sandals.

"Oh, no." Jenna grabbed the sandals and crouched in Amy's closet, shaking her head while she inspected Amy's footwear options. "You cannot wear silver sandals with a casual sundress. Here, wear these black ones. They match the flowers." Jenna swiveled around and slipped them on Amy's feet. "And I think you look like a mile-high wave. We are talking about a date with Tony, after all."

"Thanks, Jenna. So?" Amy held her hands out to her sides and looked down at her dress.

"Gorgeous. But you need earrings," Jenna said.

"I'm already on it." Bella pulled a pair of earrings out of the pocket of her dress and held her palm out flat.

Amy stared at the surfboard earrings in Bella's hand. Her stomach tumbled. "Where did you get those?" They were the earrings Tony had given her that summer. He'd bought them when they had all gone to Provincetown for an afternoon.

"When you said you were going out with Tony, I remembered you gave them to me the summer after our first year in college. Remember? I've had them in the drawer of my jewelry box ever since. Didn't he give you these?"

"Yeah. He bought them in P-town." She picked up the tiny surfboards, remembering when he'd given them to her in front of their friends and the way they'd both tried to laugh it off like she was his surfing groupie. Amy had been shocked that none of their friends had noticed the way the world spun when they were together, or the way the air sizzled and popped around them.

She put on the earrings, and the ache she'd tried to escape slowly returned. She remembered when she'd given Bella the earrings to hold for her the summer after she and Tony had broken up. She couldn't bear to see them, but she didn't want to get rid of them, either. Now she felt guilty for trusting Bella with the earrings and not trusting her with her secret.

Leanna put her arm around Amy and whispered, "Your date is here." She pointed to the bedroom window as Tony passed by. She tucked away the ache of guilt, unable to deal with it before leaving with Tony, and promised herself she'd tell them the next chance she had.

"He has flowers!" Jenna whispered loudly.

"I'm swooning already." Leanna sighed and scooted past Amy toward the bedroom door.

"Oh, Amy. You *so* deserve this." Bella hugged her, then motioned for the girls to follow her out the back door, but by the time they'd scurried out of the bedroom, Tony was already standing at the glass doors to the deck—and waving with a smile that made Amy forget that she was nervous or feeling guilty.

Bella opened the door, and Tony's eyes never left Amy's as he crossed the floor looking mouth-wateringly handsome in a pair of dark linen pants that tied at the waist and a V-neck T-shirt that hugged his arms like Amy wanted to.

"Wow. You look incredible, babe." He kissed her cheek.

Amy heard Jenna whisper too loudly to Leanna, "He called her *babe*!"

She and Tony both chuckled.

"You guys weren't trying to sneak out the back, were you?" Tony raised his brows in Bella's direction.

"Us? No. We were, um…" Bella rolled her eyes. "Of course we were. It's your first date."

"It wouldn't be a perfect first date for Amy if you guys weren't here to help her get ready, right?" Tony smiled at Amy.

First date. Wow, she loved how that sounded. They hadn't been able to date when they were younger. This felt even bigger because of that.

She knew the moment he noticed the earrings, because his eyes narrowed and met hers with an expression of disbelief.

"Well, we'll be going. You kids have fun." Leanna tugged Jenna toward the door.

"Not that we have high expectations for this date or anything, but…I wish I had my camera so I could remember this moment forever." Bella's eyes moved from Amy to Tony and back again. "Seeing two of my best friends together makes me wish I was the kind of girl who cried when she was happy." She waved on her way out the door.

Tony's eyes warmed as he reached beneath Amy's hair and touched the surfboard earrings. "You kept them."

"Not exactly." She cringed. The truth wasn't always easy, but with Tony she knew it was important. "I wasn't able to think of you for the longest time without falling to pieces. The summer after our…when we got together, I gave them to Bella and asked her to hold them for me. I never thought she would hold on to them for this long, but I'm glad she did."

"So am I. It's funny how something so small can carry so many memories." Tony held her hand as they walked down to his car. "Remember sneaking under the pier in P-town and kissing when they were at Purple Feather getting gelato?"

"How could I ever forget? That was the best summer—and the worst—of my life."

Tony didn't respond as he drove out of the complex, keeping his serious eyes trained on the road. Amy reached for his hand. She'd wanted to be able to freely touch him like a girlfriend for so many years that it didn't take much to persuade herself to go for it. He glanced over and smiled, but tension still hovered between them. She wasn't sure if it was because she mentioned that the summer was the best and worst of her life, or if it was because they had yet to discuss it in detail, but the reason didn't matter. The fact was, she hated the tension and wanted to slice it up and toss it out the window.

"I don't want our first date to have a black cloud over it," she said.

"I don't want any part of our lives to have a black cloud over it." He squeezed her hand, and she knew he understood what she was trying to say. She had matured enough over the years to realize that even if she fell apart, he'd be there to help her put the pieces back together. That didn't make it any easier to get from where she was to where they needed to be, but she wanted to try.

"So, here's the thing. It's hard for me to talk about what happened, but I know we have to deal with it." She paused to gauge his unspoken thoughts, but he wasn't giving anything away. His facial expression didn't change, but when she opened her mouth to continue, he interrupted her.

"I think we talked about that stuff enough today, don't you?" He stopped at a light and leaned across the console to kiss her.

Relief swept through her. "Thank you."

"I told you I'm going to be the guy you need. Your well-being is my priority."

"I sound like a patient."

Tony's mouth quirked up with a sexy smile. "Babe, I'd happily play doctor with you. I've got a big stethoscope."

"Yeah, I know," she mumbled, and quickly gazed out the window, earning a hearty laugh from Tony that cut through the tension and made Amy laugh.

"Where are we going, anyway? P-town?"

"For the first part of our date."

"Okay, Mr. Coy. Sounds perfect."

The rest of the ride was filled with easy conversation about the books they were reading, movies they'd seen—and hated—and Jamie and Jessica's wedding. Tony thought Jamie had looked nervous enough to wet his pants when he said his vows, and Amy thought Jamie had looked like a man in love. They had another good laugh as Tony parked at the P-town pier.

Provincetown was an artsy community located on the tip of Cape Cod, with salty sea air sweeping off the harbor and a plethora of interesting people in the streets. It was steeped with history and ripe with the arts—from street performers to comedians, photographers to painters, and every medium in between. Provincetown was the go-to destination for gays and lesbians during the summer, and on any given afternoon there were female impersonators wearing gaudy makeup and sky-high heels handing out flyers for evening shows. At night Commercial Street, the main drag that ran through P-town, was thick with diversity and good cheer. Tonight was no different.

Most of the bars, dance clubs, shops, and restaurants were located in the town center. To the east the town became more refined and polished, and to the west the nightlife seemed to never cease. Amy and Tony blended into the crowd, walking arm in arm and meandering in and out of the shops along Provincetown center.

"It's nice being with you like this," Tony said as he tipped a leather hat on his sexily tousled hair.

"Cowboy style, you mean?" Amy laughed.

He took the hat off and put it on Amy's head. "What could be sexier than Amy in leather? Now, there's a fantasy."

Amy took off the hat and picked up a pair of leather chaps. "Only if two can play at that fantasy."

Tony pulled her into his arms like they'd been dating forever and pressed his lips to hers. "I meant being with you out in public and not holding back."

Amy's stomach flipped. Her heart felt full to bursting, but her mind was stuck in the past. She took a careful step back to assess her feelings. She was rattled, yes, but more in a good way than bad. Finally able to be with Tony in the way she'd always dreamed of, she was elated, as evident in her racing heart. And she was scared. This she took ten seconds to delve a little further into. *What if I can't ever deal with the past?*

Tony brushed her hair from her eyes and smiled down at her, forcing her to think the unthinkable. *What if we find our happily ever after only to get married, pregnant...and then lose the baby again?*

That was where her head was when he leaned down and kissed her again, deepening the kiss right there in the middle of the crowded leather shop, with her heart fluttering like wings and her body molding to his. His hold on her tightened, and her mind, her beautiful, conflicted mind, gracefully relented, giving way to bliss.

TONY HAD TAKEN a chance when he kissed Amy, but ever since they'd kissed the other night, he'd been able to feel again. Really feel. Warm, mushy, gooey feelings that he was almost too embarrassed to admit to himself, as well as painful emotions brought on by haunting memories. But it felt so good to actually feel that he wanted to chase those feelings, and Amy had always been the person who could set him free. She'd freed him from the confines of his father's demeaning wrath years ago, and on the beach today, as she opened up to him with her deepest thoughts and fears, she'd once again unlocked the real Tony. The Tony who would move heaven and earth to be with her.

When their lips parted, Tony kept Amy close. He was done letting her go, pretending, or otherwise putting distance between them. Yes, he needed to be sure he would never hurt her again. Yes, he needed to be one hundred percent certain he was the right man for her, and he was 99.99 percent sure. And yes, he needed to be certain that she wasn't going to cast him aside again. But he was not going to lose her in the process of his own introspection. Not a chance.

He smiled down at her, feeling like the luckiest man on the planet. "I'm going to take that as an indication that you *don't* want me to hold back."

Amy went up on her toes and pressed her lips to his. "I have a lot of crap to deal with. I'm willing to carry the shovel if you'll carry the bucket."

Tony draped an arm over her shoulder. "All the way to Australia if I have to."

They headed back into the crowd, and Tony led her toward the patio of a restaurant with colorful umbrellas.

"I tried to make reservations, but they didn't take them."

"We could be here for a while." Amy leaned around him and gazed at the long line of people ahead of them.

"That's okay. You got a date to get to?" Tony looked across the street and remembered how much Amy loved Burger Queen, a shack with walk-up counter service.

Amy followed his gaze and her eyes lit up. She pulled him across the street.

"Please?"

"How am I supposed to wow you if we eat at Burger Queen?" He would eat on the moon if that's what Amy wanted.

"You have wowed me for twenty-plus years with little more than your dashing personality. I don't think an expensive dinner is going to win you any extra points."

They ordered lobster rolls from Burger Queen and ate as they window-shopped. Tony put his arm around Amy again and kissed her temple. "I think I've spent the last fourteen years trying not to think about what it would be like to be on a date with you. I'm on a bit of emotional overload at the moment, so if I gush and kiss you too much, or hold you too close, just push me away, okay?"

"Okay. Got it." Amy squeezed in a little closer. "But if I do any of those things—gush or kiss you too much—can you please just go with it? Because I don't handle rejection very well."

"Deal."

Amy pulled Tony into the tattoo shop.

"Oh no, really?" Tony didn't have any tattoos. Amy didn't either, but he knew how much Amy liked the way they looked.

"Hey, you guys." Much to Pete's chagrin, Sky put her art degree to use working as a tattoo artist part-time. She sat behind the counter wearing a long black cotton skirt and an army-green tank top. The silver bangles on her wrist clinked as she got up to hug them. "Are you here to get tats?"

"No needles for me." Amy crinkled her nose, but her eyes were filled with mischief. "But I thought it would be fun to try to convince Tony to get one." Amy pushed him toward Sky, who was sizing the two of them up.

"There isn't much you can't convince me of, but a tattoo? I don't know about that."

"Wait a second. Are you two *together* or here as friends?" Sky crossed her arms and smiled at Amy, who turned a cute shade of pink.

"We're on our first date, but apparently *first date* to Amy means needles and permanent ink." Tony pulled Amy against him again.

Sky drew in a breath, eyes wide. "Aw. That's great. I've got just the thing for you two." She went behind the counter and tugged out a stool. "Sit."

Tony eyed Amy and nodded to the stool. "Go ahead."

Amy pushed him forward. "Come on. You're the man."

With a feigned sigh, he sat on the stool, legs wide, and pulled Amy between them. "If I have to be tortured, you're staying right here with me."

"I won't ink against your will." Sky smiled at them. "Lucky for you, I do henna tats, too."

"A henna tattoo? On me?" Tony shook his head. "What am I, twelve?"

"No, you're thirtysomething and manly enough to pull it off." Amy kissed him, and he knew he'd do whatever she asked. A henna tattoo? Done.

"You might even like it so much that one day you'll get a permanent one," Sky added.

"I doubt that. It'll come off in a day with how much I'm in the water." He settled his hands on Amy's hips. "What am I getting? *Property of Amy* across my chest?"

"That usually goes across the hips," Sky teased.

"How about just *T* plus *A*?" Amy suggested with a sweet smile.

"You want me to have a tattoo that says *T* and *A*? You know what *T* and *A* means, right?" He glanced at Sky, who was chuckling.

Amy smacked his thigh. "You're a pig. I meant like *Tony* and *Amy*."

"Then how about I just get your name? Because I don't want my own name on my body."

"I guess that *would* look funny."

Tony brought his lips closer to hers and lowered his voice to a whisper. "I have a better idea. How about if I get *kitten* in a discreet place?"

Amy buried her face in his neck.

Kitten was a nickname he'd given her the summer of their affair because of the adorable way she cuddled up to him and how she purred with pleasure after they made love. Her affinity for kittens had begun after he'd given her the nickname.

He kissed her cheek and whispered, "You'll always be *kitten* to me."

Twenty minutes and one *kitten* tattoo located just below the waist of his pants later, they headed back toward the pier.

"I can't believe you remembered." Amy attached herself to Tony's side like Velcro, and he couldn't be happier.

"You might be surprised how much I remember." *Like how you love to be teased and the feel of your body.*

Tony nodded toward the pier. "Come on. For old times' sake."

He helped her off the boardwalk and onto the sand. They kicked off their shoes, and Tony rolled the cuffs of his pants. Then they walked hand in hand down by the edge of the water. There were a few couples sitting on the beach beneath the stars, but Tony had another place in mind, and from the look on Amy's face as he led her beneath the pier, she didn't seem to mind.

There was nothing particularly unique about the underside of the Provincetown pier. The pilings were scarred and uneven, spearing out of the ground at funky angles, bracing the ancient pier. The smell of fish, wet earth, and fried foods from the nearby eateries lingered in the darkness. But to Tony, all of that brought back a rush of memories so enticing that he could barely think past getting his arms around Amy and revisiting them. He couldn't pinpoint when things began to change, but sometime between their walk on the beach and now, the energy between them had become reminiscent of that summer so long ago. The good parts, when the mere thought of being apart felt treacherous and the air between them, no matter where they were, was thick with the pulse of desire.

Moonlight streamed through the slats of the pier. Tony pulled Amy's hips against his and buried his hands in her hair, cupping the back of her head. Her skin was hot, her eyes seductive and heavy-lidded.

"Kitten." The nickname came naturally and rolled off his tongue, laced with anticipation. He brushed his nose against hers and ran his thumb over her lower lip. "Boy, I've missed you."

"Kiss me," she whispered.

Their lips crashed together, tongues probing, searching, stroking, and pulling a greedy moan from deep in Tony's lungs. Kissing Amy had always been his undoing. She took and gave in equal measure. His hands traveled up her back, down her rib cage, and over her sexy curves, stopping at the hem of her skirt. He stroked the back of her thigh with his thumbs and captured her needy sounds of desire in his mouth. It took all his willpower not to do more. He promised to prove he was the right man for her, but kissing her, being with her again, left him no doubt.

He reluctantly drew back and touched his forehead to hers. They were both breathing hard, their bodies plastered together from thigh to chest. The backs of her thighs were hot and tense, and he knew she was feeling the flames, too.

"Kitten, I've never stopped loving you." Her body was doing it again, vibrating from the inside out. *Purring* as she snuggled in close, her cheek pressed to his chest, her hands beneath his shirt, pressing against his skin.

She gazed into his eyes with love and confidence. "I know."

Tony took her hand in his. His thumb moved in slow, circular motions over her wrist. Amy's emerald eyes darkened as he drew her mouth to his again. He kissed her softly, slow and deep, with the silent promise of all he had to give of himself, his heart, and his life.

"Tony," she said after a long while. "Take me home."

Chapter Eleven

TONY SLID HIS hands around Amy's waist and nibbled on her neck as she fumbled with the keys to the back door of her cottage.

"I love the way you taste." He loved the scent of her skin, the curve of her shoulder. The way she squirmed when he sucked her earlobe into his mouth was sinful. Her body stilled when he ran his tongue along the shell of her ear.

She exhaled loudly and pressed her back to his chest.

Tony gathered her hair over her left shoulder and lowered his mouth to the curve of her neck, grazing his teeth over her skin. He turned her in his arms and pressed her back to the door. The keys dropped to the deck as he took her lower lip in his teeth and gave it a gentle tug. She was so sexy, burying her hands in his hair and guiding his mouth back to hers. Their lips met in a deep, probing kiss, breathing air into her lungs in order to kiss her longer, deeper. When they finally parted, every muscle in his body was tight and Amy was breathless. Her hands grasped his shoulders as he crouched to retrieve the keys.

He ran his fingers lightly up her legs as he rose to his feet. He pressed his forehead to her chest, exhaling her name. "Amy."

He lifted his eyes to hers. They'd gone smoky and dark. He

could get lost in their seduction, but beneath the heat he recognized love. He hadn't seen such raw emotions in Amy's eyes for so long that it momentarily stalled him.

He managed to open the door. The cottage was dark and quiet as he set the keys on the counter and folded Amy into his arms again.

"I want to wrap you up and hold you tight." He kissed the corners of her mouth. "I want to get to know every inch of your beautiful body again, until I know how it changes when you breathe."

Their lips met in a tender kiss as he lifted her into his arms and her legs circled his waist. In a few determined steps they were in the bedroom, lips locked together. He lowered them both to the bed. The intimacy brought a rush of emotions. Not crazy, lustful stranger kind of emotions, but emotions of what they'd shared, how deeply they'd loved, and the carnal memories of how their bodies came together. He wanted to stay there and revel in the feel of them connecting on an emotional level again. He fisted his hands in her hair and deepened the kiss. Her delicate fingers traveled up and down his back.

"Kitten, I've waited so long to touch you. I need you to be sure, because if you're not, then we need to wait. I won't be able to take loving you again and then hearing that you regret it." He searched her eyes. There was no doubt in them, only love and raw desire, but he needed to hear it from her lips. "Are you sure?"

"Yes. Oh, yes. But, I haven't been with a man in a very, very long time. Fourteen years to be exact."

His heart nearly stopped.

She trapped her lip between her teeth again.

"Kitten?"

She shook her head. "I couldn't. I've done other stuff, but…you're the only man I ever wanted to be with."

"Oh, baby. That's a really long time."

She shrugged and closed her eyes. He kissed her closed lids.

"I'll make it up to you."

"You don't need to make it up to me. Just love me. Love the past away."

He lowered his forehead to hers. "The past will always be there." No lies. He'd promised to be the best man he could, and that meant pure honesty, no matter how much it hurt him to say it.

"Then love me through it."

Amy lay with him as she'd done a dozen times that summer. He breathed deeply, allowing the memories of the past and the present to coalesce.

His sweet kitten was back.

Chapter Twelve

AMY AWOKE TO an empty bedroom. She listened to the silence of her cottage and knew Tony had left. She had a fleeting thought that perhaps she'd made up last night in her hopeful mind, but when she rolled over and buried her nose in the other pillow, Tony's scent remained. She exhaled loudly and covered her eyes with her arm. *Tony.* She waited for the longing and the inevitable pain that she'd been squelching for too many years, and when it didn't come, it gave her hope that she could move forward. They'd talked about that summer, and she hadn't fallen completely apart. And he'd loved her—oh, how he'd loved her. Like they'd never been apart.

Amy heard the slider open to the front deck. Her heart leapt. *Tony.*

"Hurry up."

Jenna. Amy heard feet scurrying across the floor and turned to find Leanna, Bella, and Jenna lined up in the doorframe with stupid grins on their faces and steaming mugs in their hands—two in Leanna's.

"I saw Tony leave for his run," Jenna explained as they piled onto her bed.

"And Sky said she tatted him up last night." Bella leaned in close and whispered, "Kitten."

"Oh my gosh." She covered her eyes. "Isn't there some rule of confidentiality with tattoo artists and their clients?"

"They're *tattoos*," Bella explained. "Think of skin like a billboard. Even beneath the waist."

Amy groaned. Bella was the only one not wearing pajamas. Unless Amy counted herself, because she was quite nude beneath the blankets.

"Oh, come on, kitten. We think it's cute." Jenna curled her fingers into claws and pretended to paw at Amy while holding her mug in the other hand. "Meow."

They all laughed.

"It's not a sexual thing." *Well, it kind of is.*

"Uh-huh." Bella patted Amy's shoulder. "You keep up that lie. We'll back you up."

Leanna handed Amy a cup of coffee. "Sit up and drink up. We want the scoop."

Amy held the sheet over her chest. "Hand me a T-shirt?"

Jenna snagged a shirt from Amy's drawer and tossed it to her. After putting it on, she sheepishly added, "And underwear," to which Jenna laughed and obliged.

"Please tell me you're clean," Bella said.

"Geez, Bella." Amy felt her cheeks flush. "We showered last night."

"Oh, this is better than I was hoping for. Details?" Jenna fixed her cami, which was slipping off her shoulder. She scooted closer on the bed.

The girls formed a semicircle around Amy. She felt a little like it was sharing time at school, but no student would be grinning from ear to ear with delectably sinful memories.

Amy sipped her coffee and gave in to her friends' expectant

gazes. "It wasn't like a real first date. I mean, it's *Tony*." *The man I made love to at least once a day the summer when I was eighteen. The only man I've ever made love to.* Only they didn't know that. She bundled the guilt into a ball and mentally tucked it away.

"Well, that's true," Leanna said. "You guys have known each other forever. I'm happy for you, Amy."

"Okay, enough mushy stuff. Was it wonderful?" Jenna leaned in close, eyes wide. "Or were your expectations too high? Sometimes that happens. You know, when you've thought about being with some guy for so long and then it's like...*Oh, really? That kinda sucked.*"

"Been there, done that," Bella added.

"Usually it's the guy thinking that in my case." Leanna frowned.

"Not true." Amy had learned to cover her abstinence by embellishing what she *did* do with guys. She'd had to learn to embellish in college in order to save face with the other girls in her dorm who *hadn't* lost a baby and given up the man they loved in the course of a few hours. That bundle of guilt rolled out again, and she kicked it away.

Leanna nodded. "Totally true, but I don't care. Kurt loves how I am in bed, and he's the only man I want or need. Gosh, remember how scared I was to sleep with him? I was so awkward in bed, and my rhythm was always off."

"Kurt seems to have fixed that," Jenna said. "Night after night after night, according to the sound track of your love life...thanks to open windows."

"Remember that one guy I slept with a few years ago who said he'd *expected more* after we'd done it for nearly an hour?" Bella laughed. "What did he expect, a gold-plated coochie?"

They all laughed, while Amy wallowed in guilt. Her friends had shared their secrets over the years, but she'd kept hers close to her chest. So close it nearly smothered her.

"Right, Ames?" Bella tapped her arm.

"What?" Uh oh. She hadn't realized they were talking to her.

"Wow. Last night must have been really something. You zoned out there." Bella pushed Amy's mug toward her mouth. "Drink a little more before Tony comes back and wants to ravish you again."

Amy's mind sifted through potential outcomes of telling her friends what she'd gone through and how she'd lied to them. They'd never trust her again. How could they when she had kept such a big secret?

"Amy?" Leanna patted her leg. "Are you okay? Did things not end well last night?"

"No. It was perfect, actually." More perfect than she could have imagined.

"Does this mean you'll stay and turn down the job with Duke?" Bella asked.

"Oh no. Duke. What am I going to do?" Duke was a friend, and he was offering her an opportunity of a lifetime. Although she had accepted the job only a few days ago, she couldn't just blow him off. Maybe he'd understand. But maybe she was rushing things. What if she and Tony didn't work out? It had been a long time, and—

"Did he slip you a brain-numbing pill last night or something?" Bella asked.

"That would be called a triple orgasm," Jenna quipped.

For once in her life she could actually agree with Jenna's assessment and it would be true, but sharing those details of her and Tony's intimacy seemed like a betrayal to him. Amy's pulse sped up. There were so many things to think about, and she felt ill equipped to handle any of them.

"Okay, something is very wrong here." Bella took Amy's mug from her and set it on the bedside table. She brushed Amy's hair from her shoulders, and her voice turned serious. "Honey, what is it? We're here for you. If it's good, bad, or complicated, we can help."

"Maybe Tony couldn't...you know," Jenna whispered.

Amy shook her head. "It's nothing like that. Tony is...He's exactly who he's always been. He's a thoughtful and caring lover."

"Then what is it?" Bella asked.

I need to do this. She swallowed hard, trying to push away the sinking feeling in the pit of her stomach.

"What I'm going to tell you might change our friendships, and I just want you guys to know how much I love you and that I do trust you." Amy drew in a deep breath as the others exchanged worried glances.

"You're scaring me a little." Leanna set her coffee down and fidgeted with the edge of her pajama shorts.

"Well, it scares me a lot." She needed to come clean to her friends, no matter how much it hurt to do it. She had a momentary thought about telling Tony she was going to share their past with them, but one look at her friends and she knew she didn't need his permission. This was her burden from the start. Her secret. It had to be her decision to reveal it.

She pulled her shoulders back and sat up straighter, needing to be brave. "Do you guys remember the summer before we went away to college?"

"How could we forget?" Jenna asked. "It was amazing. Parties, learning to surf, picking up those hitchhiking surfers in your convertible on the way to the beach."

"Remember Leanna's brothers trying to hit on the female lifeguards?" Bella patted the sheets while she laughed. "That was the funniest. The guards were like, *A nerd, a musclehead, and a guy who likes fireworks a little too much. No thanks.* Little did they know how hot they'd grow up to be."

Leanna's solemn eyes were locked on Amy's, as if she saw the turmoil brewing inside her.

"What about that summer, Amy?" Leanna asked.

Amy dropped her eyes to the bed and contemplated playing off her silence as a joke, but she knew they'd never buy it. She'd had nine months to get her game face in place before returning to the Cape the summer after she'd had the miscarriage. Nine months…Long enough to have a baby, or forget you were ever going to. She'd had fourteen years to prepare for this moment, but not only had she not prepared; she'd blocked out the event entirely. There was no more hiding. If she wanted Tony, she had to accept what happened, and accepting meant honesty all around.

"Sweetie, what are we missing? Whatever it is, it's not going to change a thing. I promise." Jenna's voice was so sincere that it deepened Amy's guilt.

"I'm not so sure about that." Amy swallowed hard and stared at her hands. It was easier than looking at the women she knew she was about to hurt.

"That summer, Tony and I were together," Amy began.

"Of course. We all were," Jenna said.

"No. *Together*, together." She lifted her eyes.

"Wait." Bella drew her brows together, and a soft laugh escaped before she clamped her jaw closed and shook it off.

"You don't mean..."

Amy nodded.

"What?" Jenna practically yelled. "No way. You couldn't have kept that a secret."

Amy cocked her head. "You do know my father, don't you?"

"Yeah, but..." Jenna's eyes widened as understanding dawned on her. "You thought we'd tell him?"

"No. No, that's not why." *Was it?* Bella's arms were crossed, putting an effective barrier between them that scared Amy. *Please don't turn me away.* Leanna's brows were drawn together, her forehead streaked with worry.

"Okay, maybe that was partially why. I don't know. I was afraid of disappointing my father, and Tony's father wasn't exactly the nicest guy on earth that summer." The words fell fast, and as she shifted her eyes to each of her friends, the impact of them were evident. Bella's eyes were filled with something between worry and anger. Leanna and Jenna had empathy written all over their faces, but when they dropped their eyes to the bed, she knew she'd hurt them.

"And I was finally with Tony," Amy continued. "And he loved me. He *loved* me. And—"

"So all these years, your pining over him was what? A lie? You've been seeing him?" Bella's voice was anything but understanding.

"No. I *was* pining for him."

"Yeah," Bella snapped. "For a guy you'd already had, and here we were feeling bad for you that you loved him and he thought of you as a friend." She looked away.

"It wasn't like that. I mean, it was, but..." She wanted to slip to the floor and hide under the bed until her life rewound to ten minutes earlier, so she could *not* tell the truth. Her heart was beating so fast and hard she felt like the room was spinning. Her friends were waiting for an explanation that she wasn't sure she could give without falling apart, yet not explaining would be worse than spilling her guts.

"It was…" Tears slid down her cheeks. "I got preg—pregnant. Okay? It was—"

Silence.

Jenna stared at the blanket. Bella held Amy's gaze, and Leanna's brows knitted together as she looked from Amy to the others, then back again.

Amy's lower lip trembled. Her guilt felt magnified in their silence. Her throat was so thick no more words could pass through. And then Leanna's arms were around her. Her tears fell on Leanna's shoulder as she wept.

"Amy…" Bella's voice was thin, rattled. "Oh, Amy. I'm so sorry."

"But what happened?" Jenna reached for Amy's hand.

Amy sucked in one breath after another, as Leanna released her, giving her room to breathe. That ball of guilt she'd tucked away bowled her over. She felt raw, completely exposed.

"I…I didn't know I was pregnant until I started school in the fall, and then Tony and I snuck up to Seaside for a weekend alone. I was going to tell him, but we went surfing and…I…I lost the baby. I never told anyone. No one. And I never talked to Tony about it again." Sobs stole her voice, and in the next breath she managed, "I sent Tony away to save him from…from…ruining his surfing career. To save him from me."

Bella folded Amy into her arms. She held her in the quiet of the room for who knew how long. Long enough that Amy cried all the tears she had held in over the years. Long enough for the others to get in on the cathartic hug and weigh Amy down with a new type of heaviness. She couldn't breathe, but this time it wasn't caused by fear. She was smothered in their love, felt their tears on her skin.

"You didn't need to go through that alone." Bella's voice was just above a whisper.

"I was afraid," Amy admitted. "I nearly tanked my grades, and I could barely think, let alone talk about it." She took a deep breath, preparing herself to unveil the rest of her lies.

"All that talk about sleeping with guys..." Amy shook her head, she couldn't admit any more than she had. She felt emotionally drained and exhausted, but she'd opened the floodgates and she had to let it all out.

Jenna looked from Amy to Bella. "I don't understand."

"I do," Leanna said. "You never slept with any of them."

Amy shook her head and wiped the tears from her eyes.

"Amy," Jenna whispered. "Why would you lie about that? We don't care if you have or haven't slept with guys."

"I know. I mean, in my heart I know that, but I had been hiding my past for so long, and when we graduated from college, I just wanted to leave everything behind and be normal. And being normal meant doing all the things I didn't want to do. So I pretended." She shrugged and looked away, embarrassed.

"Amy. You are normal. You're probably the most normal of all of us," Bella said.

"You never talked to Tony about this for all these years? So you both went through it alone?" Leanna paused, and before Amy could do more than nod, she continued. "It's amazing that he doesn't hate you for turning him away, or that you don't hate him. I can't imagine the hurt you both must have gone through. How far along were you?"

"Just a few weeks."

"Well, it doesn't matter if you knew you were pregnant for a day, an hour, or a month. Once you know, you *know*." Leanna hugged Amy again. "But the other side of this tragic loss is that you and Tony missed out on all these years together. I don't even understand how you've had the close relationship you have with him without talking about what happened."

"I pushed him away. I buried the hurt so deep I pretended it had never happened, even when he tried to make things right. It was easier than facing it." Amy's chest tightened again with the memory of Tony standing in her dorm room, looking sorrowful and beaten down, while she feigned ignorance and somehow acted peppy and like he didn't matter. Just to save her own pathetic self.

"That explains why he made himself so scarce for those few years when we were in college," Leanna said. "Wow, Amy. I always thought it was his surfing career that kept him away. Remember? He only came up for a week here or there, and he almost never hung out with us."

"And that all changed after we graduated from college, remember?" Jenna added.

Amy nodded. "I remember, all right. I was so relieved that he came back and didn't hate me. I was afraid to talk to him at first, afraid he would bring up the past and then disappear again. But he never did, and we fell back into our friendship, only he'd become even more protective of me. I never understood why, but he told me the other night that it was the only way he could be close to me."

"He wears his love for you on his sleeve," Leanna said. "The way he's always looking after you, holding your hand or putting an arm around you."

"Carrying you to bed," Jenna added.

"Holding your hair when you barf," Bella said.

"What?" Amy asked.

"Yeah, when you drank too much last summer, he insisted on being the one to take you home," Bella explained. "I argued with him, but he was very protective of you. And when Jenna and I came to check on you, you were fast asleep, lying against him. Your hair was tied back in a ponytail, and he said he'd get us your barf bowl, like it was something he'd done a million times before. Apparently, you got sick that night, and he'd held your hair back and then pinned it up."

"You never told me this." How else had she embarrassed herself? "He never said anything, either. I must have been the joke of Seaside."

"No, you were the most loved woman in Seaside. None of us would have embarrassed you, and Jenna and I kind of were saving ourselves." Bella glanced at Jenna. "We thought you'd kill us if you knew that he saw you throw up because we let him take you home."

"Where do you guys stand now?" Leanna asked. "Have you talked about it?"

Amy nodded. "Some."

"And?" Jenna pushed.

"I think—no, I *know*—he loves me as much as I love him, and we're trying."

"But?" Bella asked.

"But it's scary, and I accepted that job with Duke, and Tony worries that he's not the right guy for me."

Bella rolled her eyes. "You didn't sleep with anyone else for a hundred years. He sounds like he's the only guy for you. Does he know *that*?"

Amy smiled at the disbelief that had registered on his face last night when she'd told him. "Uh-huh. He was a little shocked."

"I bet he was a little proud, too," Jenna said.

Leanna swatted her leg.

"What?" Jenna asked. "Come on. He's a guy. Of course he'd be proud. Was he your first, Ames?"

"First and only." Amy drew in another jagged breath, glad her tears had stopped. "So you guys really don't hate me for keeping it from you for all this time?" She cringed inside while waiting for their answer.

"Of course not," Leanna said.

"We love you, but I do feel bad that we weren't there for you," Jenna added. "We would have been there to make sure you were okay. Maybe we could have eased the pain and you wouldn't have had to carry the secret for so long."

"I have to admit it bothers me that you didn't trust us enough to help you through such a terrible time, but I get it. Your dad was so overprotective, and we weren't exactly careful of our dialogue back then. But we could never hate you for that, Ames. I hope you know that you don't have to face things like this alone. We're no longer teenagers with loud mouths. We're adults with loud mouths." Bella smiled, and Amy knew it was an effort to ease her discomfort.

Bella glanced out the window. "But I still can't figure out how you guys pulled off a secret relationship, and how we didn't notice."

Amy smiled, thinking about how they'd snuck around that summer and how exciting it had been. "The first time we kissed was after a bonfire at Cahoon Hollow. You guys were all hanging out on the beach, and I had gone for a walk by the dunes. You know how if you walk close to the dunes, it's really dark?"

"Mm-hmm," Bella answered.

"Well, that's where we were. Tony caught up to me. I don't know what I was thinking that night, but it wasn't that Tony and I would end up in a relationship. Especially a secret one. But when he was with me, just the two of us, he looked at me and…Gosh. It felt like this huge moment, you know? People say there are times when the earth stands still, but for me the earth didn't even exist. Nothing existed but us. His eyes were all dark and sexy, and I remember he was standing so close that our bare toes were touching. I got tingly all over just thinking about if he meant for our feet to touch or not. Gosh, I was so young and naive, but then again, I think I still get those same types of thoughts about him touching me sometimes. A lot, actually. Anyway, then I blurted out that I wanted to kiss him."

"You did not," Jenna said.

"I did. I have no idea how I got that brave. I told him I'd loved him since I was six, which was totally true."

"Oh my gosh, Amy. What did he say?" Leanna smiled. "I'm trying to remember Tony at twenty."

"He was sweet, confident, and so handsome." Amy sighed, feeling like she was eighteen and swooning all over again. "He behaved. He was afraid to kiss me because of my father, not that he didn't want to. I think we went back and forth a little about if we should or shouldn't, and boy did I want to. You know how at that age everything is magnified? I felt like if he didn't kiss me I was going to die, because then what? Would he go back to Jamie and laugh about it?"

"He never would have done that. He respected you too much, even back then," Leanna assured her.

"Yeah, but at that age, who knew, right?" Years of repressed tension rolled off as Amy confessed to her friends. "Anyway, we kissed, and let me tell you, we did *not* want to stop." She glanced at Jenna. "But someone came around collecting rocks. Ahem…"

"Yeah, that would be me. Sorry, Ames. Didn't mean to lip-block you."

Amy laughed. "That's okay. We stole time together when we could. After everyone was asleep, we'd sneak out. He had a sleeping bag he stowed in the woods by the pool and we'd go there."

"In the woods?" Jenna asked. "That's so romantic."

"Yeah, and we made out under the pier in P-town. Behind the ice-cream shop by Nauset. Behind the bathrooms at Cahoon Hollow." Amy smiled as the memories rolled in. "He was everything to me."

Leanna leaned closer. "He still is, Amy. He's always been your everything."

"Your everything brought you a little something for breakfast."

They turned at the sound of Tony's deep voice. His skin glistened with sweat from his run. He lifted his hands, in which he held a jar of Luscious Leanna's Sweet Treats jam and a box of croissants. Enough for all of them.

He caught Amy's eye, and she held her breath. He'd heard her say he was her everything, and she still had an inkling of worry that maybe she'd made last night bigger in her mind than he might have thought it was. Tony's lips curved up, his eyes warmed, and Amy knew that everything was going to be okay.

"Are you okay?" His voice was just above a whisper.

Amy nodded. "Yeah."

"I knocked, but you guys must not have heard me." He came into the room, his eyes gliding over the others.

Amy wondered what he saw. Did he see the same love and commitment from her friends that she did? Did he see the emotional discontent of the last half hour? Or did he just see women crawling across the bed and reaching into the Chocolate Sparrow box?

"I like this new *boyfriend* Tony," Jenna said. "He brings breakfast and delivers it in sexy shorts."

Amy winced. "Sorry, Tony. I never said he was my boyfriend, Jenna."

Jenna shrugged. "I just assumed."

"So did I." Tony held the box out toward Amy. "Should I not?"

Bella tapped his waistband. "Any man inked with a pet name is allowed to be called a boyfriend."

"Is everyone out to embarrass me?" Amy rose on her knees, skipping the croissant Tony offered. Instead she reached for his arm and tugged him toward her. "Do you really want to be my boyfriend? Just because we slept together doesn't mean you have to." *Please say yes. Please, please say yes.*

"You're right. Sex doesn't equate to boyfriend-girlfriend, but when you tell each other you're madly in love, that should count for something." He stared into her eyes with a serious look on his face.

Amy glanced nervously around the room. Her friends' eyes were as wide as she was sure hers were.

"I'm going to look really stupid in about three seconds if you don't acknowledge me in some way," he whispered.

"Yes. It counts for everything."

There was a collective *aww* as the girls filed out of the room.

"Bonfire at Cahoon tonight. Be there or we'll assume you're *riding the pipe*," Bella yelled on her way out.

Tony arched a brow. "Riding the pipe?"

"Don't ask."

Tony set the box down and pulled her into his arms. "You had me scared for a minute there, but I figured it was love when I saw your key chain." He held up her keys. The surfboard key chain she'd bought at the Wellfleet Market dangled from the silver ring. "Unless there's another surfer in your life?"

"That's a big leap to make over a key chain." She smiled at the devilish grin on his lips. "I think there's a rule about surfers in the girl handbook. *Only one surfer per lifetime*. You're stuck with me if you want me."

"Kitten, it's never a question of *if*."

She pressed her hands to his chest, thinking about the job with Duke, how her friends had handled her admission, and Tony. *Oh, Tony*. Could they really do this? Long-term? The nagging question left her lungs before she had a chance to check it.

"Do you think we're rushing things?" After coming clean with the girls, she felt like a weight had been lifted from her shoulders. She felt more confident, stronger, like she could handle just about anything. She was *ready* to rush, but she knew that she and Tony still had a lot of healing and rebuilding to do, and the job in Australia weighed heavily on her mind. They couldn't heal and rebuild if she was in Australia. She had to know what he was thinking before she made any final decisions about the job.

"Fourteen years *is* a little fast, isn't it?" He lowered his mouth so his lips brushed hers when he spoke. "Maybe we should rethink this whole *claim our feelings* thing."

"I'm still emotionally fragile. I think I need you to prove your love to me again." She kissed him. "And again."

Chapter Thirteen

AMY SAT ON her deck working through the notes she'd taken during her meeting with Duke. It was midafternoon, and Tony had gone to catch the waves at high tide with a few surfing buddies. She sat back and kicked her feet up on another deck chair. The Seaside complex was quiet.

She glanced at Leanna's empty cottage. She and Kurt had gone to stay at Kurt's home on the bay side, which was only a few miles from Seaside. Caden and Bella were renovating their house in Wellfleet, and they were spending the afternoon painting the living room and dining room with Evan and his friends. Pete was working on refinishing a boat at his bay-side house with his father, and Jenna and Sky were hanging out there for the day. Blue was meeting them to go to the bonfire later. Jamie and Jessica were still on their honeymoon. They were bringing Jamie's grandmother, Vera, who raised him after his parents were killed when he was six, up to the Cape with them when they returned in two weeks.

Amy's eyes drifted to Tony's cottage. She was meeting him at his cottage later, and they were going to the bonfire together to meet the others. She put her notebook on the table and leaned forward, looking down at the woods beyond the pool.

Her pulse sped up as she rose to her feet and stepped off her deck.

The gravel crunched beneath her flip-flops, reminding her of the nights long ago when she and Tony had snuck out together. She'd been so scared back then. Scared of everything, it seemed. Pleasing her father, who adored her but had high expectations, nonetheless. Scared of the emotions that felt as if they owned her. She physically ached when she thought of Tony, and that first night they'd made love, she'd been trembling so badly that Tony had nearly backed out. He'd thought she was too scared of it hurting, when in reality, she'd been even more scared of feeling as much as she did for him.

When her feet left the gravel and met the thick lawn, Amy slowed her pace and drank in the sparse woods. The trees had grown much taller, raising their full branches higher and stealing the camouflage that had made her feel safe from prying eyes. She turned and glanced up the hill at the cottages, thinking about how naive they'd been. Anyone could have heard them sneaking out, or caught them in the woods. She remembered the heady anticipation, the threat of being caught in the back of her mind, and the way she'd blocked it out as strongly as she'd blocked out that terrible night.

But she'd never blocked out her love for Tony.

She wound through the woods to the spot between the two pitch pine trees that grew closer together than other neighboring trees. *Our spot.*

She lowered herself down to her back and stared up at slices of the light blue sky through the canopy of trees.

Do you think I'm doing the wrong thing? Tony's twenty-year-old voice wrapped around her. That summer, they'd often spent an hour or more talking after making love, sometimes until the first feathers of dawn spread their wings.

You never do the wrong thing. He'd asked about going against his father's wishes and pursuing a surfing competition in Hawaii instead of finally going to college. *It's one of the things I love about you. I'm not strong like you are. I'm hiding from what I really want, which is to be with you all the time. You? You're brilliantly strong, and one day your father will understand and you'll make him so proud.*

She closed her eyes with the memory. Tony's father never had a chance to show his pride, or to make up for the way he'd treated Tony that summer. It was a mystery to her, the way his father had gone from supportive—always with a stern parental edge—to harsh and demeaning.

Amy had been there for the funeral. The warmth she'd loved in Tony's eyes had gone cold when they'd glossed over her. He'd lost weight in the weeks since they'd seen each other. Amy had wanted to hold him until he forgot why he was so sad, but she'd been too scared. Opening up to him after building a fortress around herself would have sent her spiraling back into the pain she'd finally buried deep enough to function. She had to finish college. Those first few months she was never sure what would set her off. Sometimes just thinking about Tony sent her into a world of tears. And she couldn't risk distracting Tony. He had to concentrate on being the best surfer there was. It wasn't just a silly dream, as his father had declared. It was what Tony lived for. She couldn't risk taking him down with her.

How many nights had Tony risked everything to be with her? They had no idea how her father would react, but how would any father react to his teenage daughter sneaking out to have sex—even if she was in love?

She'd been selfish.

Horrifically so.

Amy had *chosen* to go through their ordeal alone.

Tony hadn't.

And here he was, willing to put his heart at risk again, for her.

She opened her eyes and sat up, swatting leaves and twigs from her clothing and pushing away the guilt. She rose to her feet and walked around the tree to her left. The bark had split around their initials, but they were still there. She traced the ancient carving, remembering Tony's determined features as he carved their initials with his Swiss Army knife. She'd worried about someone seeing them, and Tony had looked at her with those sexy eyes that could convince her the ocean was red if he'd tried and said, *Have you ever seen any adult come into these woods?*

T + A 4 Ever.

How did she get lucky enough to have another chance at forever?

How could she possibly deserve it?

Amy walked back out to the road, thinking about how she could possibly make up for not being there when Tony needed her. She'd been so consumed in her own sadness that she hadn't taken into account that he'd lost something, too. She didn't have a magic wand, and she was pretty sure the time machine they used in *Back to the Future* wasn't real. Short of undoing the past, how did a person make up for their selfish actions? She'd like to think that love was enough. It was for her. Just being in Tony's arms again numbed her pain, and after making love earlier that morning—twice—she was beginning to think that Tony really could love the pain away. *He certainly has quite an effective magic wand.* She smiled at the thought. Not that she had any other man to compare him to, but she didn't need comparisons. When she was making love with Tony, everything felt right.

Maybe she was focusing on the wrong things. Tony certainly seemed to take as much happiness from their love as she did. Maybe it was less about going back in time and fixing the past and more about showing him that she'd always be there for him from now on. That she'd never make the mistake of hiding or pushing him away again.

She hurried up the road to her cottage and called Bella, who put her in touch with Evan. There were things about that summer that she'd never forget, and the more she thought about not being emotionally there for Tony when his father had passed away, the more she wanted to try to ease that pain, too.

AMY SAT BETWEEN Tony's legs on a blanket by the bonfire at Cahoon Hollow Beach later that evening. Caden and Bella were sitting in beach chairs across the fire from them, and Pete and Jenna were cuddled up on a single beach chair off to their left with Joey lying at their feet. Blue and Sky were cooking burgers on the hibachi, and Leanna and Kurt were huddled together on a blanket whispering to each other.

"Is that one of Hunter's hibachis?" Tony nodded toward the kidney-shaped grill. Hunter Lacroux was one of Pete's younger brothers. He was a sculptor who specialized in using raw materials such as stone, steel, and wood. He lived in New York but had grown up on the Cape, and he also made uniquely shaped, upscale hibachis that had become very popular across the Cape.

"Yeah. I told him I needed another hibachi like I needed another girlfriend, but..." Pete laughed and reached down to pet Joey.

Jenna swatted him. "I love the hibachis, and you have an excellent girlfriend."

"Nope." Pete pulled a pink plastic tiara out of his pocket and set it on Jenna's head. "I have an excellent *fiancée*, who also happens to be my marshmallow princess."

Jenna snuggled in and kissed him. Pete had deemed Jenna his marshmallow princess the summer they got engaged. She was as OCD about the way her marshmallows were roasted as she was about everything else in her life. Pete adored Jenna, and he was a clever man. He'd calculated the exact number of seconds the marshmallow needed to be held over the fire on each side and from every angle. Now he had it down pat, and Jenna was a very happy marshmallow princess.

"When did you get a pink tiara?" Sky asked. "I thought Pete bought you a clear one."

"He did, but—" Jenna pointed at her pink hoodie.

"Sky, how long have you known Jenna?" Pete teased. "Tiaras must match her outfits. They are accessories, after all."

The ache of longing and jealousy over what he wanted and thought was out of reach was gone. Tony laced his fingers with Amy's and silently thanked the heavens above that they'd crossed the bridge he never thought they would.

They ate dinner and talked about Amy's new job. Tony sensed Amy's discomfort in the way she kept dropping her eyes. This was another hurdle for them, and as much as this was her decision to make, it took all of his focus for him not to beg her to not go through with moving to Australia. He'd been the one to tell her to take the job, after all. What a big mistake that was.

Amy wasn't the type of person who accepted a job and then walked away from it. The similarity to her commitment to Tony all those years ago, even if secret, and how she'd walked away and cut him out of her life did not escape him. Was this any different? Would this time be any different?

Amy smiled at him and squeezed his hand, as if she'd read his mind. Yeah, he knew this time would be different. It had to be.

Evan, Caden's son, was walking beside the dunes, heading in their direction. Evan had just graduated from high school and was leaving for college in the fall.

"What was he doing over by the dunes?" Tony leaned closer to Amy. "I'd like to take you over by the dunes."

"I bet you would," she teased. "Evan was doing me a favor, but it's a secret." She put her finger over her lips.

Tony drew his brows together. "A favor?"

"Mm-hmm."

"That's where it all started for us. Remember?" He kissed her again. He couldn't get enough of being with her as a real couple.

"How could I ever forget?"

He never would. He remembered every second of every moment they'd ever spent together, including that last awful afternoon. He remembered the blood dripping down her legs, the rush at the hospital as they pushed her through the double doors on a gurney and left him standing in the cold, sterile hallway, feeling as though his life had just slipped through his fingertips. And he'd never forget the cold eyes of the nurse who'd glared at him and asked, *How could you let your pregnant girlfriend go surfing?*

Tony pulled Amy closer, pushing those horrible memories aside and bringing forth the memory of their first kiss, the kiss that had changed his life forever.

"Thank you, Amy," he whispered.

She cocked her head. "For what?"

"For coming back to me."

He kissed her again, and she climbed into his lap and wrapped her arms around his neck, deepening the kiss.

"Dude, I know you have years to make up for, but you've got a teenage audience." Caden smiled to soften the friendly harassment.

"Dad, I'm almost eighteen," Evan said.

Tony laughed. "Like he's never kissed a girl before?"

"Shoot. Too many to count." Evan shook his head and sat down beside Bella. Evan had been working at The Geeky Guys, a computer-repair shop in town, part-time for the past few years. This year he'd added working out to his daily regimen, broadening his once-rangy body into pre-college stud status.

Caden held his hands up. "I don't need to know."

"I think he learned from you and Bella," Jenna teased.

Caden pulled Bella closer and kissed her. "We're very discreet."

Everyone laughed at that.

"I'm almost eighteen. I think I learned on my own, thank you very much," Evan added.

"Okay, change of subject time," Leanna said. "Evan, what are you looking forward to most at college?"

Evan flashed a lopsided grin. "You really want to know?"

"No!" Bella and Caden said at once.

"What?" Evan laughed. "I was going to say surfing and better computer classes." Tony had taught Evan to surf last summer.

"Right." Caden gave him a playful shove.

"Well…and the babes, of course," Evan said with a mischievous grin. "Harborside is sixty-five-percent women. Why do you think I chose that school?"

"Because your best buddy's going there?" Caden said with a fatherly head shake.

"Yeah, Dad. Why do you think he's going there?" Evan looked at his watch. "Speaking of which, it's ten. I'm meeting Bobby at his house for a LAN party. Do you mind if I take off?"

"No. Go ahead. Drive carefully, and if you leave his house, let me know where you're going," Caden said.

Tony couldn't help but feel the sting of jealousy at how easy Caden and Evan's relationship was compared to the conflicting interactions he'd had with his own father the last summer they'd spent together at the Cape. He forced the jealousy aside, knowing he couldn't change the past.

"Okay." Evan looked at Amy. "You're all set. Just bring the stuff back with you."

"Thanks, Ev." Amy stood and hugged him. She whispered something in his ear, and he pointed to a backpack he'd left beside Bella.

Amy joined Tony again on the blanket, and it was all Tony could do not to pry her for information. It turned out he didn't need to. Within a few minutes everyone made excuses and left early. Caden and Bella were the last to leave. Being the ever-responsible police officer, Caden doused the fire with a few buckets of water before taking off, leaving Amy and Tony alone beneath the stars.

Amy rose to her feet and reached for Tony's hand.

"Where are we going?"

"You'll see. Can you grab Evan's bag, please?" Amy grabbed their blanket and folded it over her arm.

Tony picked up the backpack, and before he could reach for Amy's hand, she reached for his and led him toward the dunes. Tony's heart hammered in his chest with each step as they walked along the empty beach, past the protected area, and toward the place where they'd shared their first kiss—where it was dark and cool, and they could see the tips of houses above the dunes. Erosion had desecrated the beautiful dunes, taking away much of the buffer in front of the houses. Their decks were now visible from below. Amy stopped by a knee-high pile of towels.

Tony eyed the towels with curiosity, then set the backpack down to help Amy spread out the blanket. "What's in the backpack?" he asked.

"You'll see." She crouched beside the pile of towels and carefully folded each one, then set them aside.

Tony crouched beside her to help fold the towels, quickly unveiling the projector Caden bought Evan last Christmas so he and his friends could stream movies from his computer onto the exterior wall of their house.

Amy met his gaze with a smile that reached her eyes.

"I can't believe you got Evan to leave this out without anyone to watch it."

Amy pointed up toward the dunes, where a flashlight was waving back and forth. She pulled a flashlight from the backpack Evan had left for her and waved it up at them. The light on the dune faded into the distance.

"That's mine and Evan's clever signal. He would never leave his goodies out here alone." Amy smiled at Tony; then her eyes grew serious. "I've been thinking a lot about us and about our families." She pulled Evan's computer from the backpack and hooked it up to the projector. "I told the girls about that summer."

"I assumed you did by the looks on everyone's faces when I showed up at your place. How did they take it?"

Amy's eyes warmed. "They were great. You know how they are. It was really hard to tell them, but once I started, it got easier."

He pulled her to him. "I'm sorry you had to go through that."

"It's okay. I feel so much better having told them, but I went down to the woods this afternoon, and it made me realize something."

Tony's chest tightened. She hadn't given him any reason to worry that she'd changed her mind about them, but he didn't know what to make of her bringing up the past instead of avoiding it.

"Before what happened at the end of that summer, I had such good memories. But I think all the good memories have been clouded over by what happened. And I got to thinking. I can't change what happened, and I can't change how it affected either of us." She took his hand in hers. "And I can't change that I wasn't there for you when your father died."

"Amy."

She stepped closer and pressed her hands to his chest. "I should have been there."

"You were there." Physically at least, which was more than he could have hoped for after what they'd been through.

"Not the way I should have been. We were so young, and in some ways so selfish and naive. I mean, those woods are not exactly buffered by much, right? We could have been caught. I began to wonder what else we missed. Remember how my parents were always taking pictures?"

"Sure. We spent a lot of time ducking them." He smiled at the memory of Amy's mother asking them to *smile pretty* and the girls all making faces.

"Well, a few years back, my mom made a collage of the pictures and sent them out to everyone."

"Yeah, I got mine."

"Did you look at it?" She narrowed her eyes as if she already knew the answer.

"No. It was too painful. It was one thing to see you afterward. I mean after the first few years of avoiding you. That was hard, allowing myself to be close to you again, even as friends, but seeing my father? I couldn't do that. It was too much."

"I'm sorry." She pressed a kiss to the center of his chest. "I'm glad you didn't shut me out forever, and I know you and your father had a rough relationship that summer. I don't know how you eventually separated seeing me from everything that happened that summer. Not just between us, but between you and your father."

Tony looked away, clenching his jaw. It was a natural reaction when he thought of his father. "I couldn't fight the urge to see you any longer. When you graduated from college, it felt like you'd achieved what your father had pushed for, so I guess I thought it was an okay time to risk seeing you again. You were an adult, not relying on his support to make it through school." He shrugged. "I wanted our friendship, Amy. I needed it and couldn't deny it any longer. I missed you. But my father..."

"I'm sure he's on this disk, and I thought that since I wasn't there to help you say goodbye to him and deal with all those emotions then, that this might be a good time for us to do that together."

"I'm not sure I want to see him right now."

"I know. I thought you might say that. I realized today that we'd been so caught up in our relationship that summer that maybe we overlooked the good parts of your dad."

Tony doubted that there were many good parts to overlook from those few weeks. His father had been a whole different person from the man he'd ever been before, and his mother had become solemn, more of a peacemaker, trying to gloss over what was going on. She never spoke of it, but Tony knew she'd noticed. She had to. How could she not? But he'd never blamed her for not getting involved. Tony was a man by then. At twenty he didn't need his mother taking care of things for him.

"All I ask is that you try to watch with an open mind. We both have a lot at stake right now. I have a job I have to either give up really soon so I don't piss off Duke, or…"

"Or?" He gazed down at her, hardly able to believe what she was saying.

"I don't know. I want us to work, but you were right. We can't have a relationship where we pretend the past never happened. For us to move forward, I think we need closure on all of it. What happened between us, which we're already dealing with. Your father. My father."

"Your father?" Tony nodded, beginning to understand where she was heading with this. He touched his forehead to hers. "You're going for the clean slate."

"Yeah," she whispered. "I hope so."

WHOEVER SAID "A picture's worth a thousand words" was

wrong. Their worth was unquantifiable. Amy sat snuggled against Tony as photo after photo projected onto the side of the dune. Pictures of Amy and the girls from the time they were toddlers until they were bikini-wearing teenagers, laughing, making faces, and running away from the camera. Amy wasn't surprised to see herself smiling, but the look in her eyes was so much less guarded than the eyes that looked back at her in more recent years.

"You were always the most beautiful girl on the beach." Tony kissed her temple.

"If you liked flat-chested women with almost no shape."

"I loved a perfectly chested woman with the sexiest shape." He pulled her closer. "Still do."

The next picture was of Amy and her father when she was a little girl. They were flying a kite at Wellfleet Harbor.

"I remember that kite. My father bought it for me in Provincetown."

A picture of Amy and her parents sitting on the fishing pier in Chatham flashed on the dune; behind them were their other friends from Seaside. Tony was sitting off to the side with Jamie, looking out at the boats, and Amy, though only eleven or twelve years old, was staring at Tony.

"See?" she said. "I even loved you then."

"I think I knew it, but I wrote it off because I had just become a teenager and I wasn't supposed to like you in that way."

"Like you were ever a rule follower." She bumped her shoulder against him with the tease.

The next picture was of Tony and his father. Tony's father's hand was on Tony's shoulder, and they were both laughing, mouths open wide, eyes alit with humor.

"That was before he changed." Tony's stomach lurched. He

tried to push away the longing and resentment that were vying for his attention.

"No. That was the last summer. I remember that bathing suit you have on. See?" She pointed to the photo on the dune. "That's what I mean. There were moments that he wasn't as gruff that summer, and we've forgotten them. He was a good man, Tony. It was just a bad summer. Everyone has bad times. Gosh, if anyone knows that, it should be us, right?"

He swallowed past the lump forming in his throat. The picture changed to one of Tony standing at the edge of the water with his surfboard, wearing a pair of black board shorts, one hand on his hip, his eyes narrow and serious. Jamie was standing behind him, two boys who had turned into men over the winter and fall. Their shoulders newly broadened, the hair on their legs thicker, their cheeks unshaven and scruffy.

"I wonder what you were thinking in that picture."

Tony looked down at her. "The summer we got together? I was probably thinking that I'd better get in the water before I saw you in your bikini and sported a woody."

Amy laughed. A picture of Jenna and Amy appeared next. Their arms wrapped around each other's shoulders and their faces scrunched up in goofy expressions. Even as a teenager Jenna had a figure that could stop a clock and a mischievous light in her eyes that could light up a room.

"When I look at that picture, all I see is the way your eyes glimmered with happiness, your sweet body that I will never get enough of..." He pulled her into his lap and brushed her hair away from her face, leaving his hand on her cheek. "You're everything I've ever wanted."

Amy blushed with a sweet smile.

"Just you, kitten. It's who you are inside *and* out that I love, and it was no different back then." He kissed her as the photos flashed on the dune behind her, and when they parted, she cuddled beneath his arm again.

The next picture was of all of them—Tony, Jamie, Amy, Bella, Jenna, and Leanna—huddled together on blankets around the bonfire. Bella and Jenna were gazing into the distance. Leanna and Jamie were talking, and Tony and Amy were staring at each other with an undeniable look of lust in their eyes.

"Wow," Amy whispered.

"There's no way they didn't notice *that.*" Tony tightened his grip on Amy.

"They weren't looking for it. We are."

Another picture of Tony and his father appeared on the screen. His father held a bottle of beer in one hand and he was looking directly at the camera. Tony's eyes were drawn to his father's. He was powerless to look away, and the eye-to-eye contact nearly pulled Tony under. Anger, resentment, and confusion warred for his attention again, and at the tail end of those emotions, love held his voice at bay. The picture changed before Tony could manage to say a word, and the next picture was of him and his father, his father's arm around his shoulder.

"Can you pause it?" His voice was so quiet he barely recognized it.

Amy scrambled to pause the disk.

It was all Tony could do to stare at the image on the screen as memories flooded him. His father had never been a big drinker, but that had changed around that summer, too. How had he forgotten that? And how had he missed how much his father's appearance had also changed. Alcohol had taken away most of the man Tony had looked up to by then, leaving his once-toned muscles soft, a shadow of the strong man his father had once been evident in his six-two, broad-shouldered stance. He and his father shared the same deep-set blue eyes, though in the picture his father's had dark moons beneath them. Moons Tony had no recollection of seeing. They had the same strong jawline, though even against the peaks and valleys of the dune's rough facade, Tony could see the hollowness in his father's cheeks.

"Tony."

Tony turned at the feel of Amy trying to unfurl his fist.

"Maybe I should turn it off," she offered.

He shook his head and inched closer to the dune. "No. I need to see him."

"He was handsome. You look a lot like him."

"Beyond that, what do you see?" Tony squinted at the bigger-than-life image, which suited how he had once thought of his father. He hadn't been afraid of his father, but memories of his father's demeaning comments that summer fisted his hands a little tighter. He felt Amy touch his arm.

"He's not here, Tony."

"He's not gone, either." Tony shook his head, a million thoughts whirling through his mind at once. "Look at his smile. It looks real, right? Not forced?"

"Yeah, he smiled a lot."

"Yeah, he did. That's why it cut so deep that summer when he was such a jerk to me. I don't know what happened to my memories, but that man right there..." He pointed at the dune. "Amy, that's not the man I have in my head. I don't remember him looking so happy. In my mind I see the angry man he was toward me. I can't even begin to draw the memory of him looking like that. But he was that man. He was jovial, lighthearted."

"I know," she whispered.

"Wha—? How?"

Amy shrugged. "I guess for the same reason that the man I see in the pictures of my dad doesn't look like the image of him in my mind. That's why I wanted to see these. I think our perspectives were skewed. When I went down to the woods today, I started thinking about our parents and I wondered if they'd seen anything between us that summer. And that made me wonder what we'd seen of them. My dad was always pushing me to do well in school, make something of myself. To be my best. He had expectations—there's no doubt about that—but would he have really cared if we'd dated? I just don't know the answer to that. And your father?"

She looked up at the image of Tony's father on the dune.

"He was hard on you, and he was a real jerk with some of the things he said that summer. And for all these years I've sort of blamed him for my shutting you out of my life. I was always worried that he'd throw our relationship in your face in some way, and after…well, after what happened, I felt like he'd never let it go."

"He would have used it against me, Amy. He'd have told me that I was irresponsible and that I'd messed up your life and mine. You know that." Tony clenched his jaw.

"Maybe." She shook her head. "But what if he was just pushing you like my father pushed me, but he just handled it in a horrible way?"

"Does that make it any better?"

Amy shook her head. "Of course not, but…"

"But we can't change the past no matter how much we wish we could. Would I love to know my father was sorry for all the things he said to me? Of course I would. But the truth is, I'll never know." Tony shook his head.

"Why? Why can't you ask your mother?"

"She doesn't need to relive that summer any more than I do."

"Or maybe she does. And maybe you do, too. I think it's worth talking about. She's probably carrying around a lot of guilt, too. She was there, too, remember?"

Tony breathed deeply. "Maybe. Probably. The truth is, I'm not sure I *want* to revisit it."

"Too painful?" she asked.

Guilt poured from his lips before he could stop it. "If we hadn't gotten together, you wouldn't have spent fourteen years not allowing yourself to get close to another man. You would have fallen in love and been loved the way you deserve. My father, as difficult as he was sometimes, probably would have been right."

Amy dropped her eyes, and he lifted her chin so he could face his own demons.

"I am so deeply sorry for everything you went through, but I'll never be sorry for loving you. I'm sorry about what it did to you, but *not* for loving you."

"Tony, it wasn't just what happened that kept me from falling for some other guy. Even if I'd never gotten pregnant, I was in love with you. That never changed. Not for one second over those years. It was that love that pulled me through that hard time as much as it was that love that caused it."

"But you missed out on so much."

"Did I?" Her green eyes were serious, her brows knitted together. "How many women made you feel loved over the years? How many of the women you slept with did you want to have a future with?" She held up her hands, silencing his answer. "It's a rhetorical question. What I mean is that I've watched Bella and Jenna, Leanna, and Jessica all fall in love, and the one thing that seemed to be consistent is that when they really fell for their men, when they gave up the *fear* of falling in love, they never questioned it. They felt like the other guys were, well, not exactly meaningless, but definitely not meaningful."

Amy inched closer, so their lips were almost touching, and she stared into Tony's eyes. "I have never questioned my love for you. Not once. I could have slept with plenty of men over the years, and if I hadn't gotten pregnant and lost the baby, who knows what might have happened between us. Maybe we would have told everyone eventually and stayed together, but maybe we would have broken up. Maybe we needed those years apart so that you could sow your oats—and please don't tell me you had no oats to sow, because we both know that would be a lie."

Tony wished he could laugh at that, but he knew Amy was right. When his surfing career had first taken off, there were women throwing themselves at him day and night. It was commonplace to have young girls tossing their bikini tops in his direction at parties after a big win, and he was only human. He'd like to believe he never would have hurt her or cheated on her, but the pressures were so great. How could he be sure?

"But you didn't get to sow yours." He hadn't realized how guilty he felt about Amy never sleeping with another man until right now.

Amy shook her head, smiled. "You do know who you are talking to, right? Letting *you* see me naked is about as wild as I get. That's never going to change. The only thing I missed out on was being in your arms, so don't you ever let yourself feel guilty for something I never wanted."

"How did I get lucky enough to deserve you?" Tony pressed his lips to hers, feeling like tonight had opened several more doors to their future, and he intended to walk through them—even if the path was covered in glass.

Chapter Fourteen

THE NEXT DAY Tony took Evan surfing, and Amy spent the afternoon down by the pool with Jenna. Leanna and Kurt had gone back to their house on the bay. Leanna had received a big order for her new flavor, Sweet Heat, and she needed to work all day to fill it. Jenna was lying on a lounge chair beside Amy, baking in the hot sun.

"Did I see Theresa's car this morning?" Amy asked.

"Yeah. She got here early." Jenna stretched. "I think she went into Orleans to the grocery store."

"I haven't seen much of her this summer. It'll be nice to see her." Amy waved to Bella as she came through the pool gate. Her hair was secured at the base of her neck with an elastic band, and she had on a pair of enormous plastic sunglasses.

"Did you get your stuff done?" Amy asked.

"I can't imagine what could be more important than lying here with us," Jenna said.

Bella wiggled her eyebrows.

"What was that look for? Oh no. What do you have planned?" Amy leaned up on her elbow and shaded her eyes. Bella was the community prankster, and she had a glint of mischief in her eyes.

"Planned? Nothing." Bella tossed her towel on a chair and sauntered over to the pool.

Amy and Jenna exchanged a disbelieving eye roll and followed her in.

"Theresa should be back from the grocery store soon." Amy watched Bella's smile grow. "Oh, no. Bella. Tell me you didn't do something to Theresa. Remember how well Thong Thursday went over last summer? I think she's so far on to you that you can't do anything to surprise her anymore." The previous summer Bella had hung a sign up by the pool announcing Thong Thursday. Jessica, who had been a new renter that summer, had taken it seriously, when, in fact, thongs were forbidden according to the Homeowner Association documents, which Theresa not only adhered to, but strictly enforced for the community. Theresa had gotten the best of Bella last year by wearing a thong down to the pool herself.

"Yeah, well, this year will be better. Trust me." Bella tossed a raft to Jenna and a foam noodle to Amy, and they soaked up the rays.

"How did Tony like the slide show last night?" Jenna asked. "I was so tempted to beg you to let us stay. I wanted to watch it on the dunes."

"Well, I'm glad we were alone. It was tough to watch, because of his dad and all that's happened. But I think it helped us to deal with everything. One thing we did notice is the way we looked at each other that summer. I can't believe no one recognized it for what it was."

"You guys have always looked at each other like you were more than friends," Bella said. "I don't remember it being any different back then."

"But that never made you wonder?" Amy asked.

Jenna and Bella exchanged a glance that Amy knew meant they had a secret of their own.

"Okay, spill it." Amy narrowed her eyes and ran them between the two of them.

"Well, we did wonder sometimes," Jenna admitted.

"But you were always so proper, and he was old enough that he knew how to play it cool." Bella rolled off her raft and into the water. "Besides, we had no reason to think you'd get together with him and not tell us."

"Ouch." Amy had almost slipped out from beneath the guilt of keeping the truth from her friends. Bella's reminder brought it right back.

"Why does it matter?" Bella asked.

"It doesn't, really. Although I'm sorry, Bella. I know I've jeopardized your trust, and I am really, truly sorry."

Bella exhaled loudly. "No. It's not you, Amy. It's me. I got my feelings hurt and my attitude got the better of me. I understand why you kept it from us. It just slipped out, that's all. You know I love you."

She couldn't blame Bella for having lingering hurt feelings. If anyone knew there were no overnight fixes, it was Amy.

"Thanks, Bella. I know it'll take time for all of this to get better, and I really don't blame you for being hurt or for letting me know it. I deserve far worse than that."

"No, you don't." Bella swam over and hung on to Amy's noodle beside her. "I shouldn't be so sensitive. I just wish you'd trusted me back then so you weren't alone through it all."

"I did. But that's part of what I'm trying to sort through. I've been blaming Tony's dad and my dad, you know? Telling myself that we were protecting ourselves from them and that I was protecting Tony by shutting him out of my life. But..."

"But?" Jenna jumped off her raft and hung on to the other side of the noodle, facing Amy and Bella.

"But I'm not sure I wasn't just protecting myself. I was embarrassed to tell you guys that I was sleeping with Tony."

"What? Why were you embarrassed to tell us? Amy, we weren't exactly virginal princesses." Jenna laughed.

"No, you weren't, but you thought I was."

"Amy, we wouldn't have judged you," Bella assured her.

"Maybe not. I don't even know if that's it, but I think there were lots of things going on in my head back then, and after all this time I can only take a stab at what they really meant." Amy saw Theresa's car pull into the community, and she was relieved to change the subject. "Theresa's back."

Bella swam for the stairs. "Oh, good."

"Wait." Jenna grabbed Amy's arm and pulled her toward the steps. "What's the plan? Do you have a prank planned?"

"No plan." Bella wrapped a towel around herself and grabbed her sunglasses. "I'm going to get a drink of water."

Amy and Jenna's eyes widened as they gathered their things and hurried after Bella.

"Water. Right." Jenna pulled her sundress over her head.

"Bella, clue us in," Amy urged. "What did you do?"

"Nothing. Gosh, you guys. I don't *always* pull pranks." Bella took one determined step after another and kept her eyes trained on the ground.

Amy knew she was up to something. They followed her into her cottage, where she went directly for her cell phone and began texting.

"Spill it, girlfriend." Jenna put her hand on her hip and glared at Bella.

"Okay, fine. So maybe there's a little something brewing.

Come on. Let's get a drink and go out on the deck." Bella opened the fridge and handed them each a bottle of Mike's Hard Lemonade.

They settled into the chairs on Bella's deck and watched Theresa carry her groceries inside. Anticipation had them all leaning forward in their chairs like they were watching an action flick.

"What did you do?" Amy whispered.

"How about we just focus on you and Tony," Bella suggested. "Then if anything goes down, you won't get in trouble."

"Oh no. *Anything goes down*?" Jenna sucked down her drink. "Bella Abbascia, what did you do?"

Bella rolled her eyes.

Theresa waved when she came back outside to retrieve more groceries from the car. Jenna and Amy waved back.

"Maybe we should go help her," Amy suggested.

"I don't think so." Bella took a sip of her drink and eyed Jenna.

"Anywho..." Amy took the opportunity to continue their conversation. "As I was saying, we also never realized how differently we saw things back then."

Bella shrugged. "We all did. We were kids. But that was then and this is now, and it's time to put it behind you and move forward."

"Yeah, I agree." Jenna took a sip of her drink. "Although I don't think it would be that easy to move on after what you went through. I'm just not sure taking it apart this many years later is going to help."

"See? That's why I need you guys around. I could drive myself crazy wanting to know exactly why I acted the way I did." Amy breathed a little easier. Maybe they were right. She should focus on the future, not the past.

"Let's think about happier things, shall we?" Bella waved a hand in the air. "Like, are we going to have a quadruple wedding?"

"I think you are jumping the gun—don't you? We still have a few things to sort out." Amy could barely say it with a straight face when she really wanted to jump up and down like a fool and say, *I hope so!*

"Like…moving to Australia?" Bella leaned back in her chair. "I told you not to take the job with Duke. Now what's your plan?"

"I don't have one, beyond knowing that I can't very well move to Australia if I hope to have a relationship with Tony."

"Hope to? You have one already, chicky. But, yeah, he travels all the time," Jenna reminded her. "At least with your consulting business, you can travel with Tony and coordinate your schedule around his."

"Yeah, but I'd give anything to work with Duke. I love my freedom, but Duke's got so many great properties. And he's got huge ideas and the budget to match. I could do so much more than I can do for my current clients. Not to mention that he's a great guy to work with."

"And hot," Jenna added.

Amy rolled her eyes. "Hello? I have Tony, remember?" *Wow, it felt good to say that.*

"Hey, just pointing out the obvious." Jenna set down her drink.

"It really is an honor to have been offered the job. I mean, Duke doesn't hire just anyone, and if I renege on my commitment, what will he think of me? He's a friend, not just an employer I'll never see again. Besides, I'm not sure I want to turn it down." Amy closed her eyes and groaned. "But I definitely want a relationship with Tony." She set down her drink as a police car pulled into the development. "Um, is that one of Caden's friends?"

The side of Bella's mouth quirked up. "Let the fun begin."

The policeman parked in Theresa's driveway, then stepped from his car as Theresa came outside.

"Come on." Bella hurried across the street with the girls on her heels.

"Ma'am?" The officer looked to be in his late twenties with dirty-blond hair, ice-blue eyes, and a forced smile.

Theresa furrowed her brow. Her wide mouth was clenched in a tight line, and her eyes were narrow and serious. Theresa exuded practicality, from her closely cropped and layered brown hair to her polo shirt and long shorts. She dressed for efficiency rather than fashion, and the way she assessed the policeman was equally as efficient. Amy could see her mind working over the possibilities of why he was standing in her driveway.

"Good afternoon, Officer. What can I do for you?" She settled her hands on her hips and glanced at Bella and the girls with a pensive look.

"We've had a complaint about the cyber stalking of Bradley Cooper, and the e-mails have been linked to your IP address." He pointed to her house. "Would you mind if I take a look inside?"

"Cyber stalking? I haven't even been here for the past few days." Theresa looked back at her house, then turned worried eyes to Bella. "Have you seen anyone hanging around my house?"

"No, of course not," Bella answered. "We wouldn't let anyone near your house."

"I'm sure it's a mistake," Jenna said.

Amy couldn't say a word, because despite her one big fourteen-year lie, she really wasn't good at hiding the truth, and she was sure that if something inside was awry, it had everything to do with a certain mouthy blonde whom she adored.

They followed Theresa into her modestly furnished and tidy house. Theresa lived in the full-sized house that had belonged to the original owner of all of Seaside before the land was subdivided and the cottages were built. They followed the officer into the living room. The room was a good size, with a brown couch, white coffee table, and a peach-colored armchair. Off to the right was a small dining room with a round table and six wooden chairs. The walls were painted beige, except in the kitchen, which was just beyond the living room and fully outfitted in white. The officer picked up a framed photograph and studied it. He cleared his throat and walked across the room to another framed photo, which he also picked up and studied.

"Oh my gosh," Jenna mumbled and reached for Amy's hand. She squeezed so hard Amy had to stifle a yelp.

Amy looked at Bella, who had a wide grin on her lips, and was staring at a framed picture of Bradley Cooper hanging above the end table. Amy snapped her jaw closed to stifle a gasp. *Holy cow.*

"Ma'am?" The officer turned the two frames toward Theresa, who apparently hadn't noticed anything out of place. Both frames held pictures of Bradley Cooper with hearts drawn on them in red ink. "Would you care to explain these?"

Theresa shot a heated stare at Bella.

"Theresa, I never knew you were such a fan," Bella said with a straight face.

"I'm not." Theresa took the frames from him and glared at

Bella. "I don't have any idea how these got in here."

The cop arched a brow and raised his eyes to the photograph of the celebrity hanging on the wall. "And that one?"

"*Tsk!* What is this? I did not…Bella?"

Bella held her hands up. "Wow. This is kind of creepy."

"These are not my photographs," Theresa insisted.

The cop flashed a barely there smile to Bella that Amy would have missed had she not been watching everyone so closely.

The officer walked over to Theresa's desk, where her laptop lay closed. "May I open this?"

"Yes, of course. You'll see that this is some kind of a mistake," Theresa huffed.

The officer lifted the lid of her laptop and Bradley Cooper's picture appeared as the screen saver.

"Ma'am, I'm afraid this evidence speaks for itself. I'm going to issue you a warning, but if you don't refrain from contacting Mr. Cooper, we'll be forced to take further action."

"But I didn't do this." Theresa let out an exasperated breath.

"The evidence proves otherwise," the officer said.

Theresa's eyes narrowed. If looks could maim, Bella would be laid flat.

"I…I have to run." Amy headed for the door with Jenna right behind her.

They held hands as they ran across the quad to Amy's cottage.

"Whoa!" Jenna collapsed into a deck chair. "Bella went above and beyond her normal prankster game this time. Theresa is going to get her back so bad!"

Bella joined them a few minutes later with a satisfied smirk. "That was to get her back for ruining my Thong Thursday prank."

Amy covered her face with her hands. "All I wanted to do was talk about what to do about Tony and the job with Duke, and now I'm an accessory to a prank that she'll probably get you arrested for. Forget Australia. We'll all end up cuffed in the Wellfleet Police Barracks."

"Tony will bail you out."

Amy banged her forehead on the table. "Australia's looking pretty good right now."

"HEY, THAT WAS cool of you to set that stuff up for us last night. Thanks, man." Tony gave Evan a friendly pat on the back. They'd surfed for several hours, then hung out on the beach for the afternoon, talking. Now they were back at Seaside, getting their gear out of Tony's car.

"It was no big deal, and it seemed important to Amy." Evan shrugged.

"Well, it was a big deal to both of us. We appreciated it." He handed Evan his surfboard and took his own off the rack. "Stay out of trouble tonight."

Evan was going on a double date with his friend Bobby and two girls from high school.

"I told you it wasn't a big deal. They're just friends. We're going to the drive-in. Wanna catch some waves tomorrow?" Evan called over his shoulder on the way to Bella's cottage.

"Wish I could, but I think I'm going to spend tomorrow with Amy."

"See why I don't want a real girlfriend?" Evan teased.

"I've got more than fifteen years on you. I'm pretty lucky to have her." *And I'm not doing anything to mess it up this time.*

Tony glanced at Amy's car in her driveway. Either she was inside or at the cottage of one of the other girls. How many times had he looked across the street and wondered what Amy was doing? He loved the feeling of knowing she was finally his and that whatever she was doing, she was probably thinking of him as much as he was thinking of her. He headed inside to shower.

They had spent the night at Tony's cottage, and the bedroom still smelled like Amy. He stripped off his board shorts, went into the bathroom, and turned on the shower. He'd been thinking about the slide show all day, and darn if he wasn't even more confused than before. He had slotted his father's memory into a place in his head that he rarely visited. The breakup had not been easy to move past, and his father's death had come on its heels, magnifying his hurt and anger. At a time when Tony was doing all he could to remain sane and focused on keeping his career, he'd thrown himself into surfing and training and tried to be there for his mother as best he could. But Tony knew he'd barely made it through each day, much less been any help to her. He'd been determined to prove his father wrong about his career—and he'd hidden from that well of devastation by throwing himself into surfing—and he'd succeeded.

Or at least he'd thought he had.

Until now.

After seeing the pictures of his father last night, smiling, joking, being the man Tony had once admired so greatly, he wondered if the harsh memories had deluded him into forgetting the good ones. His father had been at his worst that last summer at the Cape. Tony hadn't even known he was a drinker. How he'd missed that, he had no idea.

After his shower he put on a pair of cargo shorts and a tank top and sank onto the bed with a loud sigh. It was time he dealt with his father's memories once and for all.

Tony grabbed his cell phone from the bedside table and called his mother. She answered on the second ring.

"Tony, how are you, honey?" Her smile was evident in her warm tone. Tony pictured her sitting in the living room of her Rhode Island waterfront home, knitting needles in hand. His mother had knitted for as long as he could remember, and since his father's death, the knitting needles seemed to be her constant companions.

"I'm okay, Ma. How are you?"

"Oh, you know me, honey. I'm fine. Knitting tonight. I'm making a baby bonnet for Lisa Cross's granddaughter. She's such a cute little thing. How're the kids this year?"

"Good, Ma, but they're not kids. We're all over thirty." He laughed.

"Honey, you'll always be kids to me. Even when you're old and gray. How was the wedding? I was so sorry to have missed it." His mother had missed the wedding because she'd had a bunion removed from her foot the week before, and her foot was still tender.

"It was wonderful. Jamie looked really happy, and Jessica was beautiful. How's your foot?"

"Oh, fine. It seems to be healing well; it just takes a little time, that's all."

"Good. Mom, I'm glad it's healing up. I have something I want to talk to you about, but if you would rather not, then just tell me, okay?"

"Don't be silly, honey. What is it?"

Tony rose from the bed and paced. "It's about Dad."

"Okay." Her voice turned serious.

"I was looking at pictures last night of our summers here at the Cape, and the pictures didn't match the image I have of him in my mind. I'm a little worried that what I remember of him is skewed." He rubbed a dull ache creeping across the back of his neck.

"Well, honey, why don't you tell me what you feel was different?"

"I don't know. Everything. The look in his eyes. I don't know when most of the pictures were taken, but—"

"Where did you see these pictures?"

"Amy's mother made a slide show a few years back."

"Yes. I received that."

"Of course you did. Sorry. Then you've watched it?"

"Yes. It was a long time ago, but of course I did. Those were wonderful memories."

"Yeah. For the most part. But..." Tony ran his hand through his hair, feeling too confined. He escaped into the living room.

"But the last year was not so good," she said softly.

"Yeah. Why was that?"

Silenced filled the airwaves.

"Mom? What I need to know is *why* he changed."

She was silent again. Tony stopped in the center of the living room, unable to think past what that silence might mean.

"Honey, are you sure you want to talk about this? You haven't brought up your father for a very long time."

"Yeah, I'm sure." When his father died, Tony's mother was heartbroken and Tony was lost. They had done all they could to hold themselves together, and Tony hadn't looked for any further explanation once he'd heard that his father had been drunk when he'd run off the road. From the sound of his mother's voice, he wondered if he was doing the wrong thing by dredging up the past again.

"Tony, your father made me promise not to tell you what had happened that spring, and I'd like to honor my word in his memory."

"Mom, he's gone. I'm…" He closed his eyes and gathered his wits about him, giving himself a silent pep talk to say what he wanted to say and deal with this once and for all. When he opened his eyes, he felt more in control.

"I wouldn't ask if it wasn't important. I know how much your word means to you, although I can't for the life of me imagine why you'd have to keep something about Dad's death from me."

She didn't respond, so Tony continued. "I'm in love with Amy Maples, and I want to move forward with my life, but I need to understand what happened with Dad. I need to know what changed that summer, why he changed."

"Amy Maples." The smile returned to her voice. "Oh, Tony. I'm so happy to hear this. She's loved you forever."

This stunned him, although after seeing the pictures last night, it shouldn't have. He saw the love written all over their faces, and it was no wonder other people had seen it, too. He wondered if his father had. Or if Amy's father had.

"Yes, she has, and I've loved her just as long." It felt so good to say that. His lips curled up despite the difficult conversation.

"Yes, I imagine you did."

He laughed a little. "Did you?"

"Oh, honey. There isn't much that gets past a mother. We notice changes in our children that no one else could ever see. The last summer we were at the Cape as a family, I thought you and Amy had finally found each other. You both seemed so happy. But it must have been wishful thinking because of what was going on with your father. Maybe I just wanted to see something good come of that summer. And then, after your father…"

He heard her inhale a loud breath. When she spoke again, her voice was weak. "Afterward, that spark I thought I'd seen in you was gone."

Tony sank down onto the couch. "You noticed?"

"How could I not? You went from a carefree kid who was surfing and loving life to a broken man. You were coiled so tight and running yourself into the ground with surfing and training and who knows what else. I was worried you'd never go back to the boy you were. I was never really sure if it was because of your father's passing or something else."

"Both, Mom." Tony rubbed his eyes with his index finger and thumb. "Tell me about Dad."

"I'm breaking a promise I made to him by telling you, but you're an adult, and I suppose you do have a right to know."

"Thank you." He leaned back and closed his eyes. "Whatever it is, it's got to shed some light on the way he changed."

"Yes, it will do that." She paused for a long moment, and when she continued, her tone was compassionate. "Honey, that spring your father was diagnosed with ALS."

Tony sat bolt upright. "What? Why would he want to keep that from me? Why would you?"

"Calm down, please. This is not easy for me to talk about." Her words were sharp, though she spoke softly.

"I'm sorry." He rose to his feet and paced again. "I'm sorry. I didn't mean to upset you. Isn't this something you should have told me?"

"I promised your father I wouldn't. He was given a year to live. He knew that was going to be his last summer with you. His health was declining, and—"

"Oh, *man.*" Tony sank back down to the couch. He couldn't imagine what his father had gone through. "When did the drinking begin?"

"I don't know exactly, but sometime soon after he received the diagnosis." His mother paused, and the answers became clearer.

"He wasn't drinking at a work party that night, was he?"

"No." A whisper.

"Mom. He…he killed himself when he crashed into that tree? It wasn't an accident?"

"I don't know." Her voice was stronger but shaky. "We'll never know. But the father you were with that last summer is not the man your father always was. Surely you know that."

"He was always tough on me."

"Yes. Because he didn't want you to make a mistake. Parents worry, honey. When your child tells you he wants to be a pro surfer, as a parent you want to protect them from failing. To parents who aren't surfers, you might as well have said you wanted to go to the moon or be a rock star. It was all so foreign to us. Your father and I were businesspeople. Straight and narrow, follow the road put forth by your elders. College, graduate school, family. Solid path. You threw us for a loop. Not that we didn't want to support your dreams, but…"

"It's okay, Ma. I get it. I know how it must have sounded, but I was driven. I lived and breathed surfing. Still do. I made it, and I hate that Dad never got a chance to see that. He never got a chance to move past the hard time he gave me and be proud of what I'd done."

"Oh, honey." Her voice trembled, as if she were crying. "Even back then your father was proud of all you'd accomplished and the fact that you were on your way to becoming the best. But he saw that summer as his last chance to make a difference and guide you in the way a father should." She paused for a beat, and when she continued, her tone was softer. "He just didn't know how to get so much out in so little time. And the alcohol didn't help."

Tony's eyes teared up. "ALS."

"It's not genetic, so you don't have to worry about that."

"It's not that, although it is a relief. I just wish I had known. Maybe I could have talked to him about…everything."

"He loved you, Tony. He loved you so much. All those times his anger got the best of him, he wasn't aiming that venom at you. He was angry about the disease, about leaving us before he was ready. You just got caught in the line of fire."

TONY TOSSED THE phone onto the couch and buried his face in his hands. Amy stood on the wrong side of the screen door with her heart in her throat. *ALS.* She'd heard him say it, and now he was falling apart. Who was he talking to? Who had ALS?

"Tony?"

Tony spun around, eyes red and watery. She read his silent plea and forced her legs to carry her inside. He didn't stand from where he sat on the couch. He simply reached a hand out, and as she took it, the air shifted, became heavier. He drew her down onto his lap, and her arms instinctively circled his neck. She held him as his breathing hitched and his grip on her tightened.

"That was my mom," he said against her shoulder. "My father…was sick."

His sadness pressed in on her through the weight of his large hands splayed on her back and his warm, stubbled cheek against her. Amy closed her eyes and hoped she could offer a modicum of the strength that he'd always offered to her.

"I'm sorry, Tony."

She felt him nod.

"He had ALS, Amy. ALS. I had no idea." His voice trailed off.

Eventually his grip eased and he gazed sadly into her eyes. "I love you."

"I love you, too."

She kissed him to soften the hurt threaded in his voice. He deepened the kiss, turning it hot and urgent, greedy for comfort she was more than willing to give. Amy was the first to draw back, wanting to show him the love she felt so deeply and to fill her own need to bring him respite from whatever was tearing him up inside.

There was nothing she could say to take away the hurt she saw in his eyes. He pulled her closer, and she knew he needed to be loved the way she'd loved him all those years ago. She needed to take away the ache of sorrow and fill him with comfort in a way only their love could. She kissed his jaw, his neck, the tender spot at the base of his neck. She pushed at his tank top, running her hands over his muscles, and he kissed her like being with her was the only place on earth he ever wanted to be.

Chapter Fifteen

OVER THE NEXT few days, Amy and Tony talked about his father's illness and the magnitude of what his father must have felt. Tony was angry at first about his parents keeping it from him. As he came to grips with his new reality, Amy gave him the time and space to deal with it in the way he dealt with most things. He threw himself into surfing and working out. He was up before dawn for morning workouts, then beat his body up for most of the day, and when he'd return, he and Amy would talk until the wee hours of the morning and then make love until the pain and confusion was once again held at bay.

Sunday morning Tony took Evan surfing while Amy, Bella, and Jenna went to help Leanna at the flea market. Luscious Leanna's Sweet Treats had taken off so much that Leanna couldn't keep up with the customers at her booth. She'd even begun leaving Pepper at home with Kurt because she needed to focus solely on sales. Sunday was the busiest day at the flea market, and today was no different. It was a gorgeous summer afternoon with temps in the mideighties and a nice cool breeze. The girls wore their typical attire of their bathing suits beneath sundresses, with the exception of Leanna, who had on her jam-streaked cutoffs and a tank top.

While Leanna and Jenna helped customers, Bella and Amy applied labels to jars sitting beside Leanna's colorful, hand-painted Volkswagen bus. She always parked behind her booth, as most of the vendors did.

"Have you had any repercussions from the stunt you pulled with Theresa?" Amy asked Bella.

"*Pfft*. No. She can't outdo me. She knows that now."

"But that was breaking and entering. You're lucky she didn't have you arrested."

"No, it wasn't. I offered to water her plants while she was gone. Besides, it's all in fun. She knows that. Let's talk about something that matters. How is Tony holding up with the news about his dad?" Bella asked.

Tony hadn't hesitated when Amy had asked him if she should share the news of his father's illness with the girls. She wasn't sure if he'd been so quick to allow it because they would be there to support them or because he was just not into keeping secrets any longer. His decision seemed to be driven by both. She'd told the girls about his father's illness, and as she'd expected, they'd been empathetic and supportive.

"You know Tony. He's keeping himself busy until he's really ready to deal with it. I think he needs closure." Amy set a jar on the table and picked up another. "Is it weird that I feel guilty about that summer? I mean, maybe if I hadn't been so attracted to Tony back then, he would have had more time for his dad or been more focused on him. Maybe he could have talked to him instead of just being upset over how he was being treated."

"It's not weird, but only because you have the biggest, most unselfish heart on the planet." Bella peeled the backing off a label and pressed it on the jar. "You hate to see anyone sad, and you want to fix it for him. But he's a guy. You can't fix anything for a guy. No one can. They're like…" Bella looked out at the sea of people walking between the booths. "I don't know what they're like, but while they want us there to listen and love them, they want to be the fixers."

"I just want to do the right thing and help him through this."

Bella set down the jar and reached for Amy's hands. "Ames, you are doing the right thing. You and Tony are together. The rest will work itself out."

"I hope so. I hate that he can't go back and work things out with his dad." She knew it was tearing Tony up that he couldn't fix this with a phone call to his father, and she worried about what would happen when keeping himself busy wasn't enough to dull the pain.

When there was a lull in the flow of customers, Jenna joined them. "Take him to his father's grave site. He can say a real goodbye, not the angry, confused twenty-year-old's goodbye of years ago."

Bella stepped in to help another round of customers so Jenna could talk with Amy, patting Amy's arm as she passed. Jenna picked up a jar and a label and went to work.

"Do you think that will help?" Amy tucked her hair behind her ear, thinking about Jenna's suggestion. Tony hadn't cried at his father's funeral. She'd never forget the way he'd looked broken and brave at the same time, when inside she'd known he must have been shattered.

"I do. His father doesn't need to be with him for Tony to come to grips with his feelings. He just needs to be present—you know what I mean?"

"Then maybe I should take him to Pelly, that psychic in P-town." Pelly was one of the best psychics in the area. When they were younger they'd heard stories of people camping overnight in Pelly's yard to be seen the following morning. Over the years Pelly had cracked down on those folks, and now he held very limited hours for readings.

"Do you remember when we went as kids?" Jenna's eyes widened as she picked up another jar.

"How could I forget? Remember how dark the room was? And everything was red. The walls, the tablecloth, even the caftan he wore was bloodred. So weird."

Jenna laughed. "Remember how nervous we were? I can't even remember what he told us. I just remember running out and laughing so hard that we tumbled onto the grass."

"Yeah, well, I remember *hoping* he'd tell me that Tony was madly in love with me, and instead he told me something stupid like, *Be true to your heart and you'll find your way.*" Amy scoffed.

"Ames..."

Amy met Jenna's wide-eyed gaze. "What?"

"Duh. You did follow your heart. And you did find your way."

Goose bumps rose on Amy's arms. "Yeah. Maybe he wasn't so far off after all, but maybe that's not the best thing for Tony. I mean, if Pelly is as good as people say, what if he really does reach Tony's dad and something's...I don't know. *Off.* Or if it doesn't offer the closure he needs. It might make things worse."

"There is that."

"I think I like your idea better anyway. Tony needs to come to grips with his own feelings on his own terms. If there's one thing I've learned this summer, it's that you can't fix the past. You can only accept it, maybe try to understand it as best you can, and find a way to move forward and leave it where it belongs. In the past." It surprised Amy that she was doling out such sage advice so readily. She of all people knew how difficult it was to leave the past behind. And now, reflecting on what she'd said, she also understood how important it was to deal with it before moving on.

It was nearly six o'clock by the time the flea market cleared out, despite the fact that it officially closed at four.

"Beachcomber tonight?" Bella asked as they pulled into Seaside and Leanna parked beside the laundry room, which she often did since her van was so big and it blocked her view of Amy's deck if she parked in her driveway.

"That sounds perfect." Amy stepped from the van and glanced over at Tony's cottage. His car was there, and she couldn't wait to see him. "I'll ask Tony. I think we could both use some fun."

"Ask Tony what?" Tony stepped from the laundry room, shirtless, tanned, and gorgeous, carrying a basket of freshly folded clothes.

"I don't think there's anything sexier than a guy doing laundry." Amy rose up on her toes and kissed him. "Especially this man."

"I don't know. Caden in his tool belt is pretty hot," Bella teased.

Amy laughed. "We were talking about going to the Beachcomber tonight."

"Sounds great." Tony slipped an arm around Amy's waist and whispered, "I need to shower. Want to join me?"

Amy felt her cheeks heat up. "Uh…yeah. Of course."

They made plans to meet the gang later and headed to Tony's cottage. Theresa pulled up as they crossed in front of her driveway. She waved, and Amy stopped to greet her.

"Hi, Theresa. We're going to the Beachcomber tonight. Would you like to come along?"

Theresa pressed her lips together in a way that made Amy feel stupid for asking. She was probably angry about Bella's prank, although Theresa never really got angry, at least not that Amy had ever witnessed.

"The Beachcomber is for you young'uns," Theresa said.

"We're not that much younger than you," Amy reminded her.

"Oh, I think anything more than ten years counts as older. You guys have fun and be safe."

"Okay, maybe next time."

Theresa made that face again. Amy waved as they crossed the quad toward Tony's cottage. Her cell phone rang as they stepped inside. It was Duke.

Time to face the music.

IT HAD BEEN a long few days, and Tony was ready to chill. He leaned back and enjoyed the view from their table at the Beachcomber restaurant. It wasn't the view of the ocean that drew his attention, although the Beachcomber was built on a bluff overlooking Cahoon Hollow Beach. It was Amy's hot little body moving seductively on the dance floor that drew his eyes. She was dancing with Bella, Jenna, Leanna, and Sky, and she was the most beautiful woman in the place.

"Dude, I'm pretty sure you can go blind staring like that," Caden joked.

"Then blind I shall be." Tony took a sip of his drink. He

could watch Amy dance all night long. He really wanted to be out there with her body pressed against his, but she was having too much fun with the girls for him to step in.

Pete patted Tony on the back. "Glad to see you guys together, man. This is the way it should be. Now Jenna and I can finally get married."

Tony shifted his eyes to Pete. "You needed me and Amy to be together so you could get married?"

Pete took a swig of his beer. "Not me." He nodded to the girls. "You really think they'd do something that big without each other? They can barely pee without holding each other's hands."

Tony laughed. "Yeah. It's one of the things I love about Amy. She's loyal to the bone."

"That's why Duke offered her the job," Blue said. He and Sky had been joining their group outings ever since last summer, when Sky had moved back into town and Blue had built Jenna's art studio. "He said she's not only one of the best logistical coordinators he's ever worked with, but that she's loyal and dedicated. In our family, loyalty trumps all."

As if Tony hadn't known that from the day he first kissed Amy so many years ago. She'd kept the secret of their relationship from their families and best friends, and if that wasn't enough, she'd gone fourteen years without being intimate with another man. She was the most loyal person he knew. Well, at least as loyal as he now knew his mother had been to his father. She'd kept a secret of her own for the same amount of time.

Tony scrubbed his hand down his face. Amy had spoken to Duke earlier in the evening and she'd scheduled a meeting with him for the following weekend, when he was coming to the Cape to look over a property that Blue was thinking of purchasing. Tony hadn't pushed her for information even though he was dying to know if she'd made a decision. But after they'd made love and showered together before coming to the Beachcomber, he'd asked if she had a plan for the job. She'd said she wasn't sure, but she'd made it real clear that she wanted their relationship to work, and Tony could only hope that meant she'd consider staying in the States.

"How do you feel about her going to Australia?" Blue asked. "You surf there, right?"

I feel like I don't want her to go. "Yeah, I do. Whatever makes her happy."

"You're a better man than me," Pete said. "I'd tell her to stay."

Kurt looked at him sideways. "And Jenna would listen?"

Pete ran his hand through his thick dark hair and shifted his eyes to Jenna, who was shimmying up Bella's body on the dance floor. "Jenna doesn't *listen.* She makes her own decisions, but I know she'd never leave me."

"If Leanna wanted to go to Australia for her work, I'd go with her," Kurt added.

"That's because you can work from anywhere," Caden pointed out. "It's a tough call."

"You're in a rough spot," Blue said to Tony. "I'm no expert on love. I mean, I haven't had a steady girl in years, but I'm not sure I could sit back and wait for a woman I loved to make that big of a decision. I'd take Pete's route and tell her to stay. Of course, Duke is my brother, so if it were me, I'd have to deal with that."

"You'd put your relationship ahead of her career?" Tony asked. Amy had already put Tony's career ahead of their relationship once. He didn't want her to do it again. While he knew Amy had been protecting herself as much as she'd been protecting him all those years ago, he couldn't deny—and would never forget—that she'd supported his success by removing herself as a distraction. Even if he hadn't wanted her to.

He watched a group of handsome twentysomething guys approach the girls. Amy smiled up at one of them. Jealousy corded Tony's muscles tight. Amy took a step back from the guy and Tony rose to his feet.

"Yeah," he mumbled to himself. The word dripped with sarcasm. "That's not happening, jerk," he mumbled as he crossed the dance floor and slid a possessive arm around Amy's waist. "May I?"

She turned in to him with a grateful smile and clenched his shirt in her fists. "I was hoping you'd come to my rescue."

Their bodies moved in perfect rhythm, hips brushing, hands wandering. He pulled her closer and whispered, "I'm not taking any chances of losing you after this many years."

She ran her hands down his biceps, and her eyes darkened. "I don't think you have to worry about that."

"I only have to worry about losing you to kangaroos and the outback?" He touched his forehead to hers, knowing it was unfair to put pressure on her to decide between him and the job, but he was unable to stop himself. He needed to know exactly how committed she was, because he was completely ready to be committed to her.

"Mr. Black, is that jealousy I hear in your voice?" Her lips curved in a playful smile.

"It would be petty to be jealous over a job."

"Oh, I meant over the hot guy—and the job."

He narrowed his eyes, took her hand in his, and led her off

the dance floor and down a narrow hallway, where he took her in a deep, hard kiss and backed her up against the wall.

"I want to put you in a position that I shouldn't," he said in a harsh whisper.

Amy's eyes widened. "Here?"

"Not a sexual position." He laughed, then lowered his voice. "Although that sounds good, too."

She trapped her lower lip between her teeth.

"You're so cute, kitten."

She hooked her finger in the waist of his pants. "You already made me purr twice today."

"Three times, but who's counting?" He kissed her neck, earning him a sexy moan.

"I know I told you to take the job with Duke, and I don't want to stand in your way, but I want you with me, Amy. Every day, every night, every single minute of my life."

Chapter Sixteen

AMY LAY ON her back in Tony's bed, listening to the calm cadence of his breathing and thinking about what he'd said the night before. *I want you with me, Amy. Every day, every night, every single minute of my life.* They'd been interrupted by Bella and Jenna about a second after he'd said it, and he hadn't brought it up again.

Tony stirred beside her and she closed her eyes. She felt the bed shift, and then his warm lips touched hers.

"How long are you going to pretend to be sleeping?" He smiled at her.

"I'm sorry. Did I keep you up?"

He looked beneath the covers and flashed a heated grin. "That would be a very happy yes."

Amy couldn't repress her smile. "I really don't want anything separating us, Tony. In any way. Just so you know, I'm on the pill."

"That's great, but I'm a little nervous about putting you in the same position you were in before."

"It wouldn't be the same position. We're adults, and the pill is ninety-nine percent effective."

His eyes grew serious. "I told you I'd always take care of

you, and a one percent chance is one percent riskier than you deserve."

"Isn't that being a little overprotective?" She ran her fingers lightly over his chest.

"Maybe." He brushed his lips over hers. "I've learned my lesson. No more taking chances where you're concerned. You're my life now, kitten." He took her in another soul-searing kiss.

"Then let me be your life. Love all of me. *Feel* all of me."

He gazed up at her. "I want to do the right thing."

"This is the absolute right thing. I want to feel *you* from now on. I want that with all my heart. I never want anything between us again."

"I don't either. Including the past. I was thinking about your suggestion, about going to my father's grave."

"Yeah?" She'd suggested it on the way to the Beachcomber last night, and he'd said he would consider it.

Tony pushed himself up on one elbow. "I think it's a good idea."

"You do?" She felt her eyes bloom wide and tried to rein in her hope that this might bring him some relief from the hurt he tried so hard to hide. He was good at putting on a brave face. Amy hadn't realized how good until she'd allowed herself to revisit the memories of that tragic summer again. Now she understood the strength it had taken for him to not only walk away from her that night at her dorm but to keep from pushing her away all these years.

"If you don't have any plans, maybe we could drive out to Rhode Island together to visit his grave."

"Tony, I would love that." She could hardly believe they'd come this far. "I've decided not to talk to my father about that summer. I think it's time I have a different talk with him. It's time for me to cut his umbilical cord. I'm going to clear the air with him, but about how he hovers over me, not about you and me. What we do is private."

"Are you sure you're okay with that? He might not like it."

"I've only remained under his thumb out of guilt. I don't feel guilty about my mom leaving anymore. I never should have. It wasn't my place, but I was never strong enough to draw that line. As we've come back together, I realized that it's time." She squeezed his hand, knowing it was the right thing to do.

"I support you any way you want to handle it. Just let me know what I can do to help." He kissed her softly. "Will you consider doing one more thing for me?"

"Anything."

He brought her hand to his lips and pressed a long, warm kiss to it; then he gazed into her eyes. She wanted to lie right there for hours. Just like that, staring into his deep blue eyes and wondering what he wanted. She loved the not knowing, and the anticipation of readily agreeing to whatever it might be. She loved pleasing him. She loved seeing the relief and love in his eyes when they found each other after a few hours apart and the way his arms engulfed her, making her feel safe and warm.

"Anything," she whispered again.

"Let's put the past where it belongs and really move forward."

"I want that."

He stared at her for a long moment with loving eyes and spoke just above a whisper. "Surf with me again."

There were a million things that Amy was ready to agree to. This wasn't anywhere near the list.

Chapter Seventeen

MONDAY MORNING HEAT beat down on Tony's back and rose from the pavement, burning from all angles as he ran toward the bay. He'd gotten up early to try to get his head around visiting his father's grave. He hadn't been to the cemetery since the year after his father died, when he'd visited with his mother on the anniversary of his father's death.

My father's death.

He pushed himself harder and kicked up his speed with the thought. *ALS.* Tony had Googled the disease last night, and by the time he'd finished reading, he felt like he could barely move. *Amyotrophic Lateral Sclerosis.* The fatal disease was also known as Lou Gehrig's disease. He couldn't fathom what must have gone through his father's mind after being diagnosed with such a vicious disease. His father had taught him to bike, to fish, to lift weights. His father had taught him to surf when he was six years old. Tony smiled at the memory as the bay came into view and sea air filled his lungs.

His father was a casual surfer. He had tried so hard to get Tony to go slow, take surfing one step at a time, but Tony would have no part of it. From the second the board was in his hands, he was a shark and the waves were his prey. He had to have them, to master them. To rule them. No one ruled waves. Tony knew that, but that didn't stop the six-year-old boy from trying—and failing—so many times that his father begged him to stop and try another day. They'd stayed in the water until Tony's entire body was numb and until he'd caught so many waves and swallowed so much sea water that it became part of who he was.

His father had been agile and strong, even if more academic in nature. He was tall and broad, with a flat stomach and a sharp mind. Tony ran down the beach trying to reconcile the image of his father then with the image he'd allowed to take over his memories. The soft-bellied man with a sharp temper, harsh nature…and ALS.

Tony pounded out step after step on the uneven sand as he thought of what he'd read about the fatal neurological disease that his father had faced. His father had been staring at the end of his life in clear view, regardless of if it was a year or two or only months away. It had become too real for him. He'd known what lay ahead: gradual degeneration and death of motor neurons. Eventually his brain's ability to control his voluntary muscle movements would have been lost completely.

Tony stewed on that thought as he ran another two miles and circled back toward Seaside. He couldn't decide if his father was a coward or the bravest man he'd ever known. Was it cowardly to leave his family without so much as a goodbye? To allow himself to fall into a bottle to escape reality? Or was it brave to leave this world on his own terms?

Coward.

His father could have talked to him. He should have talked to him. How could he have thought it was a good idea that his son believe him to be a jerk at the end of his life rather than the man he'd always been? It was a selfish thing to do. Any way Tony looked at it, it seemed like the horrifically wrong thing to do.

He sprinted up the slight incline in the road that led back to the highway, breathing hard, sweat dripping from every inch of his body, knowing that no matter how hard he ran, he'd never outrun the voice in his head that told him his father had only done the best he could. The voice that insisted it was Tony who was selfish for wanting his father to have ended things differently. Had he been so into his career that anything his father said to him would have been met with his own disgruntled stubbornness? Were his father's suggestions of getting a college degree as a backup plan *that* unreasonable?

It was the way he said it. Demeaning and demanding.

Was it?

He crossed Route 6 and ran into Seaside, slowing to a jog as he passed Bella's cottage and walking after he passed Jenna's. He listened for the girls' voices and heard Amy's laughter above the others. His lips curved up. What would his father have really thought of his relationship with Amy? He'd loved Amy like a daughter. He'd loved them all like they were his children.

As Tony passed the pool and Amy's cottage came into view, he realized the enormity of how he'd twisted his thoughts over the years. How just eight short weeks had warped his view of the man his father had been. And he wondered how much of that convoluted view had impacted Amy's desire to keep their relationship a secret that summer. Even if his father had known about them, it wouldn't have changed the outcome of her pregnancy—but it might have changed her decision to send Tony away, despite her concerns about her own father.

Chapter Eighteen

THE DRIVE TO Rhode Island was solemn. Every time Amy stole a glance at Tony, his jaw was working itself over and his brows were knitted together, as if he were deep in thought. She'd tried to make small talk with a comment about the weather and asked about his morning run, but his one-word answers only solidified her thoughts. He needed mental space for what they were about to do, which left Amy with way too much time to mull over her own predicaments.

She was finally in the position she'd always dreamed of. She and Tony were a couple, and a happy one. She'd built a successful career and managed to remain sane while being so crazy in love with him over the years that she'd doodled *Amy Black* like a schoolgirl, complete with little hearts. There were other versions, too. *Amy Maples Black, Mrs. Tony Black, Tony Black's wife*. If she didn't know herself, she'd think she had stalker tendencies. But she did know herself, and she simply loved him. Every bit of him, quirks and all. And Tony *did* have quirks.

He pushed himself harder than any man she'd ever met. He held himself to standards that seemed impossible to achieve, and yet he always seemed to make them look easy. He put her on a pedestal that she definitely did not deserve. That was a super-big quirk in her book. But she knew she couldn't change the way he viewed her any more than he could convince her that he wasn't the best and only man for her.

She gazed out the window as they turned off the highway and drove into town. She'd been to Tony's hometown and to his parents' home a few times when they were younger. Their parents had gotten together around the holidays, but around the time that Amy was nine or ten, they'd stopped making the trips. She never knew why and had never thought to ask. Now it no longer mattered.

Tony stopped at a red light and squeezed Amy's hand.

"I'm glad you suggested this, and I'm glad you came with me." The tension in his jaw eased, but his eyes were still shadowed with worry.

"Thanks. I hope it helps." She took a deep breath, thinking of the decisions she still had to make, about her job and surfing with Tony. Could she do that? She hadn't even thought of getting back on a surfboard since that horrible afternoon.

When the light changed, Tony turned his attention back to the road. His teeth clenched again, but his hand remained linked to Amy's. He'd worn a gray O'Neill T-shirt and a pair of khaki hybrid shorts, shorts made to be worn in the water as a bathing suit or on land as regular shorts. His hair was a bit unruly, which Amy loved because it suited her man so well. *My man.* She loved thinking about him in those terms. He was not what she'd call *tame.* Sometimes it surprised her that she'd been so attracted to him. Not because he wasn't more delicious than a triple-scoop ice-cream sundae, but because she was reserved and a little conservative and careful. She was plain vanilla and he was honey-jalapeno kitty-kitty bang-bang. And somehow they blended together with the perfect combination of sweet and spicy.

Sweet Heat. Leanna's new flavor. Maybe it was kismet that Leanna came up with the new flavor at the same time that she and Tony reunited. Or maybe Amy was just distracting herself from thinking about the job she'd accepted, surfing again with Tony, and visiting his father's grave.

TONY PARKED IN the lot nearest his father's grave and cut the engine. He felt Amy's eyes on him and was glad she wasn't one of those pushy women who couldn't stand silence. She seemed to know when he needed to be left alone to process his own thoughts and when to reach out. She was in tune with him in so many ways, like knowing he needed to do this when he hadn't even realized it himself.

He squeezed her hand, then silently stepped from the car and opened her door. He crouched beside her and took her hand.

"I want you to know that I can't think of another person I could do this with, or who I would want to do this with."

She smiled and touched his cheek. He loved her gentle touch.

"Thank you. There are so many things from our past that feel huge, aren't there? Like they've been looming over us forever?" Her hair fell in front of her eyes, and she tucked it behind her ear. "I'm glad we're trying to deal with them."

"Me too. I guess I never realized how present they still were." He pulled her to her feet and held her close. "All this stuff we're going through and trying to understand will only make us stronger."

They walked hand in hand down the narrow concrete path toward his father's grave. Tony's hands began to sweat. He wiped them on his shorts and tried to ignore the way his throat constricted. They stopped at the edge of the path near a large oak tree casting a shadow over his father's headstone.

Tony remembered the day of the funeral. It had rained that morning, and the ground had been wet when they'd gathered around the grave site beneath a blue awning. He'd sat beside his mother, both dressed in black, both trying to present a brave front. Tony hadn't moved during the service. Not an inch. He'd hardly remembered to breathe, and then they'd lowered his father's casket into the earth, and he'd felt a piece of himself go down with him. He'd reached for his mother's hand, to keep himself grounded in reality. He remembered wishing Amy were sitting beside him instead of so far away and feeling conflicted for thinking about her during a time when he should have been focused on the loss of his father.

Amy stroked his arm, pulling him from the painful memories.

He took her hand, and together they crossed the lawn to his father's headstone. He crouched in front of the rose-colored marble and waited for sorrow to swamp him. He felt Amy's hand on his shoulder. He reached up and touched her slender fingers and waited some more. He drew in a deep breath, anticipating the weight of sadness or anger. For tears, the inability to breathe, or the urge to scream.

Nothing changed.

Nada.

Zilch.

Amy crouched beside him and placed her hand on his thigh.

Her green eyes were full of compassion, and there he was feeling…normal.

"You okay?" she asked.

He nodded, not trusting himself to speak. He reached out and traced his father's name on the headstone. *Jack Black.* His mouth quirked up in a smile.

"Jack Frigging Black."

"Well, yeah. That was his name."

Tony covered his mouth, not wanting to seem insincere in front of Amy as his mind linked his father to the comedic actor for the first time ever, but he was barely able to cover his smile. The whole situation suddenly seemed absurd. When a laugh bubbled from his lungs, he sank down to his butt and pulled his knees up, tried again to cover his mouth, and finally gave in to the laughter.

"What is so funny?" Amy sat down beside him.

"This. All of it."

Amy's eyes grew serious. "I don't follow."

"Amy, my dad was a great guy. I mean, he really was a great guy. He taught me everything I know."

"Yeah, but that summer…"

"That summer he was a jerk, and I was probably a stubborn jackass who thought he was going to be the world's best surfer. I didn't care what he thought about my career choice." He took Amy's hand in his. "Amy, I was twenty. All I wanted was to spend time with you and surf. That was it. Anything else was an inconvenience."

"Yeah, but why is that funny?"

"Because look at the whole situation. I was twenty years old and *still* spending the summer with my family. Who does that? Twenty-year-olds are out working internships or they're spending summers drinking and hanging out with friends. And there I was, a young man, trying to live a sane summer in a three-bedroom cottage with my parents. Ridiculous."

"But..."

"Do you know why I even went to the Cape that summer?" He didn't wait for her to answer. "I went because I knew you'd be there. I went because I thought I was a mini celebrity and you'd finally notice me. And then we hid our relationship—from everyone. My head was so messed up by all of it. It's no wonder I wiped every memory I had of my father being this great guy from my mind. I blamed him for us keeping the relationship secret as much as I blamed your father. I was pissed and in love and I was *twenty*. You can't live with your parents for eight weeks at that age. Not as a man. Twenty-year-old men are all testosterone and attitude. They have no business being under the same roof as their parents for more than three days, tops."

Amy crossed her legs and folded her arms across her chest. "Well, I liked who you were, and I didn't appreciate the things I heard him say to you."

"That's because you loved me, babe. You wouldn't have wanted anyone to say things that opposed my choices, the same way that I would have gone to the ends of the earth to keep anyone from saying things that went against your dreams. I'm not saying my father isn't guilty of doing all those things we've talked about. I'm just saying that I see the situation more clearly. I understand a little more why he wasn't himself."

He smiled to let her know how much lighter he felt.

"I wasn't just avoiding dealing with my father's death all these years. I was avoiding dealing with us, who we were. Because dealing with who we were would have meant taking a chance that you really didn't want me anymore and that I was holding out hope for something that might not ever come to fruition."

Amy bumped him with her shoulder. "I call bull on you with that one. I made it clear how much I wanted you for all these years. I practically drooled every time I saw you."

"Yeah, but you were drinking every time you acted like you wanted me in that way. I didn't trust that it was real."

"*Tsk!* How can that be? I thought guys were all about taking it when they could get it." She turned away. "You turned me down so many times, it's a wonder I got up the courage to keep trying."

He ran his finger down her cheek, bringing her attention back to him.

"Because, kitten." Every hint of humor left him as his tone turned serious. "You sent me away once without ever looking back. I couldn't take a chance that you'd do that again. It would have killed me."

"Or maybe it would have saved us both," she said with a pouty frown.

Saved us both. He wasn't sure if she meant that chancing it would have saved them years of heartache because they would have worked things out, or something else, and he didn't care. He couldn't change the past, but he could build on their lightened mood.

He pulled her into his lap, his voice thick with sarcasm. "Maybe if I had gone to college I would have known that."

"Yeah, because a finance or business degree would have helped you to understand girls a little better." She batted her eyelashes playfully.

"Or a marketing degree. It takes a bit of sales knowledge to really understand things like retail therapy, which I'm sure you'll need at some point."

Amy touched her forehead to his and smiled. His world righted itself again.

She mimicked his sarcasm. "If only you'd listened to your father."

"If only…"

Their lips met, and Tony savored the kiss. They were sitting on the lawn of the cemetery beside his father's grave and making out like he had just come back from war. In a way, he felt as though he had. Fourteen years was way too long to have such a skewed view of his father. It upset him that he'd carried around all those bad feelings for so long for a man who might not have handled things well at the end of his life, but really, who was Tony to decide the appropriate way to handle one's mortality?

He had a lot of healing to do. They both did. At least now he felt as though he saw things a little more clearly. He needed to forgive his father in order to move forward with Amy. And while the path to forgiveness might be cloudy and dark, he had Amy to help him find his way.

Chapter Nineteen

OVER THE NEXT few days Amy noticed a lightening in Tony, from the way he walked to the look in his eyes. He'd shared memories of his father that made them laugh and cry. It wasn't an easy undoing of Tony's feelings from that harsh summer's end, but it was a start, and Tony seemed open to dealing with his feelings rather than repressing them. Unlike Amy, who was doing all she could to ignore her upcoming meeting with Duke and to avoid going surfing with Tony. Not to mention dealing with her father. *One thing at a time.*

She and Jenna spent Thursday morning at the Wellfleet Library, looking through the romance novels. If only life was as pretty as Nora Roberts or Susan Mallery painted it to be.

"I think I'm going to start reading erotica." Jenna set a paperback on the display table, then straightened the other books so the spines were all facing in the same direction.

"Erotica?" Amy shook her head.

"Uh-huh. You know, to make sure Pete and I don't get bored in the bedroom." Jenna reached for a copy of *Fifty Shades of Grey*.

"So, you're suddenly into bondage? Do they make leather bras that will fit your Beyoncé boobs?"

Jenna laughed. "I don't want bondage! Don't you think they have some other ideas?"

"How would I know?" Amy leaned her hip against the table. "Are you and Pete having trouble?"

"No way. We have more sex than should be legal. Good sex, too. But how do you know if you're boring a guy or not? I mean, I've never slept with a guy for a whole year before." Jenna flipped through the paperback. "I could never get bored of Pete, and he says he will never tire of me, but..." She set the book down, perfectly lined up with the others, and whispered, "I just want to make sure, you know?"

"Well, you're barking up the wrong tree. I've been with one man, so everything I know, I basically learned from him. Or, you know, hands-on research."

Jenna laughed.

"Besides, the way Pete is always all over you, I don't think you have to worry. He's so in love with you. You could lie there and not move and he'd be happy just to be close to you."

"Yeah, I am pretty incredible." Jenna threw her head back and laughed so loud two women looked up from a nearby table. She slapped her hand over her mouth. "Sorry," she whispered.

They moved to another display of books.

"Can I ask you something else?" Jenna asked.

"Sure, not that I was any help on your first question."

"Wasn't it hard for you all those years, knowing Tony was seeing other women? I mean, we've all seen the pictures of him in the surf magazines. There were always women around him."

Amy closed her eyes for a beat. That was one of her tender spots. She hated thinking about any other woman in Tony's arms, but she'd turned him away. She couldn't blame him for taking comfort in the arms of another...or many others. She took a minute to rein in her jealousy before answering.

"Every time I saw him in a magazine with a girl, I used the picture as a dart board."

Jenna laughed. "And how'd you do?"

"Let's just say that I started out as an amateur, and I'm now an expert."

"See? Spin it positive. Now you have more skills."

Amy rolled her eyes.

"You know Pete was with plenty of women before we got together. My take on it is that we should hold our heads up high. They may have played the field, but we're the ones they'll come home to for the rest of their lives."

"I agree. Besides, they've dated enough women to know what they really want." Even though Amy hadn't needed to date anyone else to know that Tony was the only man she'd ever want. She was kind of glad to know Tony'd had his choice of women before her and that he'd chosen her out of all of them.

"Ames, how are you *really* holding up?" Jenna's voice softened. "I'm here to talk if you want to talk about what happened…you know. That summer."

"I'm good, actually. I never realized how hard it was to carry around that secret for so long. I'm glad I told you guys and even happier that Tony and I have talked about it."

"But?"

Amy raised her brows.

"Come on. I see something behind those green eyes. What is it?"

"You do not. I'm fine." *Liar, liar.*

Jenna stepped closer and stared up at Amy.

"You're intimidating for a shrimp," Amy teased.

"I may be short in stature, but I'm tall in determination.

Fess up. What's going on?"

"I just..." Amy pulled Jenna over to the corner of the library. "Tony wants me to go surfing."

Jenna arched a brow. "And?"

"The last time I went surfing was when...was that last afternoon that summer. Remember? I told you I wiped out and lost the baby?"

"Oh, right. I'm sorry, Ames. I don't know what I was thinking." Jenna's eyes grew serious. "But you're not pregnant now, so..." She gasped. "Wait. Are you?"

"Goodness, no. But the whole thing is kind of scary."

"Tony won't let you get hurt."

"No, not that kind of scary. Just...I don't know how to explain it. What if it all comes back to me and I totally freak out?" Amy crossed her arms to give her wobbly legs stability. She lowered her voice again. "What if I have a panic attack or something?"

"So what if you do?" Jenna took her hand. "Honey, you'll have Tony right there with you. He's proved he loves you a million times over, hasn't he? He waited as long for you as you did for him, even after you tossed him aside like yesterday's news."

"Hey." She swatted Jenna's arm.

"I'm just teasing, but really. If you panic, you panic. So what? So he holds you and tells you everything's going to be okay, and you know what?"

"Yeah. I know *what.* Everything will be okay. In my heart I know it will be okay. I'm just overthinking again, I'm sure." Amy sighed. "We're going to the beach at high tide today, and I know he's going to ask me to surf. Thank you, Jenna. Thanks for reminding me about what I really need to focus on. Tony will be right there. Even if I freak out, I won't be freaking out alone." *Now if I could only figure out my job situation.* Baby steps.

On their way back to their car, they spotted Theresa coming out of the market.

"Oh geez. I bet she hates us," Amy said under her breath, feigning a smile as Theresa headed in their direction.

"She might hate Bella, but probably not us."

Theresa met them in front of Town Hall. "I thought you girls would be at the beach today. It's gorgeous out, isn't it?" She squinted up at the sky.

"We're going later this afternoon when the tide's in. Why aren't you enjoying the sun?" Amy couldn't remember ever seeing Theresa wearing a bathing suit besides the thong she'd worn to one-up Bella's prank last summer, and that was an image she'd like to forget. Theresa typically wore something similar to what she had on now, a pair of pleated shorts and a polo shirt.

"I just had to pick up some groceries." Theresa jiggled her grocery bag. "I thought I'd do a little weeding around the fire pit today."

"Thank you for doing that," Jenna said. "It always looks so nice."

"Are you up for a couple weeks or just a few days?" Amy asked.

"I'll be here for a few weeks this time." Theresa turned her attention toward the street. "Assuming I'm not arrested anytime soon."

Jenna and Amy exchanged a *holy cow* glance.

"Theresa, I'm sorry about Bella." Amy stepped into Theresa's field of vision as Jenna grabbed Amy's arm.

After a minute of uncomfortable silence, Theresa finally turned toward Amy with a stoic look on her face. "No need to be sorry. I love Bella's mischievous soul, but she'll get hers." She stepped off the curb and headed for the parking lot across the street, turning once to wave with a wry smile.

"Yikes," Amy said. "I think Bella's in trouble."

TONY STOOD AT the edge of the water with one arm around Amy and her surfboard in the other. She looked incredibly sexy in her blue bikini, but he felt tension rolling off of her. When they were packing for the beach, she'd told him she was ready to try to surf again. As much as he wanted to share every aspect of his life with Amy, he'd never push her toward anything that he didn't feel she could handle. He knew she was nervous about surfing again, and he also knew it had nothing to do with skill and everything to do with the memories tied to her last wipeout.

"Ames, you don't have to do this." He pulled her against his side. "We can go our whole lives without surfing together."

Her eyes pooled with emotion, causing his own to break like a tidal wave, bowling him over but not pulling him under. He felt more stable than he had since he'd lost her fourteen years ago, and he knew what he'd spent the morning planning was exactly what he wanted, regardless of how today's foray into surfing ended up.

"I know we can," Amy said. "But it's time to put our past behind us. I loved surfing with you that summer. It was invigorating, and I felt like I was sharing in the most special part of your life. I want that again."

He kissed her softly. "Babe, you're the most special and the most important part of my life."

She shifted her eyes to the water, and he felt her body stiffen. He tried to ease her tension with a distraction.

"Happy ten-day anniversary of our first kiss in fourteen years."

Her brows drew together as her eyes shifted in his direction again. "It's our ten-day anniversary of our kiss?"

He nodded. "And I'm taking you to dinner tonight to celebrate. Just the two of us."

"Tony, the fact that you even *know* how many days ago we had our first kiss feels like a celebration." She wrapped her arms around his waist and pressed her cheek to his chest. "I love you so much."

His heart swelled, knowing she was ready to move forward and they were both done hiding from the past.

With a loud exhalation, Amy stepped away and reached for the surfboard.

"Shall we get this over with?"

"Don't sound so enthusiastic," he teased.

Amy carried the long surfboard, and the sight threw Tony back in time. He pictured her at eighteen, smiling as she ran into the waves, wincing at the frigid water just as she was now.

"I told you to wear a wet suit." He shook his head. She'd refused to wear one that summer, too.

"I told you how I feel about that." She laid flat on the board and began to paddle out with Tony swimming by her side, one strong hand stabilizing the surfboard. "I look more like a seal if I'm wearing black."

"Babe, you're so hot that a shark would be too busy drooling to bite you." He pushed her out past the waves with a grin that he had no chance of stifling. *His* Amy was braving the waves again.

For him.

For us.

He loved her so much.

They were beyond the breaking point, waiting for the right wave to roll in. Tony was nervous for her, and he wondered if her mind was wrapped around that fateful day or if she was thinking only of this very second. He was going to ask, but he wanted her focused on now, and with the slight chance that she was, he didn't want to distract her. She'd need every bit of her focus to be able to stand up on the board again.

She flashed a nervous smile, and a conflicting mischievous spark filled her eyes.

Yeah, she was nervous, and excited, and he loved knowing her thrill of surfing hadn't been lost. Tony watched the waves building in strength. He touched Amy's calf and felt her trembling, probably from the cold and the fear of being away from the board for so many years.

"You okay, kitten? This one looks good."

Her green eyes took on the fierce determination that had surprised him years earlier.

"Oh, yeah. I've got this."

He hoped so. "Okay. I'll be right there with you, babe. Concentrate. You've got this."

She nodded, and he swam away, giving her room and watching her like a hawk as the wave swelled, lifting her board. Amy grabbed the edge of the board.

"Come on, baby, pop up," he urged through gritted teeth.

In one explosive motion she pushed her body up and tucked her feet beneath her. Tony held his breath. One foot slid forward as the wave rose, tipped her board, and knocked Amy into the sea. Tony swam as fast as he could, reaching her in seconds. She coughed and sputtered as he held her around her waist, keeping her head above the surface.

"It's okay. I've got you." He was so proud of her for trying. He kicked his feet to keep them afloat and snagged her board with one hand while holding her against him. "You're the bravest woman I know. That was awesome."

She laughed and pushed from his chest. "That sucked, and I'm going to do better. And yeah, I'm brave. But then again, I have a boyfriend to keep up with."

He pressed his lips to hers, trapping their laughter. "No panicky feelings?"

"None, and I'm as shocked as you are." She was breathing hard, kicking to help them stay up. "No panic other than being afraid I won't get up on the board today."

"You're amazing."

They paddled out again, and Amy tried to catch the next few waves, each time tumbling into the water with Tony there seconds later to help her.

"I'm going to get this next one," she assured him through trembling blue lips.

"Babe, I could do this all day long, but you might want to take a break and warm up." He was paddling alongside her board, and when she narrowed her eyes and glared at him, he held his hands up in surrender.

The next wave swelled much larger than the last. "Amy?" he warned.

She shooed him away, jaw clenched, eyes trained on the water. Her board lifted with the swell, and her fingers wrapped tightly around the edges of the board. She pushed her body up and her feet tucked under, left foot leading as she popped up with a little scream of joy.

"Yeah!" Tony hollered.

Amy maintained her balance, her arms loose and extended, leaning slightly forward, lowering her center of gravity just as he'd taught her. Tony punched the air in excitement. *His* Amy was back. *Really back*.

And this time he was never letting her go.

Chapter Twenty

THE NIGHT COULDN'T have been more perfect if Amy had dreamed it up. She and Tony were sitting on a blanket at the top of the dunes at Race Point, named for the fierce rip tides that came around the point of the Cape. Tony had picked up dinner from Mac's Seafood. They'd shared oysters and mussels, a plate of seafood lasagna, and were working their way through a bottle of wine. Amy was thinking about how long she'd loved Tony and what he'd come to mean to her. He was her quiet strength, the one person who really knew and understood her. Her girlfriends knew and understood her in other ways, but only Tony knew just how to touch her when she was nervous or scared or when she needed to be held. Only Tony had felt the sheer power of their love that summer and the brutal intensity of their loss.

She realized that it was more than just love that kept her from connecting with other men all this time. Their loss bound them together in a way that she now realized left a hole that only Tony could fill. Their past would always be there—a part of them. She hadn't become pregnant because she was a reckless teenager out having a one-night stand, and she didn't need to pick it apart any more than they already had. It happened. They survived it, and maybe they were better people because of it. Maybe it had to happen in order for them to come together at the right time in their lives. In any case, now it was time to move on.

As if reading her mind, Tony covered her fingers with his. He smiled, then gazed out at the water, his features more relaxed than she'd seen all summer. In fact, he looked more relaxed than he had in many summers. His white linen pants were rolled up above his ankles. His loose short-sleeve, button-down shirt revealed a tanned swatch of his chest, and his eyes—oh, how she loved the way they told of all his emotions—were no longer shadowed with grief.

"Thank you for today." She set her wineglass down and curled her fingers around his.

"You were amazing out there. I'd almost forgotten how determined you could be."

She raised her brows and tucked her hair behind her ear, trying to give him a don't-underestimate-me look but also feeling proud of herself. So very proud.

"Almost as determined as I can be." His tone was gravelly as he leaned across the blanket and kissed her.

"I did learn from the best," she teased.

They finished their wine, and Tony gathered their things in his backpack, then rose to his feet and reached for her hand.

"I have a surprise for you. I'm not sure if you're going to like it or not, but it's something I wanted to do, and it's something I wanted to share with you."

"Tony Black, you have a worried look in your eyes. Is it dirty?" She narrowed her eyes, feigning seriousness, while anticipation rushed through her veins.

He leaned so close she could smell the wine on his breath.

"No, kitten. It's not dirty. But if you'd like, I can conjure up some dirty surprises for you, too." He pressed his lips to hers again.

"I'm...open on that front. With you, I mean," she whispered, feeling embarrassed and brave at the same time.

He kissed her again. "Well, then," he said in a husky voice, "I'll have to keep that in mind." He folded her in his arms. "But for now I would like to go up to the top of the lighthouse and release a paper lantern in honor of my father."

Her body melted against him. "Tony, I would be honored to share that moment with you."

He touched his forehead to hers and closed his eyes. He smelled like man and summer and love all wrapped up in one sensual scent.

"Kitten, I also want to release a lantern for the child we lost."

Amy's breath caught in her throat. Tears dampened her eyes as she reached deep inside herself and forced her voice to work.

"Tony," she whispered.

"Too much?"

"No." Tears slipped down her cheeks. "Perfect," was all she could manage. She buried her face in his chest and soaked up his comfort and strength like a sponge.

They put their stuff in the car and Tony grabbed a bag from the backseat.

"How did you arrange this? It's only open twice a year," she asked as a young, clean-cut man opened the lighthouse for them.

As they ascended the red circular staircase toward the top of the lighthouse, the weight of Tony's protective hand on her back helped keep Amy grounded in the moment. She kept one hand on the brick wall and the other on the railing. Her heart raced as they stepped through the door and into the cool air on the balcony at the top of the lighthouse.

"Let's just say that I owe Caden big-time. He has a friend with the US Coast Guard, and they arranged for Kyle to let us in."

Tony set down the bag with the sky lanterns in it and took her in his arms again. She fisted her hands in his shirt for stability, feeling emotionally overwhelmed by what they were about to do. He brushed her hair from her shoulders and kissed her sweetly.

"You okay?"

She nodded and opened her mouth to answer, but no words came.

"It's okay. Let's take a moment and just be together." He held her close and she closed her eyes, reveling in his understanding and love.

She felt him lift his head and clung to him like she was never going to let go. She toyed with the idea of trying to get away with that and imagined herself clinging to him while he surfed. She smiled at the ridiculous thought and forced herself to ease her grip and look out over the water.

"Wow. This is just beautiful." She looked up at Tony and felt so in love that she had to hang on to him again. She realized that the love they had now was even more intense than their first love, in a more mature way. It was the type of love that she knew she could count on in good times and bad. The type of love she'd never, ever hide again, for anyone or for any reason. This was true, grown-up love.

"This whole night is beautiful. Thank you, Tony, for not forgetting about me even after I told you to go away. Thanks for loving me."

He pressed his hands to her cheeks and kissed her. "Babe, I have and always will love you, and I'll never leave you again, even if you try to push me out the door."

They embraced, and a long while later Tony retrieved the lanterns from the bag. One paper sky lantern was pale green and the other was white. They looked like regular decorative paper lanterns, but they were much larger, with something square attached by four strings on the open bottom.

Tony held up the white lantern and pointed to the square.

"This is the fuel cell. We'll light it, and the heat will carry the lantern into the sky. I bought white for my father and green for..."

"For our child." She didn't know how those words had come so easily, but as his eyes grew serious, the words felt right, and they no longer scared her. "It was a good choice."

"Yeah," he whispered. "Should we light my father's first?"

"Yes." She drew in a deep breath, feeling more and more like they were doing the right thing. She held the lantern while Tony lit the flame. Then he took the lantern from her hands and held it up to catch the air.

"Do you want to say something?" She settled her hand on his lower back, hoping to offer him the same comforting touch as he'd given her.

The muscles in his jaw bunched and his biceps flexed as he lifted the lantern higher.

"I love you, Dad, and I hope you're looking down at me and you're as proud to be my father as I am to be your son." He released the lantern, and it floated up toward the stars. The wind carried it out over the water.

Amy wrapped her arms around him again. "I'm sure he is

very proud of you."

"Yeah. I think he is."

Tony kissed the top of her head, then retrieved the other lantern.

"Time to leave the past behind and focus on our future." She meant every word.

"Our past will always be a part of us. Who knows? Maybe if we hadn't gone through such a hard time, we wouldn't be together right now. The world works in strange ways."

"Can I light this one?" Amy wanted to take an active part in letting the past go and freeing herself from the guilt and pain that came with it. Yes, it would always be a part of them, but it didn't have to outweigh who they were now or the future they were meant to have.

"Of course." He handed her the lighter and held the pale green lantern up. When it was lit, he waited for her to hold it with him, and together they waited for the wind to catch it and carry it away. When they felt the pull of gravity, they released their hold, and Tony folded her against his side as they watched it float into the night.

"I'll never forget what we went through," Amy said quietly. "But I'll never hide it or fear it again. I want to honor all the feelings we ever feel from now on."

Tony nodded. His eyes were damp as he slid a hand in his pocket, then sank to one knee.

Amy glanced down at him, wondering what he was doing. He took her hands in his and smiled up at her.

"Tony?" Her pulse sped up. "What are you doing?" *Holy cow...Are you...?*

"Exactly what you probably think I'm doing. What I wish I would have had the chance to do that summer. Amy Maples, kitten, my sweet girl." He kissed the back of her hands. "Will you marry me?"

Marry you? Marry you! Yes! Yes! Ohmygosh! She lost the ability to speak, could barely remember to breathe.

"We'll have the family we were always meant to have. We'll spend summers here with our kids."

She fell to her knees beside him, unable to stand, for her legs had turned to jelly. *Yes, I want to marry you!* She opened her mouth, but what came out wasn't what she expected. "What about the job, and...?"

His eyes darkened, full of love and hope so palpable it practically reached out and embraced her.

"You can take the job with Duke. I'll go with you. We'll make it work."

"Take the...You...I..." She blinked away tears of happiness. "We've only been together a short while and you'd change your life that much for me?"

"We've only been together a short while, but we've loved each other for a lifetime. Yes, I'll change everything for you." He kissed the corners of her mouth, then pressed a soft kiss to the center of her lips, while she sat there, numb, trembling, and elated.

"I don't want you to put your life on hold for me, babe. You've done enough of that to last a lifetime. It's your turn to follow your dreams, and I'll support whatever they are. I know we can make this work, even if you work in Australia." He kissed her knuckles. "Just say yes, and I promise you that we'll figure everything else out. I'll make sure your life is amazing."

"Yes. Yes. Oh, Tony. Yes!" She launched herself into his lap, bowling them both over as she covered his face in kisses. "Yes." She kissed him again. "Yes." And again. "Yes." And again.

He laughed against her lips and sat up with her in his arms. He took her trembling hand in his and opened his fist, which she hadn't even noticed he'd clenched. She felt her eyes widen at the sight of the rose-gold square-cut diamond ring in his hand.

"Tony, is that…?"

He nodded and slid it on her finger. It was a perfect fit. "I bought it before I went to see you at your dorm, intending to ask you to marry me."

Tears streamed down her cheeks. *You were going to ask me to marry you?* "Oh, Tony…" She looked at the ring again. They'd seen it in a little jewelry shop in Provincetown that summer, and she'd said that she hoped when she got married her husband would know to buy her that ring. She couldn't believe he'd bought it. She could barely breathe past the lump in her throat.

"When my mother gave me the cottage, I put it in the safe. It's been here ever since, waiting for you."

She wept openly, unable to speak but wanting to say so much. His mother had given him the cottage the year after his father died. She'd said the memories were too much for her. *It's been here for all these years?*

"Amy, you've made me the happiest man on earth, and I meant what I said. Whatever you decide about work, I'll be there to support you every step of the way."

She forced her brain to fire. "What…what about your competitions and…?" She paused to wipe her tears.

"I'll make it work."

The truth and worry poured out without her permission. "But I don't want to live apart while you travel and compete, and if I take that job…" She couldn't ask him not to compete. What was she saying?

"We won't, babe. We'll figure it out. I don't have to compete in every competition. I've won all there is to win. The rest is gravy. Now it's time for us. I want this more than I've ever wanted anything in my entire life." He must have seen the question in her eyes, because he added, "Including surfing."

Honesty was evident in the sincerity of his voice and the depths of his eyes.

"And I know you and the girls wanted to have a group wedding. If you want to get married with them, that's fine. If you want to go to the justice of the peace tomorrow, I'm in. If you want a big wedding on a tropical island, I'm there."

"I don't need a tropical island. A nice quiet wedding on the beach with the girls would be another dream come true."

"If that's what you want, then that's what we'll do. All I ask is that you marry me soon, because I'm not taking a chance that you change that brilliant mind of yours."

Amy touched her forehead to his, knowing there wasn't a chance that she'd change her mind.

Chapter Twenty-One

FRIDAY MORNING TONY was up before the sun, but not to run off unwanted stress. They planned on telling their friends about their engagement over breakfast, and he knew that once the news was out, the girls would monopolize Amy's time until after the wedding took place. She still hadn't spoken with her father, and he wondered when she would get around to it, but he didn't want to pressure her. He knew it was going to be a difficult conversation for her, and he also knew Amy well enough to know that when she was ready, she'd take charge of that situation just as she had of getting his attention before Jamie's wedding. Right now he wanted a few quiet minutes alone with her before the wedding became their focus.

She was lying beside him in her bed, one arm stretched out under her head, the other draped over his stomach. Her hair fell away from her face in golden streaks across the back of the pink nightshirt he'd given her over the winter. He could see the tail of the kitten that was imprinted on the front of the shirt. On the front the kitten was curled into a ball with one eye open with the words *Stroke me* above the kitty and *I'm into heavy petting* beneath.

He was already thinking about where they'd live if she took

the job with Duke. Tony owned houses on the East and West Coasts, as well as the cottage on the Cape. Adding a house in Australia was fine with him, as long as Amy was happy. He worried about her being that far away from her friends. Not that Amy saw them much between summers, but now that all the other girls were living at the Cape full-time, he wondered if she'd rather be there with them. They were as close as family to both of them. He was thinking about how to ask her without sounding as though he would rather not move to Australia when she lifted her pretty face and smiled up at him from beneath her long lashes, and his thoughts fell away.

"Tony?" She laced her hand with his.

"Hm?"

"What if we get married and I get pregnant and..." She lowered her voice. "And I lose the baby again?"

He went up on one elbow so he could look at her face. "Hopefully, that's not going to happen. We'll be more careful—no surfing if you're pregnant—and we'll talk to your doctor and see if that seems like it's something we should be worried about."

"I have. He said he didn't see any medical reason for me to be at risk of another miscarriage."

A slice of relief cut through him. "Well, does it scare you? Would you rather not try to have children? Because as much as I'd adore biological children, I'll adore adopted children just as much."

Amy smiled. "No. I want to try, but thank you. I just don't want to disappoint you."

He brought her hand to his lips and kissed her knuckles. "Babe, you could never disappoint me. My love for you is unconditional. If we have children, wonderful. If we adopt, beautiful. And if it's just you and me for the rest of our lives, it'll be just as perfect."

"You wouldn't feel like you were missing out on something?" She searched his eyes, and he hoped she saw the truth in them.

"I've missed out for fourteen years." He kissed her and held her close. "I love you, Amy. I want a life with you. Kids are a bonus."

"I want the bonus deal," she said against his chest. "A couple times over."

He leaned back and smiled. "Then you're going to get the bonus deal. As many times as you want. And, baby, if what happened before happens again, we'll deal with it together. I'm not letting you turn me away again, and there's no way I'm going anywhere. That's a promise."

BABIES, BABIES, BABIES. That was all Amy could think about after she and Tony talked about having children earlier that morning. Now, hours later, surrounded by all their friends while they ate breakfast on Bella's deck, Amy was looking at each of her girlfriends and wondering what she'd feel like if they could have babies and she couldn't. If they had baby bumps beneath their sundresses and she was the only one with a pitifully flat stomach, would she resent them? No. She'd like to believe she would never be so petty, but the heart could be petty. Her dart-board practice confirmed that much.

"I still can't believe we're all getting married," Bella said.

"Well, almost all of us," Sky said as she French braided Jenna's hair.

"No need to rush things, sis." Pete gave Sky a brotherly narrow-eyed gaze, then reached down and petted Joey.

Jenna smacked his thigh. "She's twenty-five, Pete. She can do whatever she wants."

"I'm in no rush, thank you very much. I'm having fun just hanging out." Sky finished braiding Jenna's hair and patted Jenna's back so she knew she was free to move. "When will you guys get married? My friend Lizzie owns a flower shop in P-town. I bet she'd love to handle the bouquets."

"That would be awesome," Jenna said. "We need to coordinate dresses, flowers...*shoes*."

"Uh oh, here she goes. OCD Central coming through," Bella teased. "And this one over here can't stop looking at her engagement ring." She nodded at Amy.

"Do you blame me?" Amy held her hand out and wiggled her fingers. Tony squeezed her thigh. He was sitting beside her with the same ridiculously happy grin he'd had on his face all morning.

"It is gorgeous." Sky took a closer look at the ring.

"I don't know about you guys, but I would really like a simple wedding," Leanna said. "I have to leave for the flea market, so let me just lodge my vote. Beach wedding, casual dresses, just us."

"Whoa, babe." Kurt petted Pepper, who was cuddled up in his lap. "While that sounds more than perfect to me, I think my sister and mother might have an issue with not being there." He set Pepper on the ground, and Pepper ran directly to Amy and rolled over.

Amy petted his belly and Joey nosed her way into the petting action.

"Oh, right. Well, I guess my family might want to be there,

too." Leanna looked at the others. "And I can't imagine all of y'all's families won't want to be there, too."

Pete groaned.

Sky laughed. "Yeah, they'll want to be there. Dad would be mad if he missed it. And trust me, Hunter, Matt, and Grayson will want to witness the first Lacroux to take the plunge."

"My parents, too," Caden added.

Tony took a sip of coffee and glanced at Amy. "Babe, your parents will want to be there, too. I think this wedding is getting much bigger than we thought."

"But…everyone waited for us to get married," Amy said.

"Jamie and Jessica didn't," Bella reminded her.

"Well, Jamie wasn't really included in the three of you holding out, but I think Jamie was afraid I'd never get engaged, and he was so ready to marry Jessica anyway. I think it was hard for him to wait as long as he did." Amy thought about what kind of wedding she really wanted. When she thought of marrying Tony, the only image that came to mind was all of the Seaside gang, on the beach, getting married at the same time. She looked around the table, and no matter how hard she tried to skew the wedding in her head to include all the families, it didn't work.

"I think I have an idea," she said, and all eyes turned to her. "What about if we have our private beach wedding. Just us, and Theresa, of course. She is part of Seaside. We can wait until Jamie and Jessica come back with Vera, and then we can each have another wedding with our own families."

Tony put his arm around her shoulder and tugged her in closer. "Brilliant." He kissed her cheek. "I love that. Our families are important, but you know once we get all the families together, the wedding will become a zoo. Leanna's brother Dae will want to blow something up. Grayson and Hunter will want to construct a steel sculpture to commemorate the day—"

"And you haven't met my sister, Siena," Kurt said. "Siena and my mother will want to be part of the planning, from the dresses to the food."

"Does anyone not like my plan?" Amy scanned her friends' faces. Pete raised his brows to Jenna, who smiled and nodded. Bella and Caden whispered among themselves, and Leanna and Kurt nodded in agreement.

Evan came through the cottage door with a chocolate doughnut in one hand and his cell phone in the other. "I'm all for a beach wedding." He took a bite of his doughnut.

"Well, if Evan's in agreement, it's settled." Tony held his hand up and Evan high-fived him.

"I can handle the music," Evan offered. "And I can video it if you want."

"That would be great," Bella said.

"I have to take off," Leanna said. "This sounds great to me, if Kurt's okay with it."

Kurt patted his leg and Pepper came to his side. He scooped up the pup. "Sounds perfect to me. I get to marry you twice. You guys just let me know what I can do to help, financially or coordinating, whatever. I'm heading over to the bay to write today."

After Kurt and Leanna left, Jenna went into Bella's cottage and came back out with a notepad. "Okay. I'm ready. When do we want to do this?"

Pete, Caden, and Tony exchanged a *Let's get the heck outta here* glance and rose to their feet.

"Anyone else feeling the need to go split some wood or

wrestle a bear?" Tony asked.

"Please." Pete kissed the top of Jenna's head and patted his thigh. Joey bounded to his side. "I can feel my breasts growing from all this girl talk."

"At least you weren't feeling Jenna's while we were sitting here," Sky teased. "Go on, men. We can handle this. We'll tell you where and when to show up."

"Sounds perfect," Caden said. "Come on, Evan. Let's blow this taco stand."

"I'm taking the schooner out. You guys wanna come?" Pete asked.

"Heck, yeah." Tony kissed Amy; then the men headed toward Jenna and Pete's cottage.

"There go our men," Jenna said.

"Your men, my brother," Sky reminded her. "This is going to be so fun. I was thinking, there's this great little shop by my friend Lizzie's florist shop. It's got summer dresses that are fancy enough for a beach wedding, but not crazy fancy, so you can wear them again."

"Sounds like we need a day in Provincetown to go over flowers, dresses…what else?" Jenna scribbled on the notepad.

"Oh, you know what might be fun?" Sky leaned in closer, her tone filled with excitement. "You guys could make a weekend out of it. Have your beach wedding, then take Pete's boat to Nantucket or Martha's Vineyard for a mini-honeymoon."

"We just went to Martha's Vineyard in May." Bella tapped Jenna's arm. "Remember? You and Leanna got those matching bags."

"You did? I didn't hear about that trip." What else had Amy missed out on, and why did she feel like missing out on anything was missing out on too much? She wondered if she was feeling overly sensitive because of her impending move to Australia.

"I thought we told you about it," Bella said. "Remember? We took the night ferry back?"

"And made out like teenagers on the upper deck." Jenna raised her brows in quick succession.

"Made out like teenagers?" Amy felt like she'd been excluded from the prom.

"Don't feel bad, Amy. I wasn't there either." Sky patted her hand.

"Jamie and Jessica will be back next week, but I'm not sure how long they're staying. I know they're bringing Vera," Jenna said. "She should be here with us anyway." She scribbled something on the pad. "I think Pete is meeting a new client the second weekend in August. Do we care if it's a weekend or weekday?"

"I need to check Caden's schedule, and weekends are out because of Leanna's flea-market stuff," Bella reminded her.

"I could run her booth," Sky offered. "Oh, wait, then I'd miss the wedding. But I bet Carey would." Carey ran a booth at the flea market where he sold old records and other music paraphernalia. He and Leanna were close friends.

"Is Carey here this summer?" Amy asked. "I haven't seen him."

"No, but he was up in April and said he was doing the flea market scene off Cape on Tuesdays and Wednesdays," Sky explained. "He told Leanna if she and Kurt wanted a weekend off, he'd run her booth if she'd let him sell his records, too."

April? Amy wondered what else happened in the months when she was gone. And after she married Tony and they moved to Australia, what would it be like when they all had kids? If she could have kids, of course. *Of course we'll have kids. Stop thinking like that.* She had a feeling that she'd miss out on a lot. She envisioned the others getting together to talk about their pregnancies, all round bellies and glowing cheeks. They'd probably even make sure they conceived around the same time.

"Anyway, Amy is only here through August eighteenth before she goes back to work and I guess starts to wrap up her business—right, Ames?"

"Uh-huh," she mumbled, thinking about leaving on August eighteenth. That was something else she and Tony had to discuss. She always left around that time. Would he come with her? Should she try to stay longer? Could she? What about her clients? There was too much to think about. She felt like she was drowning.

"So we'd better do it soon. And Amy's moving in December, so..." Bella tapped her fingernails on the table.

Amy banged her forehead on the table. "I'm already feeling a little like an outsider during the months when I'm not here and you guys are all together. How bad is it going to be when I live in Australia?"

"Oh, Ames. It's not that bad, and isn't it only for two years?" Jenna asked.

"It *is* that bad." Amy set sad eyes on Jenna. "I mean it's not that bad when I'm busy running my business and not thinking about it. When I *don't* know that you guys are taking fun trips and buying matching stuff."

"It's not like we're excluding you or hiding it from you," Bella reminded her.

"I know that. I just...I keep thinking about how it will be when we're having kids, you know? I want to go through all of that *with* you guys, not a million miles away." Amy sat back and fidgeted with the edge of her tank top. "I'm also a little afraid."

"What of?" Jenna's tone was full of compassion.

Amy's eyes welled with tears, and she turned away.

"Ames?" Jenna came around the table and crouched beside her. "What's wrong?"

"What if I can't have kids?" Amy said just above a whisper.

"Did your doctor say that's a possibility?" Bella asked. "If you can't, we'll surrogate for you. Or at least I will."

"Me too," Jenna offered.

Tears slid down Amy's cheeks. "You would do that so easily?"

"Of course," Bella said. "Why wouldn't we? I mean, I'm not going to sleep with Tony, but turkey basters, you know."

Amy laughed and wiped her eyes.

Sky moved her chair closer to Amy's. "Amy, just because you had a miscarriage once doesn't mean you will again. When I was living in New York, my friend Carol had one, and the next year she and her husband had a beautiful baby boy."

Amy swallowed past the lump in her throat. "I know. I just feel like I went through it once by myself. I know that was my choice, and I know Tony would be with me if it happened again, but…it's just everything. I want to be with you guys. You guys have your men, your lives, and you get to live near one another. I want to go on the ferry with you guys and make out with Tony. I want to see Carey in April. Well, not specifically him, but you know what I mean. Is that selfish of me? Because I feel like I'm being wicked selfish right now."

"I like *selfish Amy*," Bella said. "I never wanted you to take the job in the first place."

She banged her head on the table again and groaned. "The

job. I love that job. I want that job. I just want to *live* here."

Amy lifted her head at the sound of Tony's voice and saw him hurrying across the quad.

"What did you do to my fiancée?" He took the deck steps in one giant leap and crouched beside Amy. "What's wrong, babe?"

Words tumbled out, along with a new river of tears. "I don't want to move to Australia. I want to live here and make out on the ferry with you."

Tony furrowed his brow and smiled. A little laugh escaped his lips as he stroked her cheek. "I'm all for making out on the ferry, although I'm not sure how that ties into Australia. Babe, we can live wherever you want. I don't care where we call home. I told you that. I want you to choose what will make *you* the happiest."

"Aw," Jenna said.

"Is that really true, Tony?" Bella held his gaze. "I mean, do you really not care where you live? I don't mean just this second while Amy's in tears. Don't you have a traveling schedule and other things to consider?"

"My only consideration is Amy." Tony turned his attention back to Amy. "Wherever you want to live, we'll make it work. You don't have to work another day in your life if you don't want to. Neither do I, for that matter."

"Wow," Sky whispered.

"No kidding. Wow," Bella reiterated.

"I love working." Amy swiped at her tears. "I want the job with Duke, but I want to live here, with you and the girls. I want to have kids at the same time as them and listen to Jenna complain about her boobs getting too big with her pregnancy. I want to see Leanna dress like a hippie when she's pregnant, and

I want to go shopping with Bella so she can tell me it's not fair that my stomach is cuter than hers."

"Hey," Bella teased.

"You know what I mean," Amy said. "I want to go to the bay and watch Jenna paint in her studio while it's snowing outside. I want to see Evan come home for winter break and see his smiling face as he tells everyone about how his first semester of school was." Amy inhaled a deep breath and blew it out slowly.

"I'm not making any sense. I have to tell Duke I can't take the job, because I really, really want to live here with everyone more than I want the job, I think." *Do I? Yes? Maybe?* She realized she was making huge assumptions that Tony really meant what he'd said about living anywhere. She'd always wanted to live here, but she'd never considered really taking the plunge. She had a whole life to consider back home, but if she was considering moving all the way to Australia, why not move where she really wanted to be—with the friends, and the man, she really wanted to be with?

"I mean if that's okay with you," she said to Tony.

Tony pulled her in close. "Babe, it's perfect with me. This is where we became a couple. It should be where we become a family, too." He held her close until her tears dried up.

"What should I tell Duke? I hate letting him down."

"Duke's a businessman, but he's all about family. He'll understand," Tony said.

"He's here this weekend," Sky said. "He and Blue are looking at the lighthouse over on Bowers Bluff."

"I know. I have a meeting with him Sunday morning. I just don't want to disappoint him." Amy reached for Tony's hand. "Why didn't you go with the guys over to the marina?"

"I'm heading over now. I needed to grab my keys, and when I saw you banging your head on the table, I got worried."

"Aw, thank you. I'm fine. I think."

"Well, take your time and decide what you want to do. I'm sure Duke will understand either way. You sure you're okay if I take off to meet the guys?"

"Of course." She kissed him goodbye, feeling relieved and a little conflicted about the job. She and Tony wouldn't know anyone in Australia, but the job really sounded like everything she'd ever wanted in a career. The best next step she could hope for.

She looked around the table and her heart won out. She definitely wanted to live at the Cape. She was sure of that much. She just wished there were a way to have both the job and the Cape. Then again, she counted herself lucky. She was with Tony, and that was more than she could have hoped for. It was time to pull up her big-girl panties again and hope Duke didn't hate her for changing her mind.

Chapter Twenty-Two

AMY SAT IN her car Sunday morning in front of the Bookstore Restaurant, trying to get her hands to stop trembling. She'd changed her clothes three times before leaving her cottage, finally deciding on a simple floral summer dress. Duke had seen her in her bathing suit, shorts, and dressed up. They'd known each other for a few years. She shouldn't be this nervous. They may not be super-close friends, like she was with Jamie, Caden, Pete, or Kurt, but they were still friends, and that meant a great deal to Amy. He was a smart, rational man. Surely he'd understand her decision.

Wouldn't he?

He spent so much time looking after his siblings that Amy was sure at least a part of him would understand. The question was, would it be a big enough part of him to save their friendship? She gave herself a little pep talk, then headed inside, hoping for the best.

Duke was sitting on the front patio at a table for two. He waved Amy over. Even without his suit Duke had a regal air about him. He had all the hallmarks of classic good looks: broad shoulders, square jaw, intelligent eyes on the small side but offering a welcome and warm gaze. He rose to greet Amy, and she noticed that his gray T-shirt and jeans were nicely pressed. His dirty-blond hair was slightly askew, giving him a casual edge.

His embrace engulfed Amy's small frame.

"Good to see you again, Amy." He pulled out a chair for her and waited for her to settle into it before sitting down. Always the gentleman.

"It's nice to see you, too, Duke. Did you and Blue like the property?" Her pulse was racing so fast she was afraid she might blurt out, *I can't take the job!* She was doing all she could to try to distract herself with other topics.

"Yes, very much. I think it has a lot of promise, although knowing my brother, he'll keep it for himself instead of renovating it for a business. He had that look in his eyes." Duke flagged over the waiter. "Amy, would you like something to eat? Some coffee?"

"Just ice water, please." *I'm too nervous to eat.*

Duke asked the young man for a cup of black coffee, then turned back to Amy. His eyes dropped to her engagement ring, sparkling like a beacon on her left hand, and his lips curved up in a smile.

"Ah, I see congratulations are in order."

Amy felt her cheeks flush. She dropped her eyes to her ring, and a smile pressed at her lips. "Yes, thank you. Tony and I are getting married."

Duke nodded and lifted her hand to inspect the ring. "It's a beautiful ring. Tony's a lucky guy. And that explains the possessive vibe I got from him at the wedding."

"Possessive vibe?" Amy flashed back to the wedding, when Tony had seen them talking right before he'd told Amy to take the job. She swallowed the uneasy feeling the memory brought with it. Tony'd tried so hard to fight their attraction—she was so glad that it was bigger than he was.

"Sorry about that. It was a confusing time for both of us. There's a lot of history there."

"Amy, you don't have to apologize. I'm happy for both of you. Tony's a stand-up guy. I've got nothing but respect for him. And he'll love Australia."

A pang of guilt tightened her throat. Amy was relieved when the waiter brought her ice water.

"Thank you." She was afraid to pick up the glass because her hands were shaking again over the Australia comment and what she had to tell him.

"So when's the big day?" Duke asked.

She breathed a sigh of relief. This was a conversation she could handle much better than the whole *I'm not taking the job* talk looming over her. "Soon. We're thinking of having a small wedding here on the beach with the girls and then we'd each have a bigger family wedding at another time. You and Blue will come, won't you?" She couldn't believe she was actually talking about getting married to Tony and it was really happening. She'd dreamed about it for so long, and here she was, inviting Duke and his brother to their wedding.

Our wedding!

"I wouldn't miss it for the world." Duke sipped his coffee. "I'd like to gift each of you a honeymoon suite for a week at whichever Ryder Resort you'd like."

Amy's jaw dropped. "Duke, you don't have to do that."

"It's your wedding, Amy. Hopefully this day will come only once in your life—same for Bella, Leanna, and Jenna. It's my pleasure to do this."

"Really? That's so generous of you." How could she turn

down the job after he offered her *that*?

"What good is owning luxury resorts if you can't share the fun with friends?" Duke leaned back and looked out over the harbor. "I'm a sucker for love. You guys just let me know when and where you want the rooms and consider it done."

She dropped her eyes, trying to gather enough courage to tell him what she'd come there to say. She drew her shoulders back, settled her hands in her lap, and locked her fingers together in a death grip. When she met his gaze again, he was still smiling. Her stomach sank, knowing she was about to upset his apple cart.

"Duke, before I accept your generous gift, I need to talk to you about the job." *I can do this. I can do this.*

He drew his brows together. "Should I worry that we need to talk *before* you accept the gift?"

"Probably."

He leaned back in his chair and crossed an ankle over one knee, resting his elbow on the arm of the chair. "Might as well give it to me straight, Amy."

"Straight." *Right.* "Okay, well. This is really hard for me to say, because I really, really want to work with you. The position you've offered is exactly what I've been working toward all these years, and I know I'd do an excellent job." She paused, and his facial expression didn't change at all. She straightened the silverware on the table and refolded her napkin, anything to release the nervous energy buzzing beneath the weight of his steady gaze.

"It's just…All I can do is be honest with you, Duke. I don't want to ruin our friendship, and I really don't want to give up this job, but my circumstances have changed. Now that Tony and I are getting married, I'm thinking about having children and starting a family, and I want to do that here. At the Cape. With my friends." There. She'd gotten it all out in the open without passing out.

Duke didn't say a word.

Shoot. Fearing she'd ruined their friendship and given up the job, she tried to explain further.

"I'm sorry. I am not normally the type of person to back out of a commitment." *Yes, I am. I broke up with Tony all those years ago.*

I had to. Didn't I?

Duke leaned forward, hands steepled beneath his chin. "Well, that puts an interesting spin on this situation, doesn't it?"

His words pulled her back to the present. *Interesting spin?* She didn't know how to respond to that, and she was still thinking about how she'd broken up with Tony so long ago. She'd done it to save him, yes, but she'd also done it to save herself. It had been too difficult to see Tony's caring eyes looking at her with so much sadness that she'd nearly drowned in them. She'd barely been able to make it through each day, and she'd been at risk of failing her classes if she didn't pull her head together. She'd been a kid making a decision based on fear.

What was she doing now? What or who was she saving?

Her relationship with Tony? No. He'd said he'd go wherever she wanted.

Now she was making a decision as an adult. She was saving her own stupid self again, coveting the time she had to be at the Cape with her girlfriends. Was that so wrong?

Duke was looking at her with a question in his eyes.

No. It wasn't wrong. She'd waited a lifetime to marry Tony.

I've also waited a lifetime for a job like this.

"Is this an all-or-nothing decision?" Duke asked.

"I'm not sure what you mean."

"Amy, I didn't offer you the job because we're friends. I offered you the job because you're the best person for the position." He paused long enough for the weight of his words to sink in.

The best person for the position. What a nice ego stroke. Duke's eyes were dead serious. She'd been so busy worrying about saving their friendship that she hadn't considered *why* he'd hired her.

"You have the professionalism and skill set to make this conference center a success, and you have the vision to drive it into the future. Not to mention that you know how to finesse clients." Duke sat up straighter, and Amy suddenly felt as though she weren't talking to her friend Duke Ryder but to the real-estate-tycoon Duke Gerald Ryder.

And the real-estate tycoon wanted *her* for the job.

Amy sat up taller. It had been such an emotional few weeks that she'd lost sight of the fact that she was Amy Maples, President of Maples Logistical & Conference Consulting.

Her personal life was heading in the direction of her dreams, all because she'd taken a chance the night before Jamie and Jessica's wedding. She glanced at her engagement ring. Even if she'd failed miserably at being a seductress, she must have done something right, because she'd gotten Tony's attention. She'd had no idea what she was doing as a temptress, but she knew *exactly* what she was doing in her professional life.

She reveled in her realization and used that renewed confidence as she would with any client—to get what she wanted.

"Perhaps we should discuss our options."

An hour later Amy was back in her car. She drove to the end

of the Wellfleet Pier and parked by the boathouse. With her cell phone in hand, she walked down to the docks, where her father used to take her to watch the fishermen take their boats out in the mornings. She sat with her back against one of the wooden pilings and called her father.

"Princess."

She heard the smile in his voice and her determination faltered. "Hi, Dad."

"How are you, sweetie? Are you ready to discuss the business plan for next year? I've been thinking—"

"Dad!" She cut him off before she lost her courage.

"What's wrong, honey? Do you need a few minutes to get your files in order before we go over them?"

"No, Dad. I need to get my life in order. By myself."

"I…I'm sorry, princess. I'm not sure I understand." His voice grew serious.

"I know you don't, and neither did I until recently. Dad, I appreciate all of the guidance and support you've given me."

"I know you do. That's what your old man is for. To make sure you don't go down the wrong path."

Amy closed her eyes and breathed deeply. She drew her shoulders back and stared out over the boats. "Dad, remember when you used to take me to the marina?"

"Sure. Those were good times."

"Yeah, they were." She smiled with the warm memories; then her smile faded as she finished her thought. "Remember when you told me that story about you and Uncle Sal when you went on that fishing trip? The one about Grandpa not letting Uncle Sal reel in the fish because he thought he'd lose it, and how you felt bad for Uncle Sal because you knew he could do it himself?"

Her father laughed. "I can't believe *you* remembered that."

Amy wasn't laughing. She was holding her breath because what she had to say next was second only to talking about the past with Tony when it came to things that were hard to do. She swallowed her fear and blurted it out.

"I need to reel in my own fish, Dad. You taught me well, and I can manage my business and create my marketing plans on my own." She closed her eyes tightly, hoping he wouldn't get mad.

"Why, I know you can, princess. Why are you telling me this?"

How could he not understand? Did she really need to spell it out for him? His silence told her she did. She pushed to her feet and paced the dock. "I'm telling you because, you know, Dad, you kind of hover over everything I do. You asked about every test I ever took, talked to me about studying on a weekly basis, and when I started my business, you were there with me when I met with my attorney. I appreciate it all, but now it's time to cut the line. I can swim on my own, and if I sink, I sink. But I need to do it on my own, Dad."

"But you are doing it on your own, Amy. You built your business, not me. You do the work, not me. I'm only here to guide you."

Amy let out a frustrated sigh. "I'm glad you recognize that I am doing the work, but I really don't need your guidance with my business plan, Dad. Or with my contracts. I can do this."

She listened to his breathing, wishing he'd say something.

Anything.

"Dad?"

"I'm here. I'm sorry."

Guilt threatened to strangle her. "Dad…"

"No. You're right, Amy. One reason your mother left was because I was too overbearing. *In her face*, she used to say." His voice was full of regret.

"Dad, you're not in my face. I know you mean well, but—"

"But I put too much pressure on you, and I don't let you make your own decisions. I know this, Amy, and it's not because I don't trust your decisions or your abilities. You're brilliant and capable, like your mother."

"Then why do you do it?" This was news to her. Her mother had never told her that she felt her father was overbearing. Then again, Amy had always been careful not to complain to her mother about her father's being so overprotective. She'd always skated a fine line between the two of them. Now she wished she hadn't waited so long to talk to him.

He sighed. "I don't know. It's who I am, I guess. I just want the best for you. But you have to give me credit. I bit my tongue a lot when you were younger. Like when you used to sneak out to go swimming with the girls at the pool. And that summer when you dated Tony Black. And, boy, did I want to say something. Not that I don't like Tony, but I was afraid you'd get married and follow him around the country instead of going to college. But I bit my tongue then, and you had a great summer. I figured you needed a good time before you hit the books."

Amy's breath left her lungs in a rush. She sank down to the dock, her jaw agape. "You…you…knew?"

He laughed. "Honey, how could anyone not know? You two could barely stand to be away from each other that summer."

"You knew." She said it more to herself than to him. Tears welled in her eyes. "You never said anything. That summer…you just kept harping about how I would need to *hunker down* in the fall and I'd have no time for boys and dating."

"Exactly. That's why when you two had your little fling, I didn't say anything. It seemed harmless enough. I never even saw you two kiss. I figured a little infatuation was okay before you hit the books and every minute would matter."

"A little infatuation." She shook her head as tears streamed down her cheeks. Would things have been different if she'd known that he saw what was between them? She mulled that over as he rattled on about how he and the other parents thought their crush was cute and how they were surprised that Jamie and one of the other girls didn't experience the same thing.

She wanted to yell at him, to tell him that it wasn't just a crush, that she'd loved Tony with all her heart and that she still did. She wanted to tell him that she'd gone through a miscarriage alone because she was so afraid of disappointing him that she couldn't stand to tell anyone. But in the end, as she sat alone on the dock with the sun shining down on her and the soothing sounds of water splashing against the boats in the gentle breeze, she didn't say any of that. That was her business. Tony's business. It was their private heartache, and her father knowing about it wouldn't change what they'd experienced.

She drew in another deep breath, feeling as though she were living on them lately, and said what she'd been determined to say all along.

"Dad, I love you, but from here on out we need to move forward without discussing the intricacies of my business, okay?"

"Okay, princess. I promise to try, but I'm an old dog, and you know…learning new tricks and all that."

She smiled. "Yeah. I know. I'll cut you some slack. A tiny amount."

"Okay. Fair enough. I admire the courage it took for you to call me."

"Thank you. It did take courage." She didn't realize how much until now. "Dad. One more thing. I'm marrying Tony."

"You're…"

"Marrying Tony Black. I love him. I've always loved him. And if you have anything negative to say about it, don't. Because it doesn't matter to me if you don't think he's good enough or if you think I should be with some—"

"Amy, stop."

She silenced at the paternal tone he rarely took with her.

"I love Tony like I love the other kids. Uh, the other men and women. Not kids anymore, I suppose. I have nothing against him. He's always been a nice, respectable person."

She breathed a sigh of relief. "Yeah, he is."

"I just didn't want you to follow him at eighteen. I wanted you to get your degree and become self-reliant."

"That's funny, considering how much you hover over every decision I make." She couldn't believe she'd said it out loud, and she had no idea how the words escaped without her brain stopping them first.

"Wow. How long have you been holding that in, princess?"

She was relieved to hear a smile in his voice. "Um, probably for more years than I want to admit." She felt like a giant weight had fallen from her shoulders, and she couldn't wait to see what walking around without it would feel like.

"Right. Okay, that's fair, too. You are self-reliant, Amy. As I said, I was there for guidance, but you have built your own business. You're capable, and I realize I need to back off. What matters now is this. Are you happy?"

"Very."

"That's all I ever wanted for you. So I guess it wasn't an infatuation."

"Not even close," she admitted.

"I didn't even know you were dating. How long have you been seeing each other? Or I guess how long have you been in love is a better question."

Amy thought long and hard about how to respond. Seeing each other? *Every day and night in my dreams.* In love?

"Forever."

TONY CHECKED HIS cell phone for what felt like the hundredth time. Still no message from Amy.

"Dude." Pete shook his head. "She'll call when she's got something to tell you. Sit down, have a drink, and chill." Pete patted the wooden dock.

They'd spent the morning out on the schooner that Pete had refinished two summers ago, and they'd been back at the marina for about twenty minutes. Tony lowered himself to the dock beside Pete and accepted the beer he handed him. "I'm just worried about Amy. What if things didn't go well with Duke? You know her. She's sensitive. She'll feel bad about letting him down for weeks."

"She does have that whole heart-of-gold thing going on." Caden sat on Pete's other side and waved off the beer Pete offered. "Someone's got to uphold the law. I'm the designated driver."

Pete shook his head. "Always the cop."

"I'm drinking one beer, that's it." Tony held up his beer bottle.

"You guys all cool with this whole group-wedding thing?" Caden asked.

"*Pfft*. Why not?" Pete tipped his bottle back and took a long swig. "If it makes the girls happy."

"Hey, you guys and the girls are my family as much as my mom is. I'm all for it." Tony set his beer down on the dock. "Besides, weren't Bella and Jenna waiting for Amy to get engaged before they got married? Oh, and Leanna, of course."

"Yup." Caden ran his hand through his hair with a sigh. "Call me backward, but I want to get married sooner rather than later. I haven't told Evan yet, but Bella and I would like to try to have a child together."

Tony smiled. "I think Amy's biological clock is ticking pretty loud, too."

"Jenna's, too." Pete held his beer between both hands. His eyes grew serious. "Tony, um, I don't know if this is out of line or not, but Jenna told me what you guys went through."

A sharp pain cut through Tony's chest. "Yeah? That's okay."

"I'm sorry, man." Pete gave him a brotherly pat on the back. "That must have been rough."

"Yeah. I lost my mind a little back then. That's for sure." Tony finished his beer and set the bottle beside him again.

"Bella told me, too. I can tell you that raising a kid at a young age wasn't easy. I don't mean to minimize what you went through. I'm just saying…You know what I mean. I'm really sorry." Caden had taken on full responsibility of Evan when he was still in college. He'd dropped out to take care of Evan and had become a police officer because the schedule allowed him to work nights and spend more time with Evan during the day when he was a baby.

"I know. Thanks, man," Tony said. "She's worried about having another miscarriage. I think that might be one reason she wants to stay here at the Cape, to be with the girls. She needed them back then, but she'd closed herself off."

"Well, she'll have their support, that's for sure. But you'll have ours, too, Tony." Pete blew out a loud breath. "I think it's a good thing that they'll all be together. It feels like it was meant to be this way."

Tony glanced up at the sound of fast footfalls on the dock. Amy was running down the dock in her summer dress and bare feet, arms flailing, hair flying behind her like a mane. She was running too fast. Tony rose to his feet to slow her down and she plowed into him, sending both of them over the edge of the dock and into the water. Amy flapped her arms and legs. Her eyes were wide and her cheeks puffed out as she held her breath. Her hair flowed in slow motion around her face as Tony grabbed her beneath her arms and pushed her up through the surface. Both of them gasped for air.

"Are you okay?" He held her against him, kicking to keep them both afloat as she caught her breath.

"Yes." Her head kicked back with an uninhibited laugh, which made Tony laugh.

"You guys all right?" Pete threw a life jacket into the water.

"I've got her. We're fine." Tony tucked the life jacket under one of Amy's arms.

"I've got you, but hold on to that. Are you sure you're okay?"

"Fine. Fine." She pressed her lips to his. "Duke and I worked it out."

Tony grabbed the edge of the dock with one arm, keeping a

firm grip around Amy. "That's great. I think. Is it what you want?" *Are we moving to Australia?*

"Yes!" She kissed him again, a wet, sloppy kiss as she panted to catch her breath. She let go of the life jacket and wrapped her arms around his neck. "We can live here."

"Here? Here!" He gave her another wet kiss, completely forgetting that he was keeping them up. They sank below the surface, mouths sealed together. Both of their eyes opened wide under the water, and as they rose to the top, they were both smiling.

They broke through the surface again, and they laughed and kissed each other again. Pete and Caden shook their heads.

She swiped at the water in her wide eyes. "And I talked to my dad. I told him we were getting married and to back off of my work stuff."

"Amy." He searched her eyes for any signs of distress, but they were still radiating with happiness. "It went okay?"

"It went better than okay." She hugged him tight, then pushed back with a wide smile. "Clean slate."

"Clean slate. You're amazing. Truly amazing." Tony kissed her again, and this time when they sank beneath the surface, he breathed air into her lungs, just as she'd breathed new life into him.

Chapter Twenty-Three

Three weeks later…

IT MIGHT HAVE been a mistake to choose the bedroom of Jenna and Pete's bay-front property for the girls to get ready for their wedding. Amy had been staring out the window overlooking the beach for twenty minutes. Theresa had taken them all by surprise when she'd announced that she was an ordained minister and had offered to preside over the wedding. They'd been thrilled to take her up on her offer, but she hadn't arrived yet, and now Amy worried that perhaps she wasn't going to show up. Maybe this was Theresa's payback for all of Bella's pranks over the years.

Of course, Amy had another reason to be plastered to the window for the last twenty minutes—to ogle her man, who was waiting down on the beach in his dark suit with the other grooms and Jamie, Evan, Blue, and Duke. The grooms all had their suit pants rolled up, but there was something about Tony barefoot and in a suit that had Amy practically drooling. She watched as Sky's friend Lizzie, a petite brunette with more energy than the Energizer Bunny, ran around the canopy she'd erected and laced with flowers, making sure the ribbons and flowers were secure. Duke and Blue were eyeing her like she was made of wedding cake. Amy wondered if they'd get to see some brotherly competition, and she hoped Sky wouldn't be too upset.

Bella leaned against the window frame. "Loving the view?"

"Uh-huh." Amy leaned down and petted Joey, who was lying beside her feet with her tongue hanging out of her mouth. She rolled onto her back, and Amy scratched her belly.

"Maybe you could finish getting ready so we can actually go out there and marry our men."

Amy glanced up and smiled at the tease in Bella's eyes. She looked beautiful. They all did, in their matching off-white tank dresses that stopped just above their knees. Sky and Jessica wore matching pale-pink sundresses. Jessica's skin was bronze from her honeymoon. She and Jamie hadn't stopped smiling since they'd returned.

"If you didn't force me to sleep without him last night, maybe I wouldn't be drooling today." Amy reluctantly turned away from the window.

"In my day the bride and groom never saw each other the day of the wedding." Vera sat in an armchair wearing a pretty blue dress and comfortable, stable shoes that resembled sneakers. Jenna laced them with blue ribbons for her. Vera was in her mideighties, and her hair was silver and white and cut in a pixie style. Her skin looked velvety soft despite the wrinkles mapping her cheeks, and when she smiled, her gray-blue eyes warmed.

"So..." Jenna set a challenging gaze on Bella but spoke to Vera. "So you definitely didn't sneak out to see your man the night before your wedding."

"What?" Bella turned away with a grin.

Amy bit her lower lip and looked away, too. The girls had

all spent the night at Pete and Jenna's beach house, and the guys had spent the night at Kurt's, which was just a few miles down the road. Amy had snuck out last night and spent an hour in Tony's arms out in the dunes. She'd stayed in one of Jenna's guest rooms, and she didn't think anyone had known. Now she wasn't so sure.

"You snuck out," Jenna said.

Bella and Amy both spun around and said in unison, "No, I didn't."

"I might have." Leanna waved her hand. "You probably heard me. I couldn't help it. I really wanted to see Kurt, and I knew you guys wouldn't approve, so I just saw him for a few minutes." Leanna's cheeks pinked up.

"*You* snuck out?" Jenna asked.

"Uh-huh." Leanna smiled. "I'm sorry. We just shared a few minutes…in Pete's boat barn."

"In his boat barn?" Jenna's eyes widened, but it was the mischievous grin on her lips that made Amy curious.

"Where were you last night, Jenna? When I got up to go to the bathroom, I didn't see you." It was a boldface lie, but she could tell Jenna was hiding something. No need for Leanna to suffer alone.

"I was sleeping." Jenna turned away.

Vera shielded her mouth as if she were sharing a secret and said, "I smell a fib."

"Vera!" Jenna laughed. "Okay, fine. I met Pete for an hour in my art studio."

"Oh my gosh." Bella plunked down on the bed. "I met Caden at the edge of the driveway. We're all cursed."

"Yup, because that man out there met me in the dunes." Amy sat next to Bella. "And it was worth being cursed for." She burst out laughing, and the other girls did, too. Even Vera couldn't refrain from chuckling.

"Well, if we're telling secrets..." Vera looked up at the ceiling and covered her heart with her hand. "We snuck out the night before our wedding, too."

Jessica gasped. "Vera." She hugged her. "Don't worry. I won't tell Jamie. No need to ruin his image of his pristine grandmother."

"Oh, the tales I could tell," Vera said with a playful shrug.

"Well, now that we have *that* out of the way. When I get married I will just skip the whole not-seeing-the-groom routine and take the path to being cursed." Sky laughed as she grabbed a patchwork backpack from the floor.

"I made you guys something." The girls gathered around Sky as she dug through the bag and pulled out light blue garters with tiny silver starfish hanging from the lace edge. She handed one to each of the brides.

"These are so cute. You *made* them? Thank you." Amy threw her arms around Sky's neck and kissed her cheek.

"You're welcome! The starfish are from my mom's sewing stuff," Sky explained. "So I think that counts as something blue and something old."

Jenna and Bella slipped theirs on while Leanna embraced Sky. "That was so thoughtful. Thank you."

"Vera brought you guys something, too. Something *old* and *new*." Jessica handed them each a little velvet bag from her purse.

"Vera, you didn't have to give us anything," Bella said.

"I know I didn't. I had one made for Jessica before she married Jamie, and, Sky, I have one with your name on it, too." Vera reached for Sky's hand. "No rush, dear."

Leanna, Jenna, Bella, and Amy opened the bags and shared a look of disbelief.

"Vera, I don't know what to say." Amy pulled the silver necklace with a pearl charm from the velvet bag. "This is stunning."

"My uncle lived in Wellfleet. He was a fisherman, and he dove for pearls. I have a handful of them that he'd given me over the years." Vera reached for Jessica's hand and pulled her in close. "I knew when Jessica joined our family that they were meant to be shared, not stashed away in a safe."

Jessica touched her pearl necklace. "Thank you, Vera. I will always cherish mine."

"I know you will, dear." Vera looked at the others. "I've known you girls practically since you were born. You're as much family to me as Jamie is. I want you to have them. I feel so blessed to have been invited to share in your special day."

The girls moved in for a group hug, and Joey rubbed against their legs.

"You're as much our family as we are yours," Amy said. "Thank you." She and the others helped each other put on their necklaces; then Amy peeked out the window. "I still don't see Theresa out there. Do you think she's standing us up?"

"No way," Jenna said. "She'd never do that. She texted a little while ago and said that she's going to be here in time for the ceremony, but she's running a little late."

"Okay, good. If she doesn't show up, we can't get married." Amy's stomach felt queasy.

"She'll be here, Ames. Don't worry," Jenna said.

"Uh oh," Bella yelled.

"What?" Amy said.

"We have nothing borrowed. Does anyone have anything

borrowed?" Bella spun around, waving her hands frantically. "We need something borrowed."

"I know!" Leanna grabbed her purse and fished around in it. She pulled out three long ribbons—red, white, and blue—and smiled. "Jenna! Scissors!"

Jenna ran from the room and came back with a pair of scissors.

"We'll cut this up and tie our hair back," Leanna said.

"But I just did my hair," Jenna complained.

"Oh, come on." Leanna cut the ribbon. "Don't be a spoilsport. Turn around."

Jenna made a face, then snatched the red ribbon Leanna was holding in her hand and swapped it for the blue one.

"Give the red and white to someone who doesn't have OCD. This way it will match my garter." Jenna turned for Leanna to tie her hair back.

Sky tied Amy's and Bella's, and Jessica tied back Leanna's hair.

Vera rose from her chair. "You girls are lovely. Just lovely."

They all held hands and smiled like goofs.

"We're really doing this," Amy whispered. "We're brides!"

"We're beautiful brides," Leanna added.

"And we're marrying our Prince Charmings." Jenna squealed and wiggled her shoulders.

"I just want you girls to know that I can't imagine a better wedding, or people I'd rather be with on this day." Amy's eyes teared up. "You're my sisters, and I'm so happy that Duke is letting me work three weeks on-site and then four months remotely. I can't wait to start my life with Tony, and I can't wait to move here and build our lives together with you guys. I love you guys so much."

"Aw, Ames." Leanna hugged her. "I love you, too."

"Me too," Jenna said.

"Okay, okay." Bella rolled her eyes. "We love each other. Let's go get married!"

TONY'S MOUTH WENT dry when he saw Amy walking over the dune in her off-white dress. She looked elegant with the simple dress and her hair pulled away from her face. Her smile reached her eyes, and when her eyes met his, his body shuddered with the memory of making love on the dunes last night. She'd been so beautiful, naked and bathed in moonlight. He'd wanted to stay with her beneath the stars until morning, but they'd both known they were breaking tradition by seeing each other. Nothing about their romance had been traditional, and he'd tried to coerce Amy into staying with him using that logic. She'd smiled that adorable smile of hers and shut him up with a sensual kiss. He was putty in her hands, and knew he always would be.

He watched Evan recording the girls as they came over the dunes with Joey bounding beside them. Lizzie handed each of the girls a bouquet of white roses and fastened a white ribbon to Joey's collar. She was a feisty little thing flitting about as graceful and unobtrusive as a bird. Tony stole a glance at his best friends, who looked as mesmerized by their brides as he felt. Duke caught his eye and nodded, as if to say, *You're a lucky guy.* Tony was so grateful that he and Amy had worked things out. Duke had called him last week to tell him—in case he had any doubts—that he hadn't been doing Amy a favor by agreeing to the new work schedule. Amy had done him a favor. Tony had never felt as proud as he was at that moment. He knew how wonderful Amy was, but it sure felt good hearing it from someone else.

The pride he felt now was ten times the pride he'd felt then, as Amy walked across the sand in her bare feet and came to his side.

"I love you," he whispered as the others took their places beside them.

"I love you, too, but have you seen Theresa?"

Tony nodded toward the dunes.

Amy turned. "Is that Theresa? I didn't know she was bringing a date."

Everyone turned to look at the couple coming over the dunes. As they neared, there was a collective gasp from the girls.

"Holy Moses," Pete said.

"Bella, I think you've been one-upped." Caden kissed her temple.

"Oh my gosh. Is that…" Amy's jaw hung open.

"Bradley Cooper," Tony said. "Wow."

"Hello, ladies." Theresa set her eyes on Bella and smirked. "You might know my friend Brad Cooper."

"No way." Bella stepped right up to Bradley and leaned in close, looking over his face from every angle. "Are you really Bradley Cooper or a freaking awesome double?"

He flashed his famous cockeyed grin and laughed. "I'm him. Terry said you might want to meet me." Bradley held a hand out in greeting.

"Terry?" Bella raised her brows as she shook his hand.

"Yeah." He looked at Theresa. "Terry used to babysit me. Right, Ter?"

"Darn right I did." Theresa stalked past Bella with a satisfied grin on her thin lips. "Shall we get this show on the road?"

Amy turned to Tony, went up on her toes, and whispered in his ear, "You're ten times as handsome as he is."

He didn't care if it was the truth or not. Amy said it, and that was truth enough for him.

The service was short and sweet. Amy and Tony stated their vows, then Bella and Caden took their turn. Once they finished, Jenna and Pete, and then Leanna and Kurt recited their vows. After they'd all gone, the girls looked from one to the other, but Tony didn't take his eyes off of Amy during the whole service. He wanted to remember the way a few wispy tendrils of hair came loose from her ribbon and framed her face. The scent of the bay breeze as it picked up her perfume, and how her eyes took on a fiery, emerald glow in the afternoon sun. There had been a time that long-ago summer when Tony had dreamed of marrying Amy just like this, on the beach among their friends. He was thinking about how their lives had come full circle when Theresa's voice brought him back to the moment.

"Gentlemen, you may kiss your brides."

Tony folded Amy into his arms. "I don't just love you, kitten. I adore you, and I will spend every minute of my life making sure that you know it."

She went up on her toes, her warm hands circling his neck.

"If you don't kiss me soon, I might have to go see if Bradley wants to."

He laughed as their mouths connected, and he kissed her until he felt her body go soft against him and felt the strength in her grip ease. She came away breathless. Eyes still closed.

"Brad who?" she whispered.

"That's my girl." He swooped her up into his arms.

The others were hooting and hollering, and all Tony could

think about was carrying her back to his cottage and loving her as husband and wife.

"I have to throw my bouquet," she reminded him with a shy giggle.

"Where are you going?" Bella hollered when they were halfway to the dunes.

Tony groaned and carried her back to the group. He'd been hoping to steal her away, bouquet and all.

"So I wanted to carry her home. Shoot me." Tony laughed.

"Show-off," Pete said.

"Come on, girls, bouquet time!" Lizzie shooed them all into a line.

She and Sky stood behind them, arms in the air.

"Theresa, aren't you going to jump into the mix?" Bella asked.

"Oh, goodness no." Theresa took a step backward. "I think I'll watch, thank you very much."

"Girls, stand a little closer together," Evan directed.

The girls giggled as they moved in close.

"Perfect, now I can see everyone, including Blue, Brad, and Duke, who seem to be standing as far away from the bouquet throwing as possible." Evan laughed.

"This whole wedding thing might be contagious," Blue teased.

"You should be so lucky," Tony called out.

Amy, Bella, Leanna, and Jenna counted in unison. "One. Two. Three!" They tossed their bouquets over their shoulders and spun around just in time to see Lizzie catch one and Sky catch the other three bouquets.

"Looks like someone's in line to find her forever love," Jessica said.

Sky's eyes widened. She tossed all three bouquets to Lizzie as if they'd burned her hands. Lizzie fumbled to keep from dropping them.

"Nice catch." Blue put his hands beneath the bouquets in case she dropped them.

Jenna elbowed Amy and nodded at Sky, who was talking with Brad, while Blue and Lizzie were laughing about some private joke.

"Wow. Things change so fast around here. What's next?" Jenna asked.

Amy jumped into Tony's arms. "I don't know about you losers, but I'm gonna ride the longboard."

Tony carried her toward the dunes. "You are a dirty, dirty girl, Mrs. Black."

"Correction, I'm *your* dirty, dirty girl."

The End

Please enjoy a preview of the next *Sweet with Heat* novel

Nights at Seaside

Chapter One

"I CAN'T BELIEVE in a few short weeks the apartment *and* the tattoo shop will be completely renovated. Blue, you're amazing!" Sky Lacroux shoved her favorite poetry book into her patchwork purse and locked the front doors of her shop. She waited for a few people to pass before stepping back on the busy sidewalk to admire it. She still had to paint the exterior and the sign above the door and wait for the interior renovations to be done, but as she took in the narrow building she now owned, pride swelled inside her chest.

Inky Skies was located on Commercial Street, the busiest street in the artsy community of Provincetown, Massachusetts.

It was sandwiched between her friend Lizzie Barber's flower shop, P-town Petals, which was painted light blue with flowers and greenery climbing up the columns out front, and the bright purple game store, Puzzle Me This. Sky planned on painting Inky Skies bright yellow, and as Blue Ryder, one of her best friends, threw his arm around her and dragged her away from the shop, she felt like she was walking on a cloud. Now, if only the universe would magically step in and find her the perfect man to share her joy with.

Yeah, right. Like that was going to happen in a primarily gay and lesbian community, especially with the way she worked all the time. *Not likely.* Her brother Hunter fell into step on her other side. *Definitely not likely with these two guarding me closer than Fort Knox.*

"Are you still planning a big grand opening, even though the shop has been open since you bought it?" Blue asked. He'd been one of Sky's best friends since she'd moved back to the Cape from New York three summers ago, to run her father's hardware store while he went into rehab to deal with an alcohol addiction. Thankfully, her father had remained sober after rehab and was back to running his store, which had enabled Sky to move out and fulfill her dream of opening her own tattoo shop. Two months earlier she'd purchased the tattoo shop where she'd been working part-time, and Blue, a specialty builder, was renovating both the shop and the apartment above it for her.

"Heck, yes, I am. It doesn't matter that it's been open during renovations. I still need to celebrate Inky Skies—my dream, my passion, my..."

Blue groaned, and Sky laughed and poked him in the side as they crossed at the corner on their way to meet their friends.

"And you're both coming," she said. "Like it or not."

"I wouldn't miss it for the world. I'm proud of you, sis." Hunter put a hand on Sky's forearm as they came to a curb and a bike whipped past.

"Hunter, I know how to stop at a curb, thank you very much." She rolled her eyes at her protective older brother.

She was used to being watched over, considering her four older brothers—and her slightly overprotective friend, Blue—had been doing it for years, but at twenty-six, with a new business and a new apartment, she was ready to spread her wings.

"Hey, just keepin' you safe." Hunter kept his dark hair shaved close to his head, and with his dark eyes and bulky muscles, he had an edge to him, but the playful grin he flashed softened all of that edginess, revealing the bighearted brother Sky adored.

"Hey, sugar!" A friendly drag queen, who went by Marcus during the day and Maxine when he performed, waved from across the street. He'd lost his lover, Howie, to cancer a couple of years ago, and as much as Sky wished he'd fall in love again, she knew from the look in Marcus's eyes when he spoke of Howie that what they'd shared was a once-in-a-lifetime type of love.

Ever since four of her friends had gotten married last summer, she longed to experience that kind of love, too.

"Hi, Marcus," Sky called. "No show tonight?" During the day, families came to shop, sightsee, and enjoy street performers, but at night, P-town turned into a colorful world of drag queens, dance clubs, and comedians.

"My night off." Marcus said something that made the man he was with laugh. Then he hollered, "I see you have your bodyguards with you again. Hey, Blue. Hi, Hunter. When you get tired of watching over Sky, come watch over me."

Blue laughed. "You couldn't handle me, bro."

"Doesn't mean I wouldn't want to try," Marcus teased.

Blue was straight as an arrow, but Marcus loved to tease him. Sky had quickly fallen in love with the whole community when she'd begun working at the tattoo shop. It might not be conducive to meeting a guy she'd want to actually spend time getting to know in a romantic sense—it had been forever since she'd met a guy like that—but she loved the diversity of the area and the warmth of the people. Provincetown felt like home.

They weaved through throngs of people toward a crowd gathered outside of the Governor Bradford Restaurant, where Blue had handled renovations last year. At six two and six three, with linebacker shoulders and movie-star good looks, it was easy for Hunter and Blue to part the crowd as they guided Sky inside. Governor Bradford's was dimly lit, with a bar to the left, a small stage and dance floor across from the entrance, and a restaurant area to the right of the stage. The scent of fried foods and sage hung in the air.

She followed Blue around the dance floor, stopping at a table of bearded guys who had come into the shop earlier in the day for tattoos and leaned in to hug one of them. Sky got to know most of her customers while she tatted them up.

"Hey, guys. I hope you're going to sing for open mic night."

"Trust me, you don't wanna hear us sing," the burliest of them said with a laugh.

"Chicken," Sky teased as Blue took her hand and dragged her to the far side of the dance floor, where her sister-in-law, Jenna, and their friends Bella Grant and Amy Black were waiting for them.

"Finally." Jenna stood up to hug Sky. She was four foot eleven, with curves that rivaled Marilyn Monroe's, and at five months pregnant she looked even more voluptuous. "I see your bodyguards got you here safely."

Sky laughed. "I love your haircut!" Jenna had cut a few inches off of her long brown hair. It now hung just past her shoulders.

"Thanks. It's my summer cut," Jenna said, patting her hair.

Sky reached around Bella's burgeoning belly to hug her, then did the same with Amy. "You guys are like the beach-ball-belly twins. I can't believe you're both eight months pregnant—and that your hubbies are still letting you go to open mic night."

"They know we need our P-town nights. Besides, they're all out on Pete's boat with your dad." Bella looked at Hunter and Blue. "Why didn't you guys go?"

Hunter was busy ordering drinks from a raven-haired waitress.

"I worked late on Sky's renovations." Blue pulled out a chair for Sky.

"I'm sorry," Sky said, patting his back as she sat beside him. "But I do appreciate your hard work, and I even tried to get Lizzie to meet us tonight." She wiggled her brows. "I *tried* to hook you up. The way you and Duke were lusting after Lizzie at the wedding, I thought for sure you'd ask her out by now."

"She is hot," Hunter said, eyes locked on a group of blond women across the bar.

Blue ran a hand through his thick dark hair and shrugged. "I've been busy."

"For a year?" Bella asked.

"She's come out with us several times over the past year," he said as he draped an arm across the back of Sky's chair.

"Yes. *Us.* I said *you* should ask her out." Sky shook her head, and a disconcerting thought hit her as the waitress brought their drinks. "Oh, gosh, Blue. Do you think we spend too much time together? Am I monopolizing you? Have I blocked you?"

"No, you didn't block me," Blue said with a laugh. "Have I…*blocked* you?"

Relieved, she said, "No. I've just decided that the next guy I date has to be someone who's really soulful and gets me, and around here, that's slim pickin's."

Blue raised his beer with a smirk. "Guys are not exactly soulful."

"No kidding," Hunter said.

"Oh, come on. There are soulful people all around. It just takes some looking," Jenna began scanning the bar. "I'm on a manhunt for Sky."

"Okay, enough find-my-sister-a-man talk," Hunter said. "I looked at the sign-up sheet. They have a great lineup tonight. Comedians, karaoke, and see that guy over there?" He pointed to a guy sitting by himself at the bar with a guitar leaning against his leg. His dark T-shirt revealed sculpted biceps and strong forearms, and the fabric clung to the contours of his muscular chest. One arm rested casually on the arm of his chair, the other across his lap, his finger wrapped around the neck of a guitar. He had hair the color of night and thick scruff covering a strong jawline. His eyes were narrowed and locked on a group of people across the room, like he was studying them or deep in thought. Sky couldn't tell which.

"He played about two months ago, and he's amazing." Hunter glanced at his sister. "You'll love him, Sky."

"Holy mother of hotness." Jenna grabbed Bella's arm.

"Where did that guy come from?"

"You're married," Amy reminded her.

"And preggers." Bella patted Jenna's belly. "Pete would kick his butt if he even looked at you." Sky's brother was a *little* protective of his wife.

"My interest is already piqued by that handsome creature," Sky said more to herself than the others.

"I don't want to hear that. I just thought you'd like his music." Hunter eyed the man across the room. "He looks a little rough, Sky. Not your hippie, earthy type."

Sky ignored her brother's evaluation. Yes, she had an earthy style and believed in fate and destiny and all things a little bit magical, but that didn't mean she couldn't ogle a hot guy who might not be her typical type.

While Bella, Amy, and Jenna talked about their plans for their babies and Blue and Hunter talked about work and women, Sky went back to checking out the dark-eyed man who hadn't so much as shifted his position.

The host announced the next karaoke singer, and they listened to a squeaky rendition of Madonna's "Like a Virgin." People danced and sang as they moved through several other moderately talented singers. Sky was about to pull out her poetry book, which was far more interesting than the singers, when the host called out, "Sawyer Bass," and the guy with the guitar rose and stretched, giving Sky an eyeful of just how hot he really was. Black biker boots carried him across the floor. His guitar strap was slung casually over one shoulder, as if he were carrying an old piece of lumber.

Blue bumped her with his elbow and handed her a napkin.

"What's that for?" she asked, eyes still on Sawyer Bass. *He even has a hot name.*

"Drool."

She snapped the napkin from his hands, unable to tear her eyes from Sawyer as he sank onto a stool in the middle of the stage—which looked way too small for a man of his size. He was completely relaxed, shoulders and jaw soft, eyes downcast, as if sitting in front of a roomful of people was something he did every night. He rolled his thick shoulders back and cracked his neck to either side, which for some reason amped up his sexiness.

Sawyer lifted dark eyes to the crowd, scanning everything and somehow looking as though he were seeing nothing at all. His eyes skimmed over Sky, and for a beat she held her breath, but he quickly moved on, and she couldn't help but feel disappointed.

"This guy's got serious mojo." Bella's eyes moved around the room. "Half the women's eyes are on him. Heck, most of the guys are staring at him, too."

Sky sipped her drink and looked away from the guy who held everyone's attention. She reached into her purse and pulled out her C. J. Moon poetry book. Better to concentrate on something she enjoyed than to gawk at a guy everyone wanted. He probably wasn't laid-back anyway. He was probably playing it cool, the way guys did when they knew they were hot stuff.

"You're not really going to read, are you?" Blue put his arm across the back of her chair again and pulled her in closer.

"She's *mooning* again," Jenna teased. "Blue, take that away from her. She'll never meet a guy if she's *mooning*." Jenna always teased her about *mooning* over C. J. Moon's poems.

Blue leaned closer to Sky. "You seem a little out of sorts. Is it the renovations? They shouldn't take much longer."

Sky was renting a cottage from Amy down at the Seaside

community, where Bella, Jenna, and Amy all lived. Blue had found a leak in the apartment pipes a few weeks ago, and it seemed easier for her to rent there rather than be in his way on a daily basis. She loved staying at Seaside, and she loved Blue for caring enough to ask.

"You really are a great friend, Blue. It's not that. You're doing a great job. I don't know what it is."

Sky dropped her eyes to the book and began to read her favorite poem.

A moment later, a deep, impassioned voice filled the room, bringing Sky's eyes up to the man it had come from. Sawyer sat on the stool, eyes closed, strumming his guitar and singing with an intensity that sent a shiver of seduction rippling through the room. Sky watched his fingers move confidently over the strings. His brows knitted together on the longer notes, he bowed his head as the words turned sad, and the muscles in his neck grew thicker. Passion poured out of him with every verse.

"What song is this?" Sky asked, the lyrics settling into her bones like a lonely ache. *Darkness isn't enough. Miles are too close. Nothing can erase you, wipe you clean, take away the pain you're leaving behind.*

"No idea," Blue answered.

"Never heard it before." Hunter's eyes were locked on a blonde across the room.

Sky shifted her gaze back to Sawyer. His voice was getting softer as he came to the end of the song, and it drew her in deeper with every second he held that note.

To continue reading, buy NIGHTS AT SEASIDE

More Books By The Author

Sweet with Heat: Seaside Summers
(Includes future publications)

Read, Write, Love at Seaside
Dreaming at Seaside
Hearts at Seaside
Sunsets at Seaside
Secrets at Seaside
Nights at Seaside
Seized by Love at Seaside
Embrace at Seaside
Lovers at Seaside
Whispers at Seaside

Stand Alone Women's Fiction Novels
by Melissa Foster (Addison Cole's steamy alter ego)
The following titles may include some harsh language

Chasing Amanda (mystery/suspense)
Come Back to Me (mystery/suspense)
Have No Shame (historical fiction/romance)
Megan's Way (literary fiction)
Traces of Kara (psychological thriller)
Where Petals Fall (suspense)

Acknowledgments

If you follow me on Facebook, then you know writing is my greatest joy, and writing about the Seaside gang brings Cape Cod into play, which makes it even more enjoyable. I'd like to thank all of my fans who have reached out over the years and gotten involved with my writing process, offering character names, professions, and other integral parts of the stories. Word of mouth is the best way to reach readers, and I truly appreciate everyone who shares my books with their friends and family. I hope you'll continue to reach out and take part in the giveaways, snappy banter, and inspirational photos that I share on social media.

I'd like to thank Elise Sax for pedestals and statues. You're the funniest person I know, and I cherish our friendship. Readers, if you haven't read Elise's work, I urge you to pick it up. She'll have you in stitches. A big thank you to Amy Manemann, who probably doesn't realize how inspiring she was to me for our Amy Maples. No, Amy's background does not match the character Amy Maples's background, but her personality is pretty darn close.

My editorial team is like oxygen. I have no idea how I do anything without them. Kristen, Penina, Jenna, Juliette, Marlene, Lynn, and Justinn, thank you for your meticulous attention to detail.

The energy and support of bloggers, reviewers, readers, and friends, inspire me daily. Thank you for sharing your time with me.

To Les, you own me, baby. Inside and out.

Addison Cole is the sweet alter ego of *New York Times* and *USA Today* bestselling and award-winning author Melissa Foster. She enjoys writing humorous, and deeply emotional, contemporary romance without explicit sex scenes or harsh language. Addison spends her summers on Cape Cod, where she dreams up wonderful love stories in her house overlooking Cape Cod Bay.

Visit Addison on her website or chat with her on social media. Addison enjoys discussing her books with book clubs and reader groups and welcomes an invitation to your event.

Addison's books are available in paperback, digital, and audio formats.

www.AddisonCole.com

facebook.com/AddisonColeAuthor

Printed in the USA
CPSIA information can be obtained
at www.ICGtesting.com
LVHW100144080823
754547LV00008BA/223